HEART OF STONE

Also by Robert C. Fleet

Last Mountain

White Horse, Dark Dragon

The Berkley Publishing Group
An Ace Book

HEART OF STONE

a novel by

Robert C. Fleet

Red Frog Publishing is a division of Red Frog Media
112 Harvard Ave. # 43 Claremont, CA 91711.

1   2   3   4   5   6   7   8   9   10

First Edition   Literary Thriller

Book design by Starling/Berlin wall photo by AS

ISBN-13:
978-0615472836
ISBN-10:
0615472834

FLEET
Robert C.

For and with Alina and for those trying to understand.

Special Thanks
to those who helped:
Sam Miller, J.C. Williams, Jo Groebel,
Cynthia Paloromo, many people in
Poland, Germany, France and Holland
and, as always, Alina Szpak.

BEHIND THE STORY...

In that odd way that some people call "funny," and others call heartbreaking, Heart of Stone has taken thirty-nine years to earn its 2011 copyright. It started at a Frankfurt youth hostel in 1972 when I went to an impromptu concert where half the Baader-Meinhof Gang turned out to be openly in attendance. Then there was the Polish actress I eventually married in 1977, whose set designer friend disappeared in 1969, found dead months later, after being identified in a certain photo that implicated someone as the kidnapper of a rich man's son. It found its focus in 1984, when an older Jewish movie director I was working with, a man who'd spent six months during 1943 half-dead and hiding in a mausoleum, showed no sympathy for the rich man because he was a suspected Nazi collaborator, and talked about understanding the kidnapper's revenge "like Clint Eastwood." And then, because there was maybe a movie to be made, Heart of Stone languished in development purgatory and litigation hell for money reasons that had nothing to do with revenge, truth, or moral values whatsoever. But, sitting in Russia in 1992, I started writing it anyway - and, when the story finally became free a short while ago (they can own your story, you know, sort of like owning your soul), I talked with the director, now old, and his anger was still alive. This isn't a factual story, then, only true in its heart of stone.

RCF

Prologue

The heart of stone. I thought about it a lot. They had it. I had it. The heart of stone.

Didn't have to try very hard to discover the fact: it just sort of presented itself to view with that first choice of emotion over reason. In my case - their story - I chose reason. In their case, they chose murder.

So why did I miss her. Probably a look in the corner of her eyes, a look saying to me that if anyone could be talked to by me - and understood on other than a nodding level - it was her. She held up a mirror and in it I saw myself and her juxtaposed like a surrealistic cliché. Did it reflect that I was as mean-spirited in the end as her? I hope not. I don't know.

The heart of stone. Damn! It was a diamond. And if it happens that the law is glass, then let it shatter like it should.

But, no. A long time ago, before I was thinking about it, I chose to try to keep that glass intact... nostalgia for a decaying old edifice, perhaps. Didn't matter anymore. Just as they did not need any justification for their actions from an outside world that they despised for its softness, so I didn't care whether it was soft or not. I had my own stupid need to be right - and the one or two sparkles in the system were the only guidelines I had left to keep me at least parallel with the rest.

Shoot her for that. She lost that one ounce that gives life any reason. Me, it was only a speck of dust now, lost somewhere in my clothes. And if I stayed dirty, it was just to keep from accidentally washing away that last touch of good with all the rest of the dirt.

Sam Williams

Paris metro, May 1978, Les Halles

HEART OF STONE

1972

Beaches & Bars

Friday night. And the moon cast shadows with a light so bright that one could read by it. In between the shadows stood corners of a small German town. Off to a corner of this *burger-meister*'s delight sat a strip joint. Hanau.

Hanau's little corner of suburb rocked with the mellow noise of "Ma Cherie Amour" being sung by Stevie Wonder (until most recently, *Little* Stevie Wonder - time flies and people grow up), played at top volume on a jukebox of Chicago origin, eating up quarters of Washington stamp, fed by a Negro GI of Harlem neighborhood. Volkswagens, Mercedes and U.S. Army Jeeps - a few of each - sat outside the music-producing building, noses pointed toward the brick walls as if their headlights were eyes that could penetrate the solidity (as the sound could) and see inside. A strip joint.

Filled to the gills with G.I.s and townies.

Only -

The West German townies, not a one below the age of thirty, sat on one side of the room, dominating a corner of the bar, trying to look properly bourgeois as they leered at the girls' pasted-over titties and carefully shaved beavers. The American soldier boys, black and white and scarcely a one over twenty-three (only two, actually, both "ranking" corporals) crowded themselves around the runway below the bored stripper of the moment, desperately trying to root themselves into whatever eroticism might be culled from the half spectacle. A few of the soldiers were lucky, having enough money left over from buying beers to purchase a dance with the non-performing strippers. Black private from El-Lay with white ice from Han-au. A cool-eyed, blue-eyed Florida boy gettin' *down* with the curly-wigged vampette imported all the twenty klicks' distance away from Frankfurt. Havin' fun.

Outside again, the shadows cast by the moon cut even darker than if it had been a cloudy night. Walking down the street, sliding in-light, out-of-light with strobic regularity, various neighbors scurried home to their thick, comfortable German beds. They did not look with kindly eye toward the crowded strip joint that muddied their weekend nights with noise and filled the town's coffers with lucre.

"I thought you said it was only five kilometers from base?" a uniformed voice called out across the top of a battered Volks, teenage vocal cords cracking slightly in spite of its owner's attempt to sound adult.

"Five klicks, fifteen - we here, J.C.! Who cares?!"

Well, in fact, *they* did, these two soldier boys. Having made the mistake of coming *together*, this white boy from Long Island and his black Detroit bunkmate belatedly discovered that - in addition to the U.S./German split inside the strip joint - there was a clear *color* line drawn around certain territories. The dance floor and strippers runway were still neutral. But the white G.I.s laid claim to the pinball machines, while the black contingent dominated the jukebox slot. Without saying a word of farewell, the bunkmates separated. It could have been a bar in the Midwest.

Except every single fucking beer was German: not even a crap Milwaukee *Blue Ribbon* or Texas *Falstaff* to wipe away loneliness with the proper taste of foamy home. It took a good nine-twelve months to realize that the unpronounceable suds here were better than the American brew - and almost every G.I. in the bar had yet to reach the six-month mark. Instead they got the pleasure of standing in their separate groups - b & w - eyeing one another with an essential hostility that belied their daily training. Covering up their insecurity with a bravado that wavered between good-natured and obnoxious.

The new arrival of chocolate persuasion, tall and solidly built, hugged the jukebox and told his loud story with all the relish of homesickness. He did not let his nineteen years stand in the way of assuming an "experienced" point-of-view.

"Well it be Detroit, y'know, Dee-troit, my home. And I be all of maybe 'leven or twelve and it's summer vacation and I don't got no job 'cause even if they was one for a little nigger boy *this* little nigger been told by his Poppa he got to work for his uncle for free. For *free*! No movies for Samuel T. Williams that summer. 'Least not supposed to be.

"But then the brothers they start runnin' in the streets, and the Man he start beatin' on heads - an' *all* kinds a stores just open up to a little nigger kid with big cryin' eyes who just stands outside the *right* stores an' the Man say:

"'You O.K., son?'

"An' I says: 'No, sir, my daddy's store's getting ripped off and I can't stop them.' And they just go on leavin' me right there and go on to bust other brothers' heads while I do a little 'window shoppin', so to speak."

This last line always brought a burst of familiar laughter

from everybody who remembered the news coverage of the Detroit Riots - or who was there - and Sam paused, anticipating the expected response. It came.

Attention successfully captured, he resumed the story with gusto:

"'Course my Momma was mad when she saw what I got home with, but I figured it was just 'cause she could only get a black and white TV an' I got color!"

Another expected laugh.

"I *did!* I was like a hero, skinny little nigger kid risking his neck while those whitey sticks go beatin' on heads - just so my Daddy could watch *Monday Night Football* in color."

Sam was hyper now, rattling on loudly so that the sound of his own voice would keep him and the others laughing. He was not particularly trying for a lot of attention; he was afraid of having nothing to say if he stopped.

And the Detroit story was beginning to tail out. With sudden inspiration, Sam dropped his own quarter in the jukebox and re-selected the Stevie Wonder disk: he had another surefire joke from high school. As the blind singer's voice echoed through the strip joint, Sam slipped on a pair of sun-glasses and began rolling his head in lip-synced imitation -

"Hey, man! You can't make fun of a brother!"

Sam, apparently, was not the only G.I. pushing for a Stevie Wonder joke: a white kid in sunglasses standing on the dance floor was entertaining his own crowd. The very black Private First Class facing the white boy was *not* amused.

Which did not stop the performance.

"You can't make fun of a blind brother, man!" the black PFC repeated delicately at the top of his lungs. Sam took advantage of the attention drawn to the dance floor to unobtrusively remove his own shades.

"Just admiring the music of Stevie Wonder," the white performance artist explained with a smirk. *No way* he would stop now: his audience was growing, he was happy. The jukebox voice of the vocalist in question crooned on, obliviously continuing to fuel the controversy.

A violent shove. "I said stop it!"

"Lay off, private." An ancient, twenty-four year old white corporal stepped onto the dance floor to enforce a sense of discipline in the aggressive colored G.I. His order was immediately challenged by his twenty-six-year-old senior:

"Hey, corp'ral: I a corp'ral, too. You wanta order me aroun'?" The black man stepped between the two privates and the intrusive white non-com.

It was not good Regular Army form to be cowed down. Both corporals knew the routine. They also knew what they valued: their ranks, small shit that it was. A tense, very short moment of nose-to-nose confrontation was followed by the black corporal's statement of fact:

"Hell, I like my stripes." He turned away, pushing the black PFC in front of him, clearing the dance floor.

"Cowardly nigger," a lard-assed Deutschlander noted in loud German from his observation post at the far end of the bar.

"No Nazi can call our niggers 'niggers'!" the white corporal cried, betraying his understanding of the *Deutsche* language. The corporal's temper was louder and faster than his words, shoved out in a wild launch of his body toward the bar, fists first and brain somewhere half-a-room behind.

He even made contact, much to the surprise of himself and a dozen bystanders, each of whom had expected someone else to grab at the American's arms and drag him to a halt. First blood drawn (figuratively - it was a weak connect with a fat-insulated face), within seconds scores of Germans were fighting G.I.s for no particular reason other than the fact that they hated being there together.

It was a lot more fun than watching the bored strippers.

Sam, big and dangerous-looking, was having no particular problem with the situation, his fighting technique being somewhat unique. Lowering his head, football halfback style, he charged into the melee of clanging bodies - emerging on the other side of the room unbeaten and with the probable knowledge of having elbowed a few ribs and stomped on several arches viciously. Sam didn't concern himself with deep inquires as to which side he inflic-ted the most damage on.

Two out of three sorties were successfully executed in this fashion. Sam took a breath at the end of each round, congratulating himself on his acumen, before plunging in once more. The third assault, unfortunately, attracted "blockers" like a magnet: Sam's legs bogged down in a mire of fallen combatants. He sank into a goulash of G.I.s and Germans.

Lady Caroline, the ennui-filled stripper of the moment, calmly looked down from the stage at the tangle of feet and arms struggling below her. She decided then and there to leave work early. "Willy, call my husband and tell him I will meet him at Gerta's apartment," she instructed the bouncer, who remained apart from the fray, guarding the liquor supply room.

"Call him yourself, I'm busy," he answered, distracted: the jukebox was solidly built, no one worried about *its* safety, but there was a glass window…

"*Scheisskopf*," Lady Caroline (née Hilda Wurst) muttered. Couldn't he see that Armin was using the telephone?! Oh, sure, Armin was the owner, *ja*, OK - calling the police probably - but did Willy really think that she could tell *Armin* to get off the phone?

"*Scheisskopf*," she muttered again, resigned to the prospect of having to spend the money herself at a pay telephone outside in order to call her husband to pick her up early, at Gerta's. Gerta had no phone, of course: the fucking government wired up only the capitalists and bourgeoisie. Lady Caroline, good socialist that she was, scooted out of the strip joint with quick-clicking high heels and goosebumping titties. Luckily Gerta lived only fifty meters away. Caroline-née-Hilda certainly had no intentions of waiting for the police to come.

Nor did any of the Germans in the strip joint, save owner Armin and bouncer Willy. It was an odd sensation, Sam recalled later: when he disappeared under the pile of fighting bodies, the place had been full of Teutonic faces - soft faces, hard faces, angry faces - faces, anyway, that were not American and whose eyes looked at every uniformed young man through a different language than the one Sam understood. However, when he finally sifted himself out of the scramble of bodies his last football-charge had created, something *new* immediately became apparent: all of the Germans had somehow melted away - leaving only G.I.s fighting.

Black against white.

Sam shook his head to clear it. He didn't understand the full import of what he was seeing at first. His eyes focused on the nearest skirmish: the two corporals were battling away at one another hard. The white soldier with the sunglasses was stretched out cold at their feet.

The fight had taken on some ugly edges now, too. Three whites ganged up on a single black PFC, pounding him down. A blood from Chi-town edged a jagged piece of glass at a honky private's belly.

Sam decided to join the guys on the outskirts of the dance floor who were pulling out to nurse their wounds. He did not withdraw far enough: a mass of three or four soldiers - color unknown - dropped down upon his back. A lot of chroma-colored fireworks burst behind Sam's eyelids as the side of his head slammed down on the hardwood dance floor.

He did not dive totally into unconsciousness, though. Sam clearly heard the *Ee-Oh, Ee-Oh!* squawk of the German police siren cut through the Hanau night from some distance away outside. So did the majority of the strip joint's combatants: a sudden freeze made play-statues of the scene - accompanied by a concentrated, listening, silence - leaving them all free to hear the gutless Dutch song on the jukebox that had replaced Stevie's wonderful melody.

"La! La-la, la-la, la, la, la -" the lyrics began.

"TURN OFF THAT SHIT!" black and white cried in unison. No one did, but the *Ee-Oh!* sirened loud enough through the just-opened front entrance to distract everyone's attention from matters of pop culture taste.

"Looks like we be rank," the black corporal said to his white counterpart, both emerging from the hurling mass that had recently tackled Sam. "You take it or me?"

The white corporal was still busy dragging himself to his feet. "You go ahead," he grunted.

The assumption of active command required a sufficient volume of voice to shake the rafters. The black corporal shook 'em:

"All right you honky-nigger bastards: BASE!"

He allowed a second for the import of his words to sink in, then bellowed:

"DOUBLE TIME!!!"

Or perhaps it was the white corporal's wickedly-humored addendum - "DON'T LEAVE THE WOUNDED!" - that sent the assembled military forces charging for the exits.

Internecine rivalries were quickly forgotten in the face of a common foe. With a loud whoop of action to counter the ever-louder German police siren, the American army began its disordered retreat. Responsible to their duty, each corporal burdened himself with a fallen body scooped up from the dance floor. J.C., the white boy from Long Island who took the bottom bunk and a Volkswagen for the night, pulled his bunkmate off the floor.

"C'mon, Sam. You don't wanna get caught off-base by the *polizei*," he pulled *very* hard on Sam's arm at the utterance of the last word. "Don't want that *at all*."

The color war had not ended for everyone.

The black private who was holding a jagged piece of glass still wanted his weapon to find a pale belly to lodge in. (It was the same PFC who had earlier been so offended by the white boy's imitation of Stevie Wonder, Sam recalled, uncomfortably remembering his own attempted parody.) The black private cornered a beer-stupored jackass from Alabama by the front entrance and made moves to fulfill his desire. Sam pushed J.C. out the door -

"Go find the Volks, I'm behind."

- and turned to talk to the brother.

He was beaten to the draw by the black corporal, an unconscious body slung over his shoulder, who suddenly loomed in front of the PFC. The corporal growled with an angry intimacy, and grabbed the private's shoulder roughly.

"It sure as hell don't matter if you hate that ofay's guts you about to cut up - you get your asses *together* on getting out of this place FAST!"

A truly inspirational sermon, Sam thought with some panic, taking the corporal's advice before waiting around to see if the black PFC did likewise. Don't want to get caught by the *po-lit-zei*, no! Don't want -

Where's J.C.?

The streets of Hanau were no longer quiet, what with cars peeling out in all directions: some overfilled to the gills with G.I. passengers, others containing but a single cowardly driver leaving too fast to wait for the people who obviously came with them. Sam felt the bitter disappointment of one who in all likelihood would soon find himself among the latter group. Where was J.C. and the Volks?!

"Hop in, private," the white corporal ordered, pushing Sam into his own Volkswagen, a rusty green variation on the same buglike vehicle Sam had arrived in. Three West German police cars, after driving in circles around the nearby *centrum* to assemble in force, made their appearance in a honk of sirens, rounding the last corner before the strip joint.

"Sam! *You* got the car keys!"

Even as the corporal's sardine-packed car chugged into life and away from the approaching *polizei* menace, Sam saw J.C. jogging down the street after them, crying desperately. Sam felt his button-flap breast pocket. Sure enough, the car key was there - Sam forgot that *he* had driven from camp: J.C. could borrow a car, but didn't know how to drive a stickshift. Shit!

"We gotta stop!" Sam cried into the driver-corporal's ear. "J.C.'s still back there!"

Apparently the corporal thrived under stress: he answered Sam calmly, without breaking his concentration on the road ahead.

"J.C.'s gonna be black-and-blue, then, 'cause we're not going back for him."

"Why not?!"

"Boy, you're new in this neck of the woods: 'cause *he*'s gonna get caught - not us."

The truth was in the telling. When Sam strained his neck to peer back through the rusty Volkswagen's cloudy rear window, he saw J.C. running frantically. But J.C. was no longer chasing after his friends - he was running away from the *polizei*! Two of the German police cars swept up next to him, spilling a running, angry policeman each. J.C. disappeared between them.

"They're refighting World War Two," someone in the crowd of bodies surrounding Sam explained, "winning it this time."

"Shit," Sam said, losing sight of his bunkmate's assailants in a haze of pursuing headlights.

"Try being a Yankee in Arkansas: police'll pull the same crap there," the corporal shrugged without animosity.

"I a nigger in Detroit."

"Same thing." Another shrug. "Things don't change. Wherever."

J.C.'s capture apparently slowed down the German pursuit. The corporal's vehicle tore through the outskirts of Hanau into the countryside unimpeded, its nearest posse a good deal behind.

"We're makin' it!" the passengers took turns laughing to themselves.

"Yeah!"

"Oh, Lord - !"

Two German police cars were blocking the road.

"Pull over!" a pale G.I. shrieked. "We're gonna hit!"

"We're not the only ones: lookit!" Sam cried, more observant of the situation than the others: the car ahead of their Volkswagen, a Jeep, jammed on its brakes at the sight of the road block. Too late. Without even swerving, the Jeep screeched to a dead-on stop. A foot deep into the side door of a police car.

Inside the Volks, the corporal stamped his foot down on the gas pedal and turned the stiff steering wheel hard. With a roar of its underpowered engine, the Volkswagen jumped off the narrow road and half into a drainage ditch - swerving *around* the road block. Before a startled cheer could emerge from the passengers' throats, however, German policemen were jumping into the undamaged of their two cars, intent upon pursuit. A cold dread began to pluck at the G.I.s' souls.

"You think we'll make it?" Sam quietly asked the white corporal, bending into his ear not so much from intimacy as because he was sitting on another soldier's lap in the cramped back seat. For the first time, Sam actually counted how many passengers had fit themselves into the Volkswagen: eight grown men. Not a record, but it was a miracle the corporal could drive; Sam felt himself squeezed behind the steering wheel when he was the only one in a Volks. Then again, there wasn't a lot of shifting going on: the corporal had put the car into third gear within seconds of starting up and had been pushing the gas pedal to goose their speed up past one hundred-twenty klicks ever since. One hundred-twenty kilometers per hour... Sam mentally converted the number to miles... almost seventy-five miles per hour on a crap road! Oh, fuck this!

"How many klicks to base?" the corporal asked calmly, enjoying the pressure. "Anybody see a sign?"

At one hundred-twenty klicks he did not have to wait long for an answer. "Five."

At one-twenty, there's another kilometer every thirty seconds.

"Four."

Another sign. Safety near.

"Three."

"Two!"

Last sign.

"ONE!"

Push on the brakes for a little home slide to safety in through the back door of camp -

"WE GOT IT!"

- Yeah, *in* the rear door - before the *polizei* get to catch you, and beat your head, and put you in the tank for three days, and turn you over to the MPs for another three days, then a week of shit-work detail, pay cut for the fine paid to the *po-lit-zei* - home *free*, now, just a little turn here -

The gate was closed.

Gates don't get closed on a Friday night at one of the largest overseas military bases in the U.S. Army. Too much traffic. Especially the rear gates, where supplies are routinely transported - out of sight from the anti-war German groups routinely camped at the front gates, where they protested American presence in Vietnam, in Germany, and (it seemed) just about everywhere in the world, including U.S. presence in the U.S. You needed to have other entrances to the base in order to keep a small city-sized military encampment running smoothly. And they needed to be open.

The gate was closed.

Rather *specifically* closed, so it seemed to the occupants spilling out of the rusty Volkswagen: the high, metal-link double gate was padlocked shut with a thick chain wrapped once, insolently, around the metal bars.

A half-dozen vehicles were parked at skewed angles in front of the sealed entrance, each angle reflecting the astonished moment when the car's driver, having successfully eluded German pursuit, became painfully aware that *he could not get in to safety*.

"I don't believe it," the corporal groaned, slumping back against the curved hood of his Volkswagen.

Sam jumped over to the closed gate, where twenty fellow fugitives stood sullenly staring at the empty darkness behind the chain links.

"Why don't we get over to the front gate?!" he cried, seized with desperate inspiration. He already knew the answer that more than one sullen G.I. spat at him:

"'Cause it's another five klicks away -"

"- and the *po-lit-zei* are comin' -"

"- hot and heavy."

"FUCK!" a voice howled to the moon. "Fuck-fuck-fuck-fuck-fuck-fuck-fuck-fuck-FUCK!" It sounded like a wounded chicken after a while, but Sam shared the sentiment.

The *Ee-Oh! polizei* sirens wailed into hearing range now, chugging along at their legal ninety klicks per hour. The fact that they were still in hot pursuit meant only one thing: the *polizei* had cut a deal with Army brass. The G.I.s standing here, on the wrong side of the gate, had been set-up as sacrificial lambs to military-civilian public relations. Or so one desultory meathead declaimed.

Sam wasn't so certain. Or at least he wasn't prepared to give up trying.

"I'm not gonna sit here like a sardine just waitin'," he said aloud, making his personal resolve into a public challenge. Now he would be too embarrassed to back down. Displaying a visual deliberateness he did not feel, Sam elaborately thrust his hands into his pockets and walked back-and-forth in front of the closed gate, shouting inside in a mock-calm frenzy:

"Mister MPs, Mister MPs! Don't let them bad Germans get to us! Please Mister MPs, please!" He pressed his face into the chain links, shouting to the empty darkness within the camp.

"Good luck, fella," a New York-accented voice behind Sam sarcastically remarked.

Sam chose to explain his "strategy," turning back to face the assembled nineteen and twenty year-olds behind him. "Hey, y'know, maybe they got a heart. Try it with me. C'mon."

For some reason - desperation, silly giddiness - they did. On Sam's count of "One - Two - Three!" they all pleaded like kindergartners:

"Please, Mister MPs! Please!"

His chorus performing as required, Sam turned back to the gate to direct his own voice inward -

To find his nose a scant half-inch away from that of the flat, black face of A. L. McMasters, Military Police, sergeant huge extraordinaire. It was a face crisscrossed by the wires of the chain link fence: MP McMasters was on the safe side of the gate. His dark face scowled at the fugitives opposite him.

All of them, Sam no exception, began to shuffle about uncomfortably, staring at their feet, avoiding the MP sergeant's ferocious eyes.

Those eyes were no longer on the American soldiers. McMasters raised them up a quarter of an inch, to focus down the highway on the approaching, hostile German police. They were pulling their vehicles to a stop, preparatory to descending upon their intended prisoners *en masse* in force.

Sam was as tall and broad as McMasters. He stepped into

the MP's line-of-vision and endured the withering glare. "Please, Sergeant, it's not a friendly side of the fence."

McMasters must have unlatched the padlock a moment earlier: with a shove of his arm he opened the gate.

Abandoning their cars to the whims of fate, the crowd of fleeing G.I.s rushed into the gap with a speed that would have made their drill instructors proud and the Charge of the Light Brigade seem lackadaisical. When the last one was safely through, McMasters stepped in front of the gate to stand facing his German police counterparts.

Despite their numbers, in no uncertain terms the *polizei* were intimidated by McMasters' huge bulk planted not three meters away, separating them from the soldier-brawlers, not ten feet behind the gate. Sam could not see a single face: positioned behind the MP's mountainous shoulder, McMaster's head was a haloed silhouette under the multiple-glare stare of the *polizei* headlights focused on the gate. The Germans themselves were framed like scarecrows by the beams beating upon their backs. McMasters did not turn his face away from them as he held a massive paw palm-up behind his back and uttered the single-worded command:

"Keys!"

Three sets of car keys dropped into his hands.

"I left mine in the car, sarge."

"Sergeant!"

"*Sergeant*, sir!"

"There are *six* cars out there -" McMasters rumbled. No one stepped forward with an explanation for the discrepancy between cars and keys. The MP did not ask again.

Instead, with another shove of his arm, McMasters flung one-half of the chain link gate completely open: wide enough for a car to drive through, which he proceeded to do. Four times. To the G.I.s' roar of approval and laughter. Scornful laughter, aimed at the frustrated German police, left standing helplessly in front of their assembled chase vehicles. As McMasters chugged the fourth car into the compound, abandoning the keyless two remaining outside to *polizei* confiscation, shouts of "Way to go, sergeant!", "What a night!" and "Cavalry to the rescue, weehoo!" resounded through the brisk late-night air -

To be stopped by an overpowering -

"ATTEN-SHUN!"

It was recorded in Sam's mind that no single one of the bedraggled, triumphant, soldier-escapees actually came to Attention upon hearing McMasters' command. He himself most certainly did not assume the ramrod-straight, feet-forty-five, hands-to-pants-crease position. But everyone there, that moment, quite literally froze in his tracks (including a few *polizei*, caught off-guard by the sudden burst of Authority). McMasters did not appear to notice.

Calmly and quietly he began walking among the G.I.s, oozing a deadly superiority in his clear, *basso* declamation:

"Gentlemen, it is one o'clock in the morning, and I fear that there is far too much dirt on this road for me to go to sleep with a contented feeling this night. I need this road to be clean. Push-ups will help attract the dust to your already filthy clothes. And so will sit-ups."

Sam emitted an uncontrollable groan. McMaster's eyes

dived in on the source of such unwelcome comment. He strolled over to the open gate, out to the *polizei*, to stand next to his German colleagues and address the American soldiers from there:

"The option is to leave this path and re-enter base through the front gate, thus keeping *my* road clean."

No one exercised the option.

"*Le jeux sont fait,*" McMasters shrugged with French resignation. "Begin. One - two -"

He left his smiling *Deutsche* counterparts to rejoin the American contingent.

"- three. Come, come, only a few hundred more to go! - four, five -"

The *polizei*'s laughter dug in deeper than the gravel into their hands. The exercising, half-drunk, half-asleep soldiers understood Dante's concept of self-made Hell. Samuel T. Williams tried thinking of anything else in the world. All he could remember was the moldy oldie *My Guy* by Mary Wells. He got stuck on the words.

> *Nothin' you can do*
> *Nothin' you can do*

Sam knew there was a lot more to the song, but this was how he felt this crappy moment.

* * * * * * * * *

Saturday. September left a final, lingering hint of summer in the air. It made the beach not half as frigid as it should be. The North Sea, of course, was cold. Braun buried the Uzi among his blankets and laid himself down on the sand. He would watch the others. Sweating profusely from the effort of running across the dunes, not one of the half-dozen university students considered for a moment diving into the salt-icy waves crashing near their ankles with exciting regularity.

Not so Frederick: caution was not his ilk. Maybe because he wasn't a student like the others. Maybe because Frederick believed that, if a ball was thrown, it *had* to be caught, no matter where it flew. Maybe because he was a dog, and a Great Schnauzer to boot.

Or so Braun thought, admiring Frederick's bold, ultimately futile leap into the sky after another one of Alex's wild pitches. The tennis ball arced with tempting nearness just beyond the reach of the dog's iron-trap jaws. Frederick twisted his head, neck, entire body in desperate contortion to snatch the small orb from the sky - missed - then seemed to run across the air itself to jump into the whale-grey wave upon whose crest the errant missile chose to rest.

Brrrr-aaah!

Braun uttered an involuntary shudder from the cold that he knew would penetrate even a Great Schnauzer's corkscrew-curled thick fur. Frederick only bounced the faster across the beach, spurred on by his own adrenal impulse, impervious to the ice bath.

The humans all gathered round to congratulate him on his Viking-dog feat, but Frederick held tight to his prize until he could deposit the tennis ball at Birgit's feet. The Great Schnauzer fawned over Birgit with almost as much affection as his love for Braun allowed. Then, of course, he showered the assembly with a nose-to-tail shake of his body that "shared the wealth" from his recent diving expedition. Birgit squealed in delighted horror! Even Jo (and this was an accomplishment Braun took note of) – even *that* clerically-serious student barked a laugh of surprise.

It could just as easily have been a snarl, Braun reflected appreciatively. Yes, it had been a good idea to bring along Frederick this trip. For a few moments of delicious amnesia he felt that Hamburg - indeed, all of Germany - seemed as far away from their lives as ancient Baghdad and *The Arabian Nights*. Braun was content to lie flat on his dune a hundred meters above the others and let Frederick spread his canine cheer among them.

Though he needed the dog's good-humored hedonism for himself.

"I would love to stop thinking," Braun said aloud to no one present but himself. He had a tendency to repeat himself in his thoughts: "stop thinking." Immediately, Braun dismissed the complaint as a whining, middle-aged version of the students' overwrought *angst*. Twenty year-olds could indulge in self-directed tears without too much danger of appearing ridiculous. Fifty year-olds had no such excuse except nostalgia – and Braun would never allow himself to become nostalgic.

"Sit me down in front of a beer stein," he snorted contemptuously at his own attempt at weakness, "and let me cry with the other fat old men!"

Truth and the warm September day that had coaxed Braun

into removing his shirt told a different story. He was not a *fat* oldster, and - the issue of birthday aside - Braun's thoughts were as fresh, as radical, as the students' below. His thinking was clearer than theirs also - but more definitely radical. "More *True*," they said of Braun in Berlin. Where the funding came from. *"True* with a capital 'T'," Braun reflected with a smile, enjoying his hobby of repeating American slang. He was almost certain that no one in Berlin knew what the hell they were talking about. Most certainly they did not know about *his* veracity, as they had not since…

When?

Since 1945.

"Huwhar y'all from?" the Kommandant asked. (He was not titled "Kommandant" by the American army he served - but, after three years in the camp before liberation, that habit of addressing anyone in uniform was ingrained in his listener.)

"What?" the listener asked in German, then added in halting English phrases, "I don't dig your… jive." And even the Kommandant understood, though he spoke only - in his own words - "hillbilly English".

"He does not speak English" the translator explained needlessly, his own language skills taxed rather heavily by the polyglot duties thrust upon him since liberation of the camp. The translator was always "rather taxed" with his duties: the smiling skeletons facing the Allied conquerors rattled his confidence. The skeletons seemed to expect him *to understand* them, *and -and - words were not enough to explain their disassociated smiles, the echoing eyes, the stories they spewed out at him as if he, he alone, could make the camp they stood in, and the memories attached to it,*

disappear simply by translating *this atrocity to the American soldiers.*

"Baked fish," a naked skeleton had solemnly explained on the very first day, pointing to a pile of ash beside the incinerators. The translator just as solemnly converted this into English for the Arkansas captain at his side. For a minute they allowed themselves to believe the lie. Then, of course, the naked skeleton had collapsed in their arms. His veins were too withered, his belly too shriveled to drink in the C-ration soup the Arkansan soldier tried to pour down the skeleton's gullet. They wasted precious time saving the corpse's life - only to be repaid by a high command that posted the translator and his captain here permanently until the problem of what to do with this camp's inhabitants was resolved.

What to do with them...

"Where - are - you - from?" the Kommandant from Arkansas said in labored German (his three months' in the conquered Reich had not left him totally untutored). The skinny young man in front of him - a third of his weight heavier than when the camp had been liberated - struggled through the American's unruly-accented question to answer simply:

"Breslau. From Breslau."

"Breslau is on the Russian *side," the translator explained, "and they say it is now part of* Polen *- Poland. 'Wrocław' they call it. 'Vrotswaf'."*

The skinny young man shrugged, "Wrocław, I know, that is the old name." He spoke in fluent, non-Teutonic German, his eyes burning ahead to questions unasked by the Kommandant. "The Poles call it 'Wrocław', the Germans 'Breslau'. Who is they *who say it is Poland now?"*

The translator ignored the man's historical commentary and limited himself to translating only the question.

"Who's they?" *the captain repeated, relaxing back in his creaky folding chair to grow expansive. "They* sure ain't the Polacks, that's for sure.*

They *is the late, great FDR hisself, plus Churchill and Big Joe Stalin:* 'said the *Nazi's gotta pay for some a this crap -*" He waved his hand at the unseen ex-death camp behind the canvas of his command tent. *"So we done took a chunk a Germany 'n give it to the Polacks. Which are ya? Polack 'r Kraut?"*

"Ślązak - Silesian."

The captain stared blank-eyed back at the young man when the answer was translated to him.

"Yeah... So which is it? German or Polish?"

"Silesian. Not German. Not Polish."

"And I'm not a damn Yankee, but -" The captain hesitated, trying to figure out a way to help the skinny man make a decision. *"- but which do you like better, Americans or Russians?"*

"It doesn't matter."

"OK, Germans or Polish?"

"It doesn't matter."

"You speak German."
I speak Polish, too."

"So which are you? Polish or German!?"

"Silesian." And now it was time for the young man to ask: *"Why does it matter?"*

"Because the Ruskies are kickin' the butts of all the Germans outta Wro-, outta there, *uh, no offense if you're German,"* he added hurriedly to placate the large-eyed man in front of him, ignoring the fact that his translation was running half-a-paragraph behind. *"Ah mean, if you're German you're no Nazi - being in here 'n all I can figure that out pretty well - but ya gotta know ya can't go back: only Polacks get to go there."*

Braun thought carefully about what he heard the Kommandant say. There had been rumors of all this. Rumors were not the same as hearing *it from the American captain's lips. It did not surprise him that no one gave a moment's concern for the Silesians who had lived in Wrocław since before Poles and Germans.*

"May I go there to see my city, then decide?"

The Kommandant sighed, "Fraid it's a one-way ticket, friend: the Ruskies'll let ya in, no telling if they let ya out." This, too, had been one of the rumors.

Braun's dark eyes calculated the odds.

"German," he said at last, "I am German."

"I am German," Braun repeated, mimicking the rhythm of Berlin he had picked up in the twenty-seven years since 1945. "I am German," he said again with a Hamburg accent. He repeated the phrase with the music of an Alsatian and again with the waltz of a Viennese. He wanted to stop repeating the memories, but they would not go away, even when he fell into a near doze upon the sand. His eyes were open, his sight and hearing stuck in thoughts far away.

With the annoyance of a busy man, the farmer stalked away from his open green field to the seclusion of the dunes. "I need a crap!" he called back to his son, knowing full well that nothing useful would get done unless he was there to give instructions.

"Just tell me which rows?" the teenager asked, displaying an unexpected initiative. Of course, when the boy abandoned the tractor to follow his father, the end result was the same: nothing got done.

Still, the boy's gesture pleased the farmer. He almost began to answer in detail which rows need to be plowed for beets - and which for winter cabbage - and which for…

Then he remembered what he was about to do. The farmer waved his son back to the tractor even as he stepped behind a dune to relieve himself.

"You go wait: I'm not talking with my pants pulled down-"

The farmer recognized the dangerous small dark open hole for what it was -

The barrel of a gun.

- and did not move.

Braun pushed the Uzi's barrel a centimeter closer to the man's face. He was angry with himself for dozing, for allowing someone to stumble upon him unaware. He transferred that anger into a productive demand:

"How many are with you?" Brown asked, carefully replicating the farmer's rough, North German accent.

"Just my son," was the answer slowly given.

"Tell him to come here."

"You are Black September?" the farmer asked fearfully.

Braun shook his head *No*.

"They are in Munich, we are here." No, he was not allied with the Black September terrorists holding twenty Israeli hostages at the Olympic games.

"Call your son. You will be safe if you don't act stupid."

The farmer reluctantly obeyed the command. As soon as the teenager appeared - and froze at the sight of the Uzi - Braun pursed his lips together and emitted a high-pitched, piercing whistle.

On the beach below, Frederick gave a joyous leap of recognition at his master's call. Jo, Birgit, Alex, Wolf and Karl froze in their places, looking up at the dune expectantly.

Braun put two fingers to his lips and let out a second, stronger whistling call. A moment later Frederick scrambled up the steep sand cliff to join him. The others followed only seconds behind – startled to find Braun holding a farmer and his excited son at bay, Braun's semi-automatic machine pistol sweeping in small arcs between their stomachs.

"Don't move," Braun cautioned the prisoners, as the Great Schnauzer clambered across the dunes and directly to him. Frederick was rewarded with a grasp of affection deep into his fur.

"It is time to leave," Braun explained tersely to the later-arriving students. They hustled without question toward the van hidden behind yet another dune. Their brief respite from revolution was over.

"You never saw us," Braun cautioned the farmer. He waved the two prisoners back to their field.

"Can I have your autograph?" the farmer's teenage son asked. In West Germany, 1972, knowing a terrorist was almost as good as having sex with a rock star.

Dresden Figurines

It was always music, in fact, in 1972. Sam could never erase the hum of a melody from his thoughts for long. Whenever he tried (infrequently), the music was playing somewhere else, outside, to be heard and heard and heard. Not that Sam objected. It was just as often *his* music playing as anything else: from the tinny pocket transistor radio purchased at the base PX, or the small cassette tape player he carried everywhere they would let him. True, the radio only broadcast Army frequency programming - hence the "Moldy Oldies" that the brass considered safe enough for G.I. ears. (Didn't they think every kid in the world *knew* that John and Yoko were sitting naked in bed singing *Give Peace A Chance*? *I Wanna Hold Your Hand* was so ancient as to be dead, just like Paul McCartney and the Beatles in general.)

The tape deck was better than the radio, even if it wasn't 8-track quality. A week before shipping out to Germany, Sam had plugged it into a homegrown radio station and recorded as many hours of *real* American soul as he could remember to change ninety-minute cassettes. They were getting scratchy now, those two dozen tapes, played to death filling Sam's homesick ears with deejay noises, commercials and - just to change the pace - a song every once in a while. Sam was going broke buying batteries for the damn thing! Every night, after lights out, he'd snap in the earplug and pop in a cassette for his own repeated hour of home. Fall asleep that way. Wake up next morning with six brand-new, drained-out C-cell batteries, tape wound tight to the end - still trying to play some tunes.

You could make fun of the commercials, but they were home, too. At least that's what Sam always thought. Like today, trucking down a street in Frankfurt on a 12 hour pass, somewhere off the main *strasse*s.

"Wantoo watari - use Afro-Sheen!" the chorus chanted, and Sam thought of the decent 'fro he'd left behind at boot camp. Home. Not like right now - on a street you and your G.I. Joe fellow troopers could find in almost any European city - but rarely did - simply by taking one step out of the mainstream and turning left. This weren't home.

And everybody else was someplace else by now.

Sam's eyes had been glued to the display window, his focus somewhere miles beyond, as the band of G.I.s jostled one another down *Zeilstrasse* searching for tapes and electric wristwatches in the discount (read: "tourist") stores. A minute later, five minutes perhaps, Sam looked up from the display window to discover that he was abandoned.

It didn't matter. They'd all of them wind up at the U.S.O., that was a given, for the 2300-hours bus back to base. (It was free - and why hassle with the effort of trying to *Spreichen zie Deutsche* by using the German trolleys?) Anyway, Sam had his piece of home hanging from his left hand: he popped in the earplug and flicked the "play" switch to Dark Soul's finest "Midnight Hour."

"You are here, brothers and sisters, you are here…" Dark Soul cooed, leaving Samuel T. Williams free to take that step off the broad expanse of *Zeilstrasse* and follow tiny display windows down the winding, narrow street.

They held objects he did not even comprehend.

Small figurines from cultures past.

A blown-glass crystal of infinite depths.

Why did Dark Soul play *Angie* now? Those Stones were white boys?

But Angie, Angie, ain't it good to be alive?

The Dresden figurines stood frozen in their centuries-old poses, the formal dance about to begin: a gentleman's tentative bow, his intended's rejecting (but not quite) poise of her fan - and a spark-ling eye. Sam stared down at them, shrugged them off. Wandering aimlessly.

"Soldier, halt!"

Instinctively, Sam ceased to move upon hearing the familiar tone of command, his body drawing up straight to attention. (Not quite a *snap* - it *was* free time off base, after all.) Sam hesitated a brief moment to wait for further command - none - then right-faced to the direction of the voice.

Master Sergeant A. L. McMasters, Military Police.

Was not in uniform. Was not standing behind Sam. Was, in fact, sitting at a small table in a quiet beer garden, separated from the street by a low but impassable hedge of rose bushes. A chess board was set out on the table. The dark black, very large man sitting there was not in uniform as Sam was, but dressed in civvies that would pass as German style if he were white. Not a pretense, just a passing, comfortable nod to the locale - in which McMasters seemed fairly comfortable.

"You doing anything, soldier?"

Sam felt the universal guilt of everyone when asked that type of question by the police - particularly by an MP one has trespassed only a week before.

"No, sir," he answered after an obvious hesitation.

McMasters stared up at the cloud-mottled sky before asking his next question:

"You got anything better to do?"

He heard only silence in response. McMasters was forced to shift his gaze back down to the fresh meat recruit.

"I need a partner. You're it," he said with awkward curtness, fully aware that - to the young private's ears - it came across as a martial command.

Well, not precisely. Sam did not exactly gawk at the sergeant, but his eyes indicated clearly that he was searching hard in the back of his mind for some data on what this situation was all about. McMasters was not unperceptive: his next words came as a suggestion firmly patient in tone:

"Sit down. I'll pay for the beer." Neither friendly nor aggressive. It still sounded like a command to the fresh meat private.

And it didn't pay to cross the police. Sam understood too clear the predicament he was in. Uncomfortably, he followed the rose hedge down the street to the beer garden's entrance.

It was a restaurant's entrance, actually, one whose rear door opened onto the beer garden. Not an elegant place, but also not the fast food/immigrant food/serviceman bar-type of place Sam had ever been to in Germany before. Already disconcerted by the MP sergeant's unexpected appearance and invitation, Sam stopped mid-way through the entrance to get his bearings. It was heavy: no strong music or crowds to shove past - and no one who looked like he or she particularly spoke English. The young Detroit émigré felt very alone suddenly. He hurried through the restaurant as soon as he caught sight of McMasters through the rear door.

"They's only Germans here!" he exclaimed in a conspiratorial whisper, as if McMasters needed to be let-in on the heretofore hidden secret of the place.

"Um-hmm," McMasters nodded in agreement while signalling "two" to the waitress following in Sam's nervous wake. With the same hand he gestured for the private to sit down. Sam obeyed with a clang of his chair against the back of a neighbor's.

"How you talk to 'em?" he asked in amazement. McMasters' equanimity in the face of such, such "foreign"-ness contradicted almost every G.I. maxim Sam had learned to date.

The hulking black man - he made Sam look almost pale enough to "pass" by comparison - merely shrugged, arranging hand-carved wooden figures in mysterious formation upon the checkered game board.

"Some of them speak English, I suppose. I speak German." He looked up from his task. "How do *you* talk to them when you're getting around, private?"

There was a distracted air about McMasters' gaze, as if everything he looked at he was not seeing as it was. Sam did not totally notice this when he confidentially explained his experienced methodology:

"That's different. You can yell at 'em. They understand then."

McMasters' eyes saw Sam as he was now; they severely focused on the nineteen year-old's face.

"Where you from, …Williams?" he asked, reading Sam's name for the first time from the I.D. tag above the private's uniform breast pocket.

"Detroit." It didn't enter Sam's mind to call the sergeant by name.

"Finish high school?"

Sam's turn to shrug. "Sort of, you know, 'blood." He smiled to the brother across the table

McMasters knew. He held up a piece from the chessboard, the smallest piece, plainly carved, of which there were many:

"This is a Pawn. It's like you: a nothin' G.I. - But you're gonna have to think like a King here to keep my afternoon interesting."

The waitress, addressing McMasters in German, fortunately brought two full steins of beer at that moment. *Real* steins. Full of *real* beer: hand-drawn lagers excellent even by German standard. McMasters plowed into the afternoon, semi-reconciled to his fate. This awkward hour was an investment in his future. If it paid off, not every Saturday would have to be as tedious as this.

* * * * * * * * *

It requires time and dedicated inquiry to understand the roots of a war, of a specific national hatred. Who has the patience? Certainly no one in the world connected with Vietnam ever did, certainly not in 1972.

To Sam Williams, Vietnam was - well - not something to think too hard about. 'Nam was the backdrop to all his memories for the past eight years, almost half his life. Always was and always will be. There. The draft snatch you up, Vietnam where you land. Luck only to be here in Frankfurt for a tour of duty.

It was not much different for Hals or Jens or Gerta or the other three thousand nineteen year-olds from Heidelberg marching through Frankfurt this weekend between classes. Vietnam was always there. Or, perhaps maybe, the German teens had a slightly wider perspective (if equally impatient with detail): the United States was in Southeast Asia aided by the compliant silence of its Common Market allies in Europe. Yet another reason to reject their parents. First the Nazis, now the Americans - the German *bourgeoisie* was hopelessly corrupted by imperialism.

You could see it in their parents' automobiles: prosperous Mercedes and shiny polished new BMWs. Too many Porches, admittedly sleek and sexy, but didn't Hitler subsidize the Porsche firm? "I hate American imperialism," Franz (a friend of Gerta's) could say with sincerity, his passion whipped up by repeated listenings to the Jefferson Airplane song - oh, that Grace Slick!

> *Volunteers:*
> *Got a revolution*
> *GOT a revoluTION!*
> Oh, Grace! I love you: get the hell out of Vietnam,

GET THE HELL OUT OF VIET NAM!

> *We're volunteers of Ameri-ka*
> *Volunteers of Ameri-ka*
> *Volunteers of Ameri-ka*
> *Volunteers of Ameri-*

Ka-aah...
Why does *mein* Daddy look so smug?
Why DOES *mein* Daddy look so smug?
We're dirty, cor-rupt, helpless slugs
Why does *mein* Daddy...

The U.S. Army's presence in West Germany was impressive. As part of the front line NATO defense against imminent Soviet invasion via East Germany, hundreds of thousands of American soldiers stood ready to defend this foreign soil with their lives. The same defense they gave to the South Vietnamese against the encroachments of the Communist North.

A base the size of a small German city squatted on the edge of Frankfurt, the green-grey barracks and clean, brown streets a comforting presence for the vulnerable Bonn government. Oh, sure, politicians like Willy Brandt talked about *rapprochement* with their relatives on the Soviet-controlled side of Germany, mimicking the *detente* policies of Henry Kissinger, the American President Richard Nixon's pet Secretary of State. (German-born, of course. A Jew, *ja?*) But *realpolitik* dictated a different reality. The North Atlantic Treaty Organization required the United States to defend her European allies: we would stand by our promises, even if the children of our allies misunderstood the purpose.

Hals, Jens, Gerta and Franz and their three thousand friends milled outside the front entrance to the base, screaming their misunderstanding of NATO at the tops of their voices.

Which did not trouble Sam's mind this Sunday morning. Strolling down Company A Street with a bellyful of scrambled eggs and potatoes, only a small inkling of homesickness pricked at Sam's heart.

His bunkmate, J.C., had returned from a week's work detail (courtesy of the unfortunate strip joint episode). Sam was happily recounting the escapees' adventure at the camp gate - and the unexpected freebie meal from McMasters it led to for Sam just yesterday. The protesters' chants echoed like a sports arena cheer over the treetops, to reach the young soldiers' ears stripped of violent emotion. A reassuring sound in some ways: it was very easy for the G.I.s to imagine that a German soccer game was in progress, the Frankfurt home team winning. Reality is how an event is perceived.

A.L. McMasters did not perceive the muffled screams as anything other than what they were intended. In four tours of Germany since his enlistment in '51, McMasters had practiced the *Deutsche* language to the point where the students' taunts were understood now with ease. The sergeant didn't pass on an interpretation of their obscenities to the twenty MPs standing guard at the front gate under his command. They all felt the tension clearly enough without benefit of literal translation.

Perception. To the MPs, the shouting protestors wore an expression of cowlike unanimity. For a vague moment McMasters saw a horde of Chinese charging down on him from a hill in Korea…

Then he refocused again on the earnest, immature faces standing behind the wooden barricade only a few feet away - and he heard the truth of some of their protestations, despite the ugly simplicity imposed upon it.

Can't they see the other truth?, the dark man asked himself.

Don't they fear the fields of plowed earth sown with land mines cutting like a wall only a hundred kilometers to the east?

No, they didn't. McMasters did not waste another moment on the question, the answer being so obvious. From their white-bread safety, they couldn't see that prison for the East Germans. Couldn't see it any more than LBJ had never understood how a nigger fighting a gook had every right to feel betrayed by his country when he looked back and saw pale boys sitting up in Washington calling all the shots.

My country, right or wrong. Even that sentiment didn't play well when you were thinking about it in Germany.

"You keep cool, cowboys," McMasters reminded his MPs, walking down the guard line to reassure them of his support. He wasn't worried. Experience told him it would be a calm demonstration.

Besides, all of the German liberals were somewhat off-balance at the moment, anxious to re-establish a moral center after the fiasco of initially supporting the Black September terrorists at the Olympics - and then watching with horror the unexpected violence that ensued. Just as important to McMasters' immediate concern, these students were out-of-towners: kids ready to have a little fun in Frankfurt after a few hours' conscience relief. The MP sergeant headed into camp to let the Officer of the Day know that everything was under control.

The two G.I.s passed only a yard in front of McMasters.

The white boy jerked a quick salute at the unexpected appearance of a superior. The black kid saw him, too, but sauntered past.

"Soldier, halt!"

McMasters' voice held none of the patience for Sam Williams it had carried the afternoon before.

"What the hell do you think you're doing, soldier?!"

It was something of a relief to the twenty-one year veteran to take out his political frustrations on Private Samuel T. Williams of Deetroit. Master Sergeant A.L. McMasters, Military Police, explained in *blistering* detail the entire lexicon of military protocol. It was a tirade worthy of his days as a drill instructor, guaranteed to wither ears and private parts.

And to J.C. Levitt, also of private rank, formerly of Long Island, New York, came the budding realization that his bunkmate was full of bull: that MP sergeant was no "best buddy of Sam T. Williams - let me get away with shit." That MP sergeant was the Non-Com From Hell.

* * * * * * * * *

If you think of chess, you think of war. Not as a helpless participant, but as Napoleon must have felt it: an abstraction - with real losses.

McMasters had explained this to Sam three times that first Saturday afternoon, a dozen times in the week since. The Sunday morning dressing-down had led to an hour-a-day punishment detail: janitorial clean-up of the sergeant's office. In reality it became for Sam a daily lesson in the mechanics of the game.

"Why you making me learn this stuff?" Sam asked in annoyance somewhere between McMasters' third and sixth lectures on strategy.

McMasters turned his angry-looking eyes on the PFC and thought about whether he should level with the kid or not. Truth: the MP had only recently developed a passion for the game, then sadly discovered that none of his non-com colleagues shared the obsession.

Answer: "I give orders, private, I don't ask for questions about those orders." McMasters was nothing if not willing to abuse his authority and cow a private into becoming his regular chess partner.

But first you had to learn the game, the "hows" and (more important) "whys."

Which, for some reason, caused Sam to think of how a Knight moved across the chessboard - even as the enemy's tank was bearing down upon his position.

This was a game, too: war game. Not much different than chess in its way. Field exercises against supposed Russian tanks rolling across the German countryside in armored superiority to the NATO defenders. Ground rules: Air power is not a factor - the two forces cancel out each other. Ignore the probability of nuclear arms - the Ruskies wouldn't send their own tanks into a target area. Assume that you have survived up to this point - a big "if", but the basic assumption that all land soldiers must make if they are to keep their sanity -

An abstraction with real losses.

They marked you "dead" at random in these games.

The lieutenant was dead, the captain... was wherever captains get to at times like this, officially "regrouping" somewhere further back on the other side of an open field. Sam and his seven fellow lost souls were supposed to either scramble back to the regrouping point - or get "killed" in the process.

An "enemy" tank was bearing down upon them.

J.C., like he always did in these exercises, played John Wayne: he leaped to his feet, "shot" a dozen rounds at the steel armored monster, and was promptly tagged "dead" by the referees. The remaining six dogfaces cowered behind various trees. Sam dived under a thick bush.

Without intending to, Sam found himself admiring the lush, autumn-colored countryside. It was impossible to imagine such deep reds and oranges. *Vermillion.* The word crept into Sam's mind from eighth grade art class. The colors were vermillion.

The tank was olive drab.

A Knight moves two spaces forward, then one space to the side. Or one space, then two spaces. A sideways "L".

Always a bit of a ruse, Knight moves, McMasters said: your opponent never really can tell where a Knight will go. The tank's driver would see his direction of retreat clearly if Sam was not careful and accidentally rustled the bushes.

Very clearly. The lieutenant commanding the "enemy" tank laughed at the clumsy G.I.'s retreat. Even if he couldn't actually see the man, it was easy for the tank commander to follow the rustling bushes. According to the map there was another field on the opposite side of this stand of forest, easy enough to score a few more "victims", just follow the -

The tank lieutenant let out a voluble "Damn!"

A referee had just flagged him to a halt and was drawing a large "X" in chalk across his turret. Blown up. Destructo. Wasted.

"Why? Goddammit, why?!"

Sam tried to drop down into the cover of the hedges behind the tank, his anti-tank weapon successfully "fired" into the vehicle's ass end - but his fellow squad members crowded around him with congratulations:

"Good goin', bro! Down 'em!" Even poor, "dead" J.C. shouted his enthusiastic appreciation.

Sam pushed them away, ducked down, and began running like mad. "Move it! They comin'!" he urged between strides.

"Hey, man, it's only practice!"

Sam did not look back to shout, "You practice! I be playin'!", disappearing into the next tangle of hedges as he did so.

A moment later, six G.I.s were "captured" by a superior "enemy" force. Private Samuel T. Williams was the only survivor to explain this to his captain back at the regrouping rendezvous. His achievement earned him an overnight pass. It was only fair: Sam was the only one in his entire company who came through the day "alive."

He didn't take the pass: it wasn't enough to do anything but go out and get drunk. Alone. Wednesday nights no one got passes except officers and a few non-coms and - this Wednesday night - a few "heroes" like Private Samuel T. Williams.

Besides, it was more fun to listen to them tell "war stories" about his heroics.

"Pow, pow, pow! Five, count 'em, FIVE!" (It was three, actually.) "Another cow-boy!"

The PX Serviceman's Canteen echoed with the linoleum-bounced sound of Sam's "dead" friends' praise. J.C., adding his own John Wayne twist to Sam's exploits, crawled under table after table, popping up holding an invisible anti-tank weapon (which fantastically became a multi-firing marvel), destroying tank after tank: "Kablowee, pil-grim!"

"No, man: Sam be 'Super Fly'," disagreed a Chicago brother who tolerated Sam's bunkmate only grudgingly. "The Man be in the tank, the Sam brother got the power - the tank be gone. Super Fly!" Despite the attempt at cool, the enthusiasm was just as grade-school excited as J.C.'s. In either version, they might have been making fun of Sam, except that their eyes all shone with uncomprehending admiration.

Which Sam did not notice.

He laughed good-naturedly, instead, enjoying the camaraderie, but surprised at his own displacement from it. Gradually, the conversation moved to other topics and, after a trip to the service bar for a fresh round of Cokes, slid down the long cafeteria table away from the Man of the Day.

Still smiling at the new stories cropping up, Sam unconsciously let his left hand trace an "L" on the formica tabletop. Repeatedly. Noticing the gesture at last, he gave it a definite hop-hop - turn left - hop definition: Knight takes Rook. Three times.

'Never work in chess, he realized. *Only two Rooks, not three. Overkill don't win games against opponents not there.* It was McMasters talking in his mind.

No, it wasn't - it was something Sam thought up on his own. He smiled.

It was a weird two weeks following, and Sam never quite

remembered the way things happened in quite the same order. First thing he remembered, always (even if it didn't happened first), was flopping on his bunk, in a comfortable half-sleep early one night, when McMasters slapped a ham-hand down on his belly, its weight added to by a compact wooden box that rattled. Resisting the urge to cry out in surprise - no small accomplishment - Sam looked up uncertainly.

"Open it and read the rules," McMasters ordered, then turned and walked away down the long barracks aisle. Inside the wooden box was a portable chessboard with magnetic pieces - and a rule book.

"Then forget the rules and play," McMasters' voice resounded back at Sam from one of their conversations, always attaching itself to that particular evening's memory.

"Left! Left! Left, right, left!"

Parade drills became a part of that two weeks. There were always parade drills, since the first day in boot camp, but now Sam saw himself as a little chess piece, moving -

"Left! Left! Left, right, HALT!" It was time for the ritual bawling out. "How many the hell left feet is it possible to have!? How many the hell times is it how the damn hell possible to screw up this drill?! Williams!"

- pick on the first face nearby -

"There's not enough concentration out here! What're you thinking of?!" It was important to scream all of this crap at the top of one's lungs.

"I said, 'WHAT ARE YOU THINKING OF, PRIVATE!?'"

Startled, the three-monther stuttered the truth.

"M-maneuvers, sir."

"Maneuvers?!" This was not the answer expected. Still, it was one not unpleasing to another aspect of a non-com officer's pride. "What kind of maneuvers, Williams?"

"Uh," Sam was still too nervous to lie: this was the end. "A... a... a quee-"

"C'MON, WILLIAMS!"

"A Queen take a Bishop 'n it be Check ...sir."

* * * * * * * * *

What is the difference between Germany and Poland, Braun thought, when everyone is gone? Rachel, Lisabet, Dani, Elise... even Josef. He even missed Josef, who had never been much more than a coworker, and, in the end, became a desperately needed friend. What did it matter that the friend's attempt failed? For months that Braun had stopped counting, he'd lived on the hope that Josef had succeeded.

And, by the time Braun walked out of the American liberation camp and became "German," he had known too much ugliness to cry when he learned that ashes were all that remained of his life. His hope died too late to kill him. Braun owed Josef his life for giving him that false hope.

"What are you thinking?" Birgit asked, her little finger tracing the tired crease from the corner of his right eye.

"About dogs."

"Frederick? He is sleeping on the couch. He is a couch dragon." She pressed closer to him, both naked under the heavy down comforter and lightly starched sheets. Wherever the night air touched exposed skin, a patch of gooseflesh prickled with the cold.

"No, I am thinking of 'The King'."

"Elvis - he is old and fat and singing Las Vegas songs."

"He was young and alive once, but I am thinking of another king. The King of Mutts."

"Oh, a *kundel*, a street dog."

"Not just a kundel - a king. Are you going to record this like a good journalist, or listen like a good wife in bed?"

"I am neither, Herr Braun: I am a journalist, but I am not very good - too subjective, they say - and I am good in bed, but I am not your wife."

"Dialectics, dialectics…"

"Tell your dog story."

"He was not a dog - he was the King of Mutts."

How do you tell when feeling returns?

"It was 1946 or '47 – I'm not very interested in years - and I was part of the crew rebuilding Berlin."

"On the western side or the eastern side?"

"I never stayed on one side or the other long enough to determine."

He needed to build, the young Silesian knew that, only that. Wherever he saw bricks – in an organized stacking, in a pile, in a heap of rubble - he obsessively began transporting those building blocks to the nearest reconstruction. No one over complained about an extra pair of hands helping to erect a wall.

"I found the King of Mutts inside a burned-out bunker we were ripping apart for building material. He sat on the skull of a dead SS officer as if he owned the pile of bones attached to it. I had to honor his sense of disrespect for the German master race."

"Braun," the foreman shouted across the ditch, "get rid of the dog and bury the body."

Reflexively, Braun started to obey - and then the mutt growled at him. It was a typical Berliner kundel: ten kilograms at best and mud-colored. A swat with the flat end of a shovel would easily send him on his insouciant way. Instead, Braun bent his knees and tried reasoning:

"Bitte schön, mein herr, but this skeletal corpse was once an honored captain in Der Fuhrer's corps. He was far too much of a piece of shit for your fine paws to soil themselves touching."

The King of Mutts cocked his head at this, regarding Braun carefully. With a regal stretch and a yawn, he raised himself from atop the skull, lifted a leg, and pissed on it. He turned his ass-end to Braun, swished his stump of a tail twice, and trotted into Berlin. Braun began to laugh —

"He made me laugh."

- for the first time in seven years.

* * * * * * * * *

Mystery meat und rippchen mit sauerkraut. The thought flashed through Sam's brain and buried itself deep within the pillowed comfort of his bed.

Bed? This should be a cot.

No, it was a bed: cool, white-crisp sheets.

Where's my itchy green blanket? - Clean smell with too much chemical something, not the B.O. of J.C. on the bunk below and -

Where's J.C.?! - I'm not on my bunk, I'm in a bed!

A comfortable, sleep-calling bed.

Don't even need to raise your head to find out where you be… Just - did I ever open my eyes? - just sink in deeper…

A hospital bed.

Sam tried to wake up, to be startled by the realization - he couldn't. His head sank deeper into the pillow. He sank deeper into the memory of only a few days before.

Damn if McMasters don't know how to eat, though…

* * * * * * * * * *

"This don't be no mystery meat like at the chow line," Sam explained with relish, as if the man sitting opposite him had not partaken of Army food particulars for longer than Sam T. Williams was alive. McMasters looked around the German restaurant where he and Sam comprised the only two black faces. McMasters didn't care. And Sam was too busy being impressed.

"*Das is 'rippchen'*" McMasters replied at last, repeating the word for Sam's benefit. "*Rippchen mit sauerkraut.*"

"Yeah, I heard of it," Sam agreed, tactfully avoid the MP's subtle attempt at language lessons. "An' this be a Rhine wine, *Liebfraumilch,' ja?*"

"*Ja,*" McMasters laughed, surprised at the private's mastery of difficult words despite an almost total ignorance of simple verbs and phrases.

Sam laughed, too, pleased that he had scored a point with the sergeant. You never could tell, though: McMasters was weird.

"'You voting?" McMasters asked Sam back at the end of September. "New law, you know, eighteen and up can vote. Makes sense. 'You registered?"

"Yeah," Sam replied indifferently. "They give us all the forms when we marshaled in. Had us fill out the absent-from-home stuff just before we shipped out t' here."

"'You know who you want to elect?" Despite the short-ness of his interrogation, McMasters' dark, always-scowling face (real *Afri-can*! Sam thought) revealed a true interest in what Sam had to say.

Which wasn't much.

"Y'know... Nixon be there already. There's ol' white-ass Wallace down to the South... Course Democrats got McDonalds-"

"Mc*Govern*."

"Yeah, that dude... One of 'em... - probably Democrat, 'course."

"Don't vote."

Sam was surprised by McMasters' curt advice.

"Hey, I got the vote!" he laughed, figuring the MP sergeant was kidding.

"Don't."

McMasters wasn't joking.

"You don't know what you're doing. Don't screw it up. Don't waste my vote. Don't vote."

"It's my-"

"Don't be a 'nigger vote': you want somebody, know *why*. Nobody owns you."

"You a Nixon man, right? Figures, Regular Army."

"Fuck Nixon!" McMasters roared. "Maybe I don't *choose* to vote for anybody! Or maybe I vote Commie, for Gus Hall - ha! - whatever I do, I *know* why, I don't just screw around. You're just a street nigger!"

And he stalked away from Sam, out of his own office, away from the chessboard.

Sam sat there staring at his hands for five minutes. McMasters didn't come back. Earlier in the evening, tramwaying into the city, McMasters had said something about a "peace treaty" negotiating in Paris, about 'Nam. Sam said he heard the rumors, too. McMasters said to "Read news-papers, dammit! They're screwing us around just for the elections." Sam figured the MP was having his period.

Not tonight, though. The night in Frankfurt town was running smooth like a McMasters Special: cool wine, *rippchen mit sauerkraut*, tight game 'a chess -

Sam was having fun, and - although his voice and gestures were still a little too large for the German society they were surrounded by - he was much more comfortably a part of it than he had been at the beer garden three weekends earlier.

This was the fourth time Sam had gone off-base with McMasters. Some dudes in barrack said the MP was queer for Sam, but Sam played it cool and knew by now that McMasters' hands only touched two things with lust: food and chess pieces. Each time out together involved a few hard-nosed rounds of chess, of course, but the MP paid for his afternoon amusements with excellent meals. (Not hard to figure out why, considering the size of his gut!) McMasters avoided G.I.-patronized establishments like the plague and, as a result, Sam's exposure to the German lifestyle increased by four hundred percent over his first three months stationed in Frankfurt.

Rhine wine weren't no Detroit *Thunderbird*, neither. Rhine caught up on you slower, made your brain light - like hash (an attribute which Sam did not figure he should mention to an MP sergeant). It was a *good* high, pleasant to the taste.

McMasters came back to the table after five minutes of stalking around the *strasses* and acting like he cared about white folk politics. *Rippchen mit sauerkraut* was on the dark nigger's mind tonight. Sam thought he saw a strategy for taking the sergeant's Queen and challenged him to a new game after dessert. Some Viennese *crème* thing. 'Not Detroit.

* * * * * * * * * *

Delicate hands make delicate objects. Or so intellectuals would love to believe. The reality of creation has more mundane requirements: callused thumbs and scratched palms, hardened skin, strength - controlled, to be sure - measured out in careful segments of movement.

A fingernail torn - Jo bit it off with a taste of disgust. Birgit looked across the workbench and smiled her superiority, holding up a hand displaying five, trimmed-to-the-quick nails.

"That is from typing!" Jo protested, adding another gesture of spit-out distaste. "Journalism!"

"It is work with hands and mind," Birgit continued to smile, "something more difficult than simply *mouth* and mind."

"Bitch."

The doctoral student muttered this last epithet under his breath, attempting once again to fit the well-oiled parts back together without jamming them.

"All of us are," she cooed without malice.

Jo stuttered, trying to pretend he did not understand her reference.

"All of us are bitches, *mein* comrade," the blond-haired woman said simply. "Here, give me that -" Birgit reached across and gently pried the machine from Jo's fingers.

"It is not your fault that the mechanism sticks," she explained, carefully working the safety latch back and forth. "It is slightly dented here. See?"

Birgit pointed out the delicate pressure of metal upon metal where a clumsy spill had indented the handle. The twenty-five year-old man had to bend his head close to the thirty year-old woman's in order to see past the glare of the single overhead light they shared at the workbench.

"See?" she prodded, unaggressive, secure in her position as Braun's woman. "We women are all bitch-mothers, there is nothing you can do about that - except, maybe, to fight it - to fight the revolution. Or acceptance." For a brief instant of unthinking sensual jealousy, her warm breath made Jo hate Braun. Then he remembered that he despised Birgit and was saved.

As he drew back, Birgit knew what was in his thoughts from the unmasked emotions cornering his lips. She handed back the weapon without ceremony.

"It has to be reloaded slowly and carefully, this one. Better to use another if you can manage it."

They went back to practicing the assemble-disassemble drill, working long into the night until their fingers had memorized the motions. They did not know if this would ever be necessary, such precision, but the enemy did it; hence, so must they. It required a craftsman's skill, this art of violence.

Bank Transactions

Braun allowed himself a moment alone. Birgit understood and did not hover in the doorway, perhaps even making it a face-saving gesture: *her* choice to precede him to the van, there to wait in the crowded, nervous dark with Alex, Karl, Wolf - and Jo. They could believe that Braun needed to be alone at such a time, the last moment, really, in which to review his plans. They would not understand that his moments with her were equally as solitary. Birgit did not begrudge him this distance: Braun's touch was gentle and, if he did not ever need her, perhaps, at least, he valued her.

It was now November. Because of Black September, Braun had decided that his own group would wait an extra month.

Braun made no apologies for the fact that he did not consider himself allied with Black September. Their Olympics debacle set the radical movement behind a year and, worse, it was stupid public relations strategy, Braun argued. But he would not compromise their chance at freedom. After the Palestinian commandos took Israeli athletes hostage at the Olympic Village in Munich, then proceeded to get themselves killed or captured in the ensuing escape attempt, supporters in the Middle East had hijacked a Lufthansa airliner a few weeks later, demanding a trade from the phlegmatic West German government: "prisoner of war" for "prisoner of war". It was a successful tactic, resulting in the release of key September leaders.

Which would have failed if Braun had not postponed his own action: the expected public outcry would have hardened the resolve of the political leadership in Bonn, destroying all chance of the Palestinians' negotiated release.

Personally, Braun could not care less if the Arabs rotted in a West German prison. (What a "rot"! They ate better in jail than when free.) Braun's sponsors would not have cared, either. But it would have mattered to the students. Braun needed their belief.

And he could wait. Nothing lessened by waiting. He could wait.

November was cool and hard this night. He could wait.

Wolf hit the headlights a moment too soon, while Braun was rounding the front of the van to join the others. The beams hit him with the square force of their bright glare. Braun's throat grabbed at the instant memory of other harsh lights flashed in his face. A deep, cutting panic - but he did not let this show. You could never let it show. This lesson he learned well.

* * * * * * * * *

If I coulda told McMasters it would be no good, if I could have told him -

The hospital sheets twisted around Sam's body.

"You will have to be still, Mr. Williams, very still, your arm -

Who the hell calls me "Mister"? This ain't no po-lite Army!

"- is moving. We will have to put you under sedation again, Mr. Williams, if you continue to move."

The pinprick felt impossibly like - nothing. *I'm afraid of needles an' it feels like nothing.* Sam rolled his eyes up and tried to keep the pictures from printing themselves in his brain. But Frankfurt still kept appearing. He could see himself walking down the strasse with McMasters. Damn McMasters!

* * * * * * * * *

"I never done this before, y'know, but it's gonna cause a sen-sa-tion back home!" Sam motor-mouthed at a speed that had his legs walking faster and the master sergeant alongside panting slightly for breath. They were both in uniform this fine weekday morning on the streets of Frankfurt, the sweat beginning to prickle under the combined efforts of exertion and sunshine. "I mean, when I telegram this money to m'Mom, y'know, they gonna be surprised! They only figure telegrams mean somethin' bad's happened."

"Usually does," McMasters grunted.

"Not this time."

McMasters didn't answer. He was mildly regretting his suggestion that Sam put aside some pay every month for his family. Now the sergeant was stuck with the attendant obligation of showing the private how to deal with German banks. It would be easier if the kid would shut up, which he wouldn't.

"Nearly got you beat last night, didn't I? I've got one hundred here - shit, I don't need it."

"I need your passport, *bitte.*"

The teller stared glassy-eyed blank at the American Negro.

Sam refused to believe the man, even though the German spoke flawless English. "I don't need my passport."

"I *need* your passport - *bitte* - for identification."

Sam turned to McMasters, frantic. "How do I do this? What's going wrong?"

The master sergeant had expected Sam to stumble on the German bureaucracy. Now for the solution -

"You don't need a passport," he explained calmly. "*We*'ve got military travel documents. It amounts to the same thing. Show him your I.D. He'll be happy." The huge, dark MP smiled down at the teller and explained the private's misunderstanding - in German - to ensure that the teller did not take it upon himself to add another layer of difficulty to the transaction.

Instead, *Sam* made it difficult.

"I don't got no papers," he said in a tiny voice.

A hiss escaped McMasters' lips.

"Didn't you bring any I.D.?"

"What I need I.D. for? I'm in uniform, they can see my name here," Sam pointed at his name patch. "They takin' *my* money!"

Despite the irrefutable logic of that argument, McMasters managed a weak smile to the teller - "*Danke schön*, we'll be right back" - and pulled Sam away from the window.

"You didn't bring *any* I.D.?" he accused in a muttered undertone, pushing Sam over to an open counter.

"Well, no - I told you it was my first time doing this."

"What's the first rule of any soldier off-base, private? If you don't have proper identification you're in violation of regulations."

"Yeah, well the first rule of G.I. survival, sergeant, is don't let the whores 'n drunks get your I.D. I don't take nothin' into town 'cept my pass an' the money in my pocket!" It didn't matter if McMasters was a non-com *or* an MP, Sam wasn't going to let himself be pushed around over a common sense situation. Bullshit! That German knew who he was: look just at the uniform, then the name tag, then the money - weren't no two ways about it! Except maybe facin' the fact that McMasters was still Regular Army, and R.A. was always rules without reason.

McMasters was ready to blast Sam right out of his socks - and didn't. The Detroit boy was right, as far as common sense went. Common sense, for anybody still young enough (or old and stupid enough) to hit the regular soldier-boy hangouts, said exactly what Sam just said. Every MP knew it: look at the uniform and the pass, don't screw around looking for I.D. papers from the dogfaces going out on leave.

Of course, common sense didn't work on people like German bank tellers - or certain officers - or Pentagon defense budgets and the like - or half of life. But Sam T. Williams didn't have the experience to know that yet. McMasters surprised the defensive private by toning down his reaction to a look of mild annoyance and the proposal of a solution.

"Give me the money, I'll send it under my I.D."

"You?" Sam was reluctant to avoid a confrontation so easily: it had taken a few gallons of adrenaline to work himself up to talking back to McMasters. "You know, I was kinda hopin' to write this off my taxes…"

McMasters answered Sam with a withering stare that said it all. "Son, you're not going to be paying any tax-"

A shower of pitched debris: the entrance door burst open from the force of the van rear-ending into it!

McMasters dived to the floor, seeking cover, dragging Sam down as well. Sam's arms were still protecting his face from flying splinters when the van's rear doors sprang open: to a dozen gawking eyes there was almost no separation between the explosion of glass and the appearance of the three men.

Braun stood slightly in front of the others, weaponless.

At Braun's left shoulder, Karl swept an Uzi's gun barrel in a threatening arc toward the tellers' counter. Jo ran forward and commandeered the half of the lobby on Braun's right, jabbing his own automatic weapon in angry punctuation of his words:

"NO ONE HAS TO BE HURT!

DOWN TO THE FLOOR! Your collaboration will be punished only by confiscation of -"

"- a people's blow against the capitalist structure," Karl explained to his half of the bank, his voice incredibly high-pitched to his own ears, "a structure killing babies in -"

By instinct, McMasters withdrew his service automatic from its holster. Weapon once in hand, he was compelled to finish the action -

"*Nein!*" he roared, leveling his weapon at the youngster nearest him.

Karl felt impregnable: he swiveled his Uzi toward the impertinent voice.

McMasters fired twice, striking the down-bearded terrorist in the stomach and chest. As McMasters expected, the second armed terrorist, inexperienced and aghast, turned to face his fallen comrade rather than take immediate action.

Braun did not waste time resenting Jo's moment of indecision: already the Negro soldier was pointing his gun at the young man - at the obvious threat. Leaving Braun free to crouch down to the fallen Karl's side.

It was a natural movement, much the same as Jo's appeared to be, actually. The Negro's eyes wavered between Braun and Karl, chose the weapon-holding Karl again - and gave Braun the second's opportunity he needed.

Braun grabbed the Uzi from the dead boy's fingers, pulling the trigger as he did so, sending a hail of bullets in the soldier's direction.

McMasters bought it in the face first. Then, as the German took control of his aim, the Uzi's bullets raked down McMasters' body, sending the huge MP tumbling backward as if he were a spineless doll.

Behind Braun, Karl belatedly woke up to his duty. Turning his own automatic weapon on the attacker's corner, Karl fired wildly, heedless of aim. That was the beauty of automatic weapons: one did not have to be a marksman.

Sam took Karl's first shot in the fleshy part of his forearm, a bloody but minimal-damage blow that sent him spinning. And probably saved his life: the impact threw Sam's body against a wall, stunning him - safely out of Karl's subsequent line-of-fire.

Sam only heard the next gunshots anyway. His sight was filled with the repeated image of shattering metal and glass. The world turned grey, dust-choked. Half-conscious, half-protected by a fallen table, the wounded private witnessed the remaining moments of the attack in unconnected fragments.

Others had joined the shooting terrorists. One man with glasses and long, long hair was shouting words at the terrified bank patrons - and at McMasters. The young nearsighted German kept screaming in English so that the fallen MP would understand.

Don't he know McMasters talks German?

"- Your sweat will go to the freedom-loving organizations in the south! Be happy, friends, for soon your exploited wages will be sitting in Paris, drinking *café au lait*, -"

Don't he know McMasters be dead?

"- resting on its way before joining the forces of another revolutionary freedom army." Alex bent down to shout closer into McMasters' shattered face:

"MAYBE IN VIETNAM, MURDERER! OR -"

The firing had long since stopped. Jo with embarrassment attempted to replace his empty ammunition clip with a full one. It jammed, then (thankfully) slipped in. Braun covered the bank counter - while Birgit and Wolf swept out of the van to collect the tellers' cash in expandable mesh shopping sacks.

And Alex could not stop talking.

"- or... or to fight the Jew imperialists. Do you believe that?! We give these people a country and they sell out to Amerika, TO - BEGIN - EXPLOITING yet another people! We will fight -"

Birgit selectively gutted the large, walk-in safe, grabbing only 100-*mark* bundles.

Wolf, meanwhile, had destruction on his schedule. He stepped inside the walk-in safe and dropped smoldering, gasoline-soaked rags among the remaining paper valuables. Everyone began to take note that Alex had grown increasingly hysterical, tears rolling in huge globs from his eyes into his beard.

"- we will fight, we will fight, any oppressors of the people…" He ran out of words to say.

The dead Negro soldier did not respond to Alex's accusations. The young German turned to the fallen Karl and knelt down to comfort his friend.

"*Nein,*" Braun said simply, a consoling sigh. With a nod of his head, Alex remembered his duty.

Jo and Birgit stood by Braun, too, expectant.

"We start here."

Braun nodded to Wolf, who returned to the van and his post at the steering wheel. Alex stepped back into the rear of the van, to cover the bank lobby from there. Wordlessly, Braun directed Jo and Birgit to follow him, Birgit replacing Karl - as they had planned as a back-up if either Karl or Jo were put out of action. (No one had considered continuing if *Braun* were to be hurt. There would be no plan if Braun was gone, everyone knew that, and so they simply ignored thinking of such a drastic contingency).

Braun led Jo and Birgit in a straight line path across the lobby, past the tellers' counter, to a door marked with elaborate lettering:

GESHÄFTSFÜHRER
E. Sinder

The bank manager's door had already been blown open by gunfire, an inadvertent benefit of Jo's earlier inaccuracy. The office occupants - like all others in the bank - crouched on the thickly carpeted floor in submissive positions.

Braun uttered a single phrase - a question:

"Ernst Sinder?"

The thirty-five year old bank manager, prematurely graying, fluid eyes terrified behind fashionable aviator-style photogray glasses, rose to his feet - surprise at being so specifically singled out overcoming the desire to deny his identity.

Before the man could utter a sound, Jo threw him against the wall. Ernst Sinder watched, bewildered, as the blond woman terrorist roughly pulled his right arm straight, locking his wrist to the wall, palm-outward, between the fork made by her thumb and forefinger. Braun produced a hammer and a long nail from the rucksack draped across his shoulder.

Mein kinder, moje dzieci - the Silesian's thoughts never lingered in one language for long - "Flacker, feuer, flacker: Flamen in der hoyt" - maybe those were the words, maybe not. Rachel knew Yiddish words, she taught them to the kinder.

"Dreydl, dreydl, dreydl," she would sing, laughing. Even Josef's little son Ernst knew the Yiddish words when put to tune. All of the kinder *knew Yiddish words, because the Jews made good songs: Didn't you listen to them at every campout? Every* kinder....

Braun drove the nail through Ernst Sinder's right hand with a heavy blow of his hammer.

Jo held Sinder's left arm straight, but turned his own head

away from the sight: Braun reached across the bank manager's body with one step and pounded in a second nail. Only now did the fashionable young *burgher*'s pain begin to overwhelm his shock. A low moan echoed deep inside his chest, pushing upward in a crescendo leading to a scream -

Cut off by the rake of gunfire dragged across his chest by Braun's long burst of automatic weaponry.

Without comment, Braun, Jo and Birgit turned and ran from the room. They were not ashamed, nor frightened, by what they had just done - there was simply no more time to linger at the bank. They had crashed into the bank at 10:20 A.M. By the time the first carloads of Frankfurt police began arriving at the scene, only seven minutes later, the terrorists had been gone by two.

Which did not stop the *polizei* from cordoning-off the street at each end of the block, detaining everyone within the perimeter, sending out Alert warnings to all units yet to arrive. Precious minutes were lost entering the bank carefully, always attuned to the possibility that some terrorists might remain inside.

They were in full riot gear, those first scared officers to rush in. Heavily armed, carrying thick shields, the *polizei* were met immediately by dozens of bank customers hysterically greeting them and describing the atrocity - losing precious more minutes in the race to mount an effective pursuit of the terrorists.

Sam didn't care about pursuits. Even if he'd tried to concern himself with the *polizei*'s problems, the nineteen-year-old lacked the strength to concentrate upon more than one thing at a time. At the moment Sam was caught between holding onto

McMasters to check if the sergeant was alright - and clutching the man's huge bulk for support.

Sam knew that the MP was dead. 'Man had no face! 'Didn't change the fact that it was a private's duty - a *friend*'s - to see that a Sergeant, a *Master* Sergeant, looks good for the civilians when he's decked out in full of-fi-cial uniform. Sam gave a furious tug at the body with his right hand (his left still kept hangin' there, bleedin'), trying to bring Master Sergeant A.L. McMasters, Military Police, to an upright position.

Instead, Sam fainted into McMasters' lap.

Funny how, when you're trying to learn a language, nothing comes through for weeks and weeks. Words, maybe, are memorized, but they're almost divorced of meaning. Independent.

And then, one dreaming moment, you start to *think* in the other language. Full-fledged, crystal clear understanding. Sam heard the scattered German phrases, or he dreamed them, or they drilled into his faint, and the words always seemed clearly in English when he remembered them -

"...the man with glasses said 'to France'..."

"...six of them, no, seven, maybe only four..."

They had *to be speaking German, didn't they?*

"...I am not hurt too badly..."

"...the Negro has been killed..."

And maybe only now did Sam understand that McMasters was dead. He couldn't move to do anything about it, but it was perversely comforting to know that his dreams agreed with reality.

The policeman was uncertain which Negro was supposed to be alive: they both looked dead. The big one had no face left -

but the young one? He squatted next to the Negro soldier and carefully lifted the young man's head from the corpse's lap.

"You are in pain?" he asked the flickering eyelids that failed to reveal an iris. "We will help you."

The policeman remembered only after he motioned over the doctor that he had not spoken in English to the American. Oh, well: it was too late to worry about it now.

"How many are dead?" he asked the doctor.

"Only two," came the tense reply, "and this is the fortunate one."

Sam's pupils dropped back into sight at this: he heard the word "fortunate" as "happy".

McMasters is the happy one.

Sam could not bring his eyes into focus on the doctor leaning over him. The white-coated man was blurry. Sam only saw things that happened across the lobby. He saw them lead a shrieking woman out of an office. A cloud of smoke billowed from the walk-in vault -

"They have destroyed everything they did not take!" shouted a policeman ineffectively trying to put out the hidden fire with a hand extinguisher. It only made the smoke cloud thicker.

Suddenly Sam felt himself being lifted into the air! With frantic effort he raised his head - the still-blurry doctor gently pushed Sam back down onto the stretcher being carried between two thick-shouldered policemen.

"Why did they do it?!" Sam heard himself asking the indefinite white man. "Why they do it?!"

His eyes were blasted by a shot of sunshine as the *polizei* brought his stretcher out to an ambulance. A crowd of onlookers stared back at Sam's searching eyes as if they knew something he didn't.

"You speak English?" he cried out to the nearest of the curious. "*Sprechen sie Deutsche Englisch!?* Why they do it?!"

A warm fire spread up his wounded arm. The ambulance attendant pressing the needle full of morphine into Sam's veins answered in careful English:

"They are terrorists. Maybe from France."

"They spoke German," Sam protested dully, the warm fire spreading its consoling numbness into his brain.

The attendant altered his opinion - "Maybe from Switzerland then" - anticipating the indecision that was to characterize Official Opinion.

* * * * * * * * *

Braun took over driving of the van from Wolf at the third corner. An impatient Mercedes Benz taxi honked behind them. Birgit, sitting beside Braun, turned quickly to look around. All of them jumped a little, craning their necks to see if the horn preluded a more ominous sound.

Except Braun. His eyes remained glued to the road, calmly considering the traffic - something Wolf had been unable to do. Had Wolf still been seated behind the steering wheel, the van would have attracted unwanted attention with his fitful driving antics. Braun did not hold it against Wolf. The others - sitting on the floor of the van, Karl's body between their feet, were too nervous themselves to care.

The taxi honked again.

"It's nothing," Jo said to Birgit after a moment of uncomfortable silence, remembering that impatient taxis always honked at stoplights, especially the Turkish *gastarbeit* drivers. It was probably a Turk.

Probably.

Another moment of uncomfortable silence settled among them - until Birgit added the rejoinder:

"It's never nothing - it was a solid blow for liberation. And *we* did it!"

Wolf and Alex nodded agreement with this, a little too enthusiastically.

Jo, somewhat jealously, picked up on Birgit's theme:

"Of course we did it! *Action*, not words! Let them talk in the universities. Let the politicians babble away. *We - Do.*"

Braun continued driving, making no comment. The uncomfortable silence settled in again.

Jo needed to hear words.

"They kill people," he said at last. "They burn whole villages - and they will call *us* 'criminals'." There was an honest moment of silence now as the thought burned in, until - truly, naively outraged - Jo cried through clenched teeth:

"Just because a child has slanted eyes and yellow skin does not make him any less human than us! They buy their lives with dollars and marks and francs!"

Shallow breaths and shining eyes flashed ready agreement.

Birgit's hands felt very cold and she could not warm them up.

Braun heard their talk only vaguely. His attention was occupied by the right turn he needed to make - made - then found itself concerned with the necessity of segueing into traffic leading toward the *autobahn*.

"A pity about that Negro," Alex said in quiet deference to Jo's reasoning.

"A pity about that Negro," Jo agreed, suddenly filled with a veteran freedom fighter's weary wisdom. "But he was a soldier, a mercenary in the American imperialist army. He -"

The van was on the *autobahn* now, speeding away from Frankfurt. North.

"- should have joined us, not fought for his oppressors."

Alex disagreed. "But he had to fight us."

"Nobody -" Jo became very consciously aware again of Karl's dead body touching his foot, "- nobody had to fight us, nobody"

It was so hard to think that Karl would not be making dinner for them tonight: Karl was the best cook of the group.

"- he could have stayed down, like the others. He could have…"

Braun did not agree with Jo - and did not say a word. They had done this for him today, Braun was grateful: he would not contest their pride today. What was the Yiddish word for how they handled themselves today? *Chutzpah*. And the Poles would say it *Wielka chutzpah* - better than could be expected from any German.

* * * * * * * * * *

Rippchen mit sauerkraut, McMasters - an' don't you go puttin' no mystery meat on my plate. Don't go puttin' your hamburger face there, neither! No, neither! You're supposed to know all about tactics, mo-fo, so how you dead so much on me? How come you so dead? Whyn't you just lay down quiet like me in this bed - real bed, Mister MP, not no Regular Army spring cot or crap bunk. Why, I don't even wanta open my eyes from it...

They read his medical chart with a disregard for Sam's presence that was typical Regular Army - even here, in a civilian German hospital. A military doctor and a captain huddled around the German surgeon and discussed such private matters as blood count and muscle trauma without a thought of explaining them to Sam. A reed-thin Bavarian nurse acted as translator, supplying to the Americans a heavily-accented summary of Sam's condition. It all reminded Sam of a bad comedy routine on the TV back home. What was that show? *Laugh In?*

"Ve sink he iss doingk verrry interestingk -"

Yeah, *Laugh In.* - Wasn't that canceled?

"- tells us the wound is superficial, but you'll be on the inactive list for thirty days. Do you want to go home?" The captain was looking down at Sam, wearing his best professionally paternal expression.

"Huh..." Sam shook the clouds from his brain. "Uh, how many days?"

"Thirty, son. Do you want to go home?"

"Home?"

Words seemed to take a long time to have meaning.

"No," Sam answered with matter-of-fact simplicity. *No,* the word took root in his thoughts. *No, not home. Not right now.* Sam didn't think to question why.

"The bullets were of a small caliber, so they passed easily through -" The pros were discussing Sam's condition again, forgetting the patient.

"What really happened?" Sam interrupted, catching the captain's ear.

"What do you mean?"

"I - saw them kill - the sergeant. And then I - I musta been out've it - looked like they… they… used hammers…?"

What was it they did? A word from Baptist Sunday school mornings - *Jesus Christ, shit: They* crucified *him!*

The captain answered to a different train of thought, long processions of words bearing down on Sam without thought, emphasis or consideration: "There were twelve wounded, of which you were one, and two fatalities. The terrorists were judged to be six to ten strong, engaging in what appears to have been a symbolic act of crime to, quote 'prove to the people' unquote, their seriousness."

"… ?"

Sam could not think of what to ask. It made no sense, what he heard the captain saying. "About the people…?"

Before the captain could answer, though, the Army doctor interrupted to explain a bureaucratic problem that put paying for Sam's medical treatment about on a par with ordering pork rinds for the PX. The Army physician took his German colleague in-arm and faded away from Sam's bedside.

"Fine," the captain nodded to them. "I'm right behind."

He turned his divided attention momentarily back to Sam: "The thirty days are still yours. You sure you don't want to go home?"

Sam was certain.

"No."

The captain responded with a friendly smile that put a *But* - to his inflection: "'No, *sir*', private: don't forget that when you come back." He was halfway to the others when Sam remembered:

"Captain!"

His voice was weaker than intended, but in the silent hospital the word reached its mark. The captain spun on his heel to face Sam.

"Captain, my mother know about this?"

"Your mother! *Ach*!" the captain remembered, mimicking his German house cleaner as he hurried back to the bedside. "Forgot to give you this."

He tossed a heavy, sealed envelope down on Sam.

"Your hundred dollars never made it, needless to say. See you in thirty days, soldier." With a crisp salute, the captain attempted to make his escape once again.

"About my mom…?"

The captain only graced Sam with a walking half-turn to answer this question - "Yes, she knows" - meanwhile shifting into an accelerated gear to catch up with the others far down the hallway.

"We sent her a telegram."

Sam rubbed his face rapidly. An almost-angry chuckle

stuck in his throat. *Bad news again - sorry, Mom.*

Sam had accumulated his hundred dollars to send home in fits and starts; the envelope was heavy with one dollar bills. A simple flick of the wrist tossed it over to the small nightstand beside Sam's bed - where it knocked against the portable chess board. Board and envelope teetered precariously on the edge of the stand, threatening to spill onto the floor, probably taking an empty water glass with them. Involuntarily, Sam reached out with his left arm to save them -

"Damn!" he winced, drawing back quickly from the sharp stabbing pain in his forearm. "Damn you, McMasters! You even taught me to act *fast* like a fool!"

Nothing fell.

Sam watched the imperiled items wobble, then find a point of balance. A heavy footstep would send them crashing to the floor.

With nothing else to do, Sam waited with malicious patience to see who would be responsible for the mess.

'French Connection' Terrorists in Frankfurt

The headline banner of the *Herald American* tugged at Sam's attention for the umpteenth time that day. The English-language European newspaper had been left on his nightstand some time during the night, while he slept. They probably thought Sam wanted to read about what had happened to him. So far he'd resisted the temptation. He didn't want to think about it. *Wanting* did not stop the thinking from happening.

"Why do you not to go home?"

The Bavarian nurse was returning Sam's medical chart to a hook at the foot of his bed. Without missing a beat, she deftly rescued the envelope, chessboard and water glass from their dangerous imbalance. Sam was defeated.

And she was someone to talk to - whatever it was she'd said. *Why do you not to go home?* She stood there waiting for an answer.

"I don't know. Maybe if I thought about it before the cap'n asked me I'd a said 'yes'. Too late now."

The incredibly skinny girl asked the next question more from professional politeness - she was busy straightening Sam's bedspread - than from any real interest:

"You will go on to vacation then? Somewhere else?"

"Yeah…" He hadn't thought about that, either. "I guess…"

That answer was all the nurse had time for. She quick-stepped lightly to her next task of the day, arranging the *Herald American* comfortably on top of the other items, to ensure that they would not be spilled if Sam decided to read.

"Vacation… Maybe south."

Not Detroit

It had begun like this, *in a café.* It was 1955, probably. Braun could never remember. Was Elvis invented yet, or not? The day Elvis was created, the world of the young changed everywhere, not just in faraway America, and Braun found himself more caught in the race of its pulse than in the staid melody of his own time. But Elvis had nothing to do with that day, sitting in the café off the Kurfürstendamm.

> *Braun saw Josef Sinder for the first time in… fifteen years.*
> *He should have been dead, Josef.*

When he had agreed to help disguise Braun's children as good little Aryans - and they had been caught - Josef Sinder would have been one of the first tortured by the Gestapo. Unless the *kinder* were discovered at school ("You must make their routines seem normal, Josef. Make them seem like any German."). Or, more probably, Josef had placed them with another family - that family had been discovered first - and Josef had gone underground. *That was it! Oh, it took too long to think straight!* Braun hurried to race after Josef and - But first throw down some money on the table, and - *Where had Josef gone?*

Although Braun searched around the neighborhood for an hour, he already knew the answer: Josef had taken one of the public transports during the stupid seconds Braun wasted thinking, letting his eyes wander and his back turn. Still, he had *seen* Josef: if his friend was living in Berlin now, Braun would find him and talk. After so many years without feeling, he was ready to take the pain of learning how close his children had come to surviving.

Josef did not live in Berlin. It would be another ten years before Braun learned that "Sinder & Sons" was a growing banking concern spreading out to West Germany from a home base in Hamburg. In the meantime, ironically, Braun himself was expanding his horizons in opposite political directions that would eventually lead him to know everything about Josef Sinder. Everything and nothing.

He had fallen in love with rock and roll music to fill the vacuum of numbness. Elvis, Little Richard, Haley - later the Beatles, Stones, Who, Cream, Velvet Underground, Hendrix (especially Hendrix) - all who pushed his adrenaline into high gear and with a thumping bass to give his heart the illusion of feeling. Or maybe because the songs were in English. English represented the language of his release. By that logic, as a displaced person, Braun should have gone to America or England. But he knew there was not enough to rebuild there. By default, then, he found himself associating more and more with university students and others of their age, those who did not try to find false nostalgia in the past. Everything that they had was future. Even youth, though, could grasp at nostalgia with boring desperation. Braun grew impatient with those who latched onto the '50s decade, then with those who thought all life began and ended with the '60s. He did not try to capture the style of the ever-elusive *now*, he only knew from his time in the camps how to live it. How to live *now*. Without intending to lead, he found many following.

And recruiting. Braun's obsession with rebuilding had

crossed East and West Berlin too many times to count. It was not so hard to make this crisscross in the first postwar years. Braun's official "residence" was in the French sector, and they were such slipshod administrators that no one questioned his equally slipshod documentation as long as it had a stamp from *La Républic Francaise*. Besides, for the Nazi-disciplined officials of the Soviet sector, Braun was, in a practical way, living their professed socialist ideal: working for the community good without self-interested possessiveness. The Stasi, East Germany's bastard child of the KGB and Gestapo, took a malicious interest in him, of course. Over the late 1940s and 1950s there were five or six abortive and heavy-handed attempts to pressure Braun into committing to the East. However, with no family or other connections to pressure, the Stasi found the death camp survivor a poor candidate for intimidation.

They switched tactics when the Wall was erected. Noting Braun's influence among the young, the Stasi offered him continued East-West passage - for whatever his own purposes (they could always *always* watch) – in return for which he would bring young West Berliners with along him to "see the truth." A simple recruitment arrangement, really.

Until Braun asked them for help in finding his old friend, Josef Sinder.

Braun never had money: the search for Josef proceeded in fits and starts that ended always with his very small amount of saved funds going kaput. There was also the problem of Braun's *ennui*. Outside of his obsession with rebuilding things and a need to lose his thoughts in rock music, Braun found it difficult to become involved with anything else. To survive the camp, he had been forced to sever the nerve endings of his emotions; now Braun felt things only in unexpected, short-lived flashes. There was never a persistence of feeling.

In searching for Josef, Braun had also miscalculated, assuming that - since he had seen Josef in Berlin - Josef lived somewhere in the vicinity. It was so easy, Braun decided, to ask his Stasi contacts to find out if Josef Sinder resided in East Germany: unlike the more freewheeling West division of the country, the Soviet client-state kept very close tabs on its inhabitants.

It was, as Braun's Stasi minder noted in her voluminous log books, a too-easy task to move the immovable "builder" into covert duty for the cause of world communism.

Simply put, the minder found no record of Josef Sinder in East Germany - and located him at once in Hamburg, the West German Baltic seaport. And she did not tell Braun this latter half of her findings. Instead, the woman shared with Braun a rumor - a horrible rumor - about Josef Sinder. It could not be proved: if it could have been, the Stasi would have forced Sinder into becoming their agent years earlier. As a rising star in the financial world of capitalist West Germany, Josef Sinder meant more to the East than the unambitious, unambiguously honest Braun ever could.

That which cannot be compromised should, at the least, be utilized.

The Stasi minder - an unremarkable woman who, when later prosecuted in a periodic power skirmish within the Party, admitted to an attraction for Braun - she told him the ugly rumor about his friend: that Josef Sinder had collaborated with the Gestapo. She let the implications of that sink in without comment (her own KGB minder had taught her the value of patience), but she did ask the obvious questions: Where had Josef Sinder come up with the cash funds to start his banking operation not long after the war's end? Given his professed non-Nazi sympathies, how had Sinder survived the Nazi clampdowns on subversives? Sinder "helped" many Jews during the war - and yet *he* is the only survivor?

And then, of course, the woman who was Braun's minder slept with him, eventually "confessing" her frustration at being unable to locate Sinder in the West in order to confirm the rumors and help Braun. Only Braun himself could do the searching. The Stasi would train him how to do it, would provide funding, but only if Braun became more actively involved in their covert operations. It wasn't a question of spying, or of politics: it was important to find out the *truth* – and do something about a system that protected the lies.

* * * * * * * * *

Paris. Left Bank. Winding streets and lights and crowds of people as different from Frankfurt and Detroit as day is from night. Sam's left forearm ached from inactivity and healing: the doctors had taped it to his chest to keep Sam from moving it, then released him to the world. But overnight on a second-class train seat jostled everything in Sam enough to send the nerve endings screaming into France. Somewhere between a town ending in an *é* and another milk run village closing its name with an R (Sam made no pretense of knowing where the train stopped every fifteen midnight minutes), he retreated to the minuscule WC and ripped off the medical tape. The little hairs on his chest and forearm came off, too, bringing a few unintended tears to Sam's eyes. Yeah, this trip to France was a real blast so far.

So he tried not to move his left arm as he wandered down the *Rue Saint Jacques* now - night again - after a day of walking from one famous monument to another (the Eiffel Tower had looked so *close*, so had the Arch of Triumph - ha!) - crowded among its mélange of students and North Africans, a mist of lights curving off into side-upon-side streets. Looming behind the lights, across the river, the huge Cathedral de Notre Dame, her flying buttresses pouffed out impressively, looked down on Sam's meanderings but did not beckon: perhaps one or two of Our Lady's gargoyles noted that the young American soldier had become lost in the immediate attractions of the streets. As so many did.

Sore arm and worried feet notwithstanding, Sam was overwhelmed by a seductive fascination with it all - coupled with an equally strong, less attractive reaction: an incredible feeling of distance from everything he saw. There was nothing the young stranger from Detroit could latch on to as *real*; this was like being stuck watching one of those documentaries in Social Studies class that the teacher'd bring in whenever she got tired of talking. Except this was taking a lot longer to get through and there was nobody talking on the soundtrack to explain what Sam was seeing. Every corner of the sidewalk was crowded: nut-sellers tempted with their over-priced wares, next to Tunisians with their blankets spread out on the ground, selling the interlocking puzzle rings - in competition with dozens of others selling the same rings - all pressed for space by the open book stalls thrust out onto the sidewalks. No sidewalk cafes here: those that would have been were glass-enclosed at this time of year: *SERVICE NON COMPRIS 15f.*

Sam's stomach joined his aching arm and feet to growl in protest: You fool, eat something! Sam had been afraid to enter the expensive places lining the *Champs-Elysées* earlier in the day. Now, just ahead of him, three jet-black Africans turned into an inexpensive-looking North African bakery; Sam followed.

But, instead of warm and inviting, the bakery was lit by the harsh glow of uncovered lightbulbs. The selection of digestibles consisted largely of things that looked either fishy or sticky. An Arab behind the counter ran over to Sam.

"*Et tu? Et tu!*" he shouted.

Sam shouted "Yeah!" and pointed at something that looked like a flat coil - maybe it was a kinda cinnamon roll.

"*Deux! Deux!*" the Arab shouted back, holding up two fingers, then rubbing them together in the universal sign language for money. Sam forked over two francs.

The - noise!

And yet it was meaningless sound to Sam. Traffic outside on the street was so crowded that there was no whoosh of passing cars - though honking was heard regularly enough. A wrapping of constant, busy noise surrounded Sam as he stepped out of the bakery.

His hunger had overcome his reservations by now: imagination made the brown pastry he held in his hand appear positively scrumptious. With eager anticipation Sam took a huge bite into the sticky, sweet-looking delicacy. Disappointment. Whatever glaze was poured over the coil, it held no flavor; the cooked dough inside even blander. Sam looked at the delicacy in his hand with a sense of betrayal. Following the lead of every third person on the street, he let the garbage drop to the sidewalk.

It was only then, oddly, that Sam noticed he had gravitated to a quarter where the majority were colored: brown or black, they were almost all Africans. But, aside from skin tone, there was no kinship here that Sam could relate to. He felt more different among the Africans than he did among the whites of Paris. Unlike Sam (who, even with mouth shut, was betrayed as an American by the civvies he wore), the Africans spoke French fluently and dressed accordingly. It was weird.

Finally, though, Notre Dame condescended to beckon Sam, drawing the young foreigner away from the Left Bank and onto the *Ile de la Cité*. The combination of dark night and half-light from the surrounding city gave the island-lodged cathedral a seductively warm aura. Indeed, it was virtually hot within, compared to the autumn river dampness outside the centuries-thick walls; Sam could feel the heated air flow out from the front portals. He did not enter: a wedding was in progress inside, with about a hundred people in attendance, oblivious to the other hundred people, tourists, milling about the cathedral in constant movement. Instead of joining the intrusive throng, Sam's interest lingered on the bas-relief statues carved into the front facade of Notre Dame - there was one beheaded saint, holding his severed head in his hands.

Despite the early fall of darkness in November, it was still early evening. Sam plodded slowly back to the Right Bank, hanging a left just over the bridge from the *Ile*, following the path of least population. He was very shortly inside the *Jardin des Tuileries*, or so the sign said, a park unlike any he had ever seen, with the grass marked-off to be looked at, not touched. Large statues and fountains appeared everywhere - not the clumsy or patriotic structures of home - pieces of stone and metal with a wildness of life about them.

He was back on the *Champs-Elysées* - after a suicidal run across the Concorde Place, where putt-putt Citroens vied with Renaults for the honor of striking down any pedestrian foolish enough to think that a crosswalk was anything other than a target area. The broad avenue was more imposing at night than under mid-day grey skies, somehow filled with even more automobiles and people, looked down upon from brilliantly lit display windows by severe mannequins in more severe fashions, sidewalk cafes enclosed against the night jutting out into the sidewalks. Truly exhaustive hunger pulled Sam into one, to sit reluctantly at a small dot of an unoccupied table by the open door.

"*Ein bier*," Sam indicated to the instantly-appearing waiter, holding up one finger to emphasize the precision of his order.

"You are German?" the waiter asked with good-humored insolence, whistling his *S*s and growling every *R*. He held up his index finger in imitation of Sam: "Just do this, I will understand - never *this*," he replaced the index finger with an aggressive middle finger, "*n'est-ce pas?* Just this." He held up his index finger again - then wagged it mock-pedantically: "Don't speak German here."

And then he disappeared. Vanished. Sam realized that he had dozed off for a moment, sitting up. He was cramped between conflicting perfumes seated shoulder-to-shoulder behind him at their own respective dots. Every single chair was occupied by costumed, style-conscious patrons - a sharp contrast to the Rue Saint Jacques denizens. The waiter reappeared at Sam's table, depositing a bottle of beer and a glass in front of the young American.

"How much?" Sam asked, shaking himself awake again.

With a smile the waiter spread the fingers of both hands wide to indicate the number.

"Ten?!" Sam exclaimed.

A shrug was added: "You are here!"

The book had said *Europe on $5 A Day*: Sam was $2.40 in the hole and still had an empty stomach - *before* finding a place to sleep.

* * * * * * * * *

"So he hold up this finger and say: 'Not like this - like this!" The expected laugh. Sam appreciated the response.

"They all like that! Crazy!" An L.A. with Coke agreed.

"Yeah!" A Queens with Pepsi laughed. "Keep'em away from me, brother! Sure wish I was home!"

A nod from Atlanta. "Better to be with your own kind - not a buncha strangers."

"Righteous," Sam nodded. The U.S.O. cafeteria rang with the four teenagers' simultaneous pounding of soda cans on the table top. A twenty year-old sailor looked over with disapproval at the nineteen year-olds' immaturity. "Where you from?" he asked, his intention to put them down sidetracked by a tidal wave of hunger for companionship.

Pepsi answered first: "Queens."

"Me, too, that's what I figgered."

Pepsi and Navy were lost to the others now, delving into New York City lore, using any excuse possible to establish a connection; finding one, finally, at a pizza joint under the Jamaica Avenue train station.

"Shit, wish I was there, too. But not too far you can go on a three-day pass."

"Damn straight."

Sam cut in, eager to hear himself talk: "I got a thirty. They even said I could go home."

A buncha pairs of eyes stared at him.

"Well, whyn't you go back?" L.A. with Coke asked incredulously.

"I just... didn't." Sam saw the faces around him lose their familiarity: they looked like his own face. What did his own face look like?

"Damn! I'd a given anything to get away from here!" Queens Pepsi muttered, shaking his head, seconded by Queens Navy.

The jukebox was started up - again. They played it fifteen minutes on, fifteen minutes off at the Paris U.S.O. Half-a-hundred other Sams sat around the small room and listened to the same music they would in Kansas, Frankfurt or Thailand. *Black Is Black*, another moldy oldie. The music intro, though, with its steadily increasing tempo vamp stirred things in Sam's insides.

"- sitting in with people I know, not strangers like here. Food I know -"

"I was in Italy last month: why they don't even have American pizza there!"

"Things look good about home…"

"Yeah."

Sam walked away from L.A., Atlanta and Queens, heading for the exit; they hardly noticed his departure.

"Y'all stay back in Detroit."

He couldn't get the tempo out of his heart, and the fast-paced emotion forced him to try things he had avoided all day. Sam paid across a dozen francs to a teller at the *Metro* ticket booth, got a handful of *billets* in return, and hoped that he wasn't being ripped off. But he didn't begrudge the teller either way. Instead, just guessing at the names he had seen that day, he dived down into the Paris subway system, *Le Metro*, and flew underground for a whirling fifteen minutes. At one stop - the *Louvre* - glass-encased works of art appeared in the walls as if the underground train had wandered into a different city. Sam almost stepped out onto the platform, but there were only a few passengers getting on the train and the doors closed too quickly for his decision to be finalized. Two stops later he was disgorged from the *Metro* through an Art Nouveau wrought-iron gate lit by giant tulip lanterns to join the thinning crowds of Left Bankers on the *Boul' Mich*.

There was an Algerian bar almost directly opposite: inside there were others with skin like Sam's, and speakers of French. But they, too, were something of outsiders here. Sam took one look around and left the Algerians as he had the G.I.s

Sorbonne. The sign struck a chord in Sam's memory and produced a responding thought: McMasters had said the word more than once. Beyond that, Sam remembered nothing more. Nevertheless, he gravitated toward where the sign's arrow pointed.

There were more people of Sam's age on the street here, *Rue des Écoles* - and less street life than on the brighter boulevards closer to the river. Also more sense of direction: people were either going in - or coming out of - the dozen cafes that seemed to populate each block. Sam chose one at random.

And regretted his decision almost immediately, although for a totally new reason than his earlier rejections: the music stank. It was a typical French song (which Sam did not know was typical until he had heard almost the same variation for thirty minutes straight), a love ballad with almost no melody, certainly no danceable beat, only rapid words and heavy emotions. Maybe it made sense in French, Sam couldn't tell, but it appeared from listening that the singer of the moment vied with the Godfather of Soul himself, Mister James Brown, in seeing how intensely he could strain his vocal chords. To little effect: almost no one in the cafe was listening - which was why Sam chose to stay there despite the miserable music - grouped as they were in twos and fours, talking animatedly over cups of coffee and bottles of wine crowded onto tables smaller than the chairs upon which the patrons sat. A heavy pall of cigarette smoke hung on every piece of clothing. There were enough black faces to make Sam feel inconspicuous, enough white faces to assure him the cafe was really French.

For all the sense of denseness about the place, it was not crowded; Sam had no trouble finding a free table. After a decent waiting period - he noticed that the cafe's waiters seemed to have an important conversation going on that they only intermittently interrupted by servicing customers - a short-legged waiter (who still managed to slouch) loped over to Sam's table. Sam sat back in his chair. Not over-confidently, but with no hesitation, he held up an index finger in front of his face.

"Coffee," he said with definition - and not the slightest trace of Germanic accent.

"*Café?*" the waiter prompted.

That was the word: "*Café*," Sam agreed.

The waiter took a short-legged step away from the table, then half-turned to ask, "*Africain.*"

"American," Sam answered, adding an ever-so-slight French twang to the word.

The waiter's face twisted into an angry scowl: "Viet Nam!"

Sam did not react. To himself he counted quietly "*Ein, zwei, drei…*", then said clearly and quietly to the waiter: "American. Black… *Café.*"

The waiter continued to look at Sam, still in his half-turn, back still crooked in his slouch, with no particular expression animating his face. Finally he said in a British-tinged English: "This is your first night in Paris?"

"Yes," Sam answered warily.

The waiter lifted a bottle of wine from the counter behind him, plopped it in front of Sam.

"Drink wine on your first night in Paris, coffee in the morning."

The chalkboard behind the counter showed the cafe's menu and prices: a bottle of wine cost 20 francs - four dollars! The waiter saw Sam's immediate anxiety.

"It is on me. *Service compris*." He returned to the other waiters and resumed his important conversation.

It took a full minute for Sam to comprehend what had just happened, staring slack-faced at the bottle until a smile and a small, interior, laugh overtook him. He poured a glass of wine - red, he knew not what - waited until he caught the waiter's eye - then offered a relaxed military salute with his right hand and a wine glass salute with the left.

"You're a nigger, aren't you? Well -"

The face was white and feminine.

"- the Brits have made me an Irish nigger and I don't even believe in the bloody Pope. We might as well consider ourselves on the same side. -"

Sam did not want to have a thing to do with her.

"- My name is Ann Shea and I -"

"Go away!" Sam cut her off, caught decidedly off-guard himself by the young woman's introduction. Ann Shea ignored him and sat down at his table.

"A bit strong for you? You never heard the word 'nigger' before?"

"I heard it."

"You're supposed to use it, too, that's what the others say."

"I use it."

"Then why shouldn't I use- oh..." She let her eyes widen in disingenuous innocence. "You're not a racist, are you? You're not one of them blacks that are ashamed of being black, are you?"

Sam still had his glass poised in mid-air. He managed to place it back down on the table without further comment from the Irishwoman.

"You talk fast," he said, deliberately slowing the pace.

"Well of course I talk fast, if I didn't talk fast I wouldn't survive in this godforsaken beautiful city, would I?, where you and I are the only two people in this room who speak English naturally. May I share your wine, I buy the next bottle?"

Same was vaguely aware of nodding 'yes' - or at least Ann Shea grabbed at the bottle as if he had - while asking: "Was that supposed to mean something?"

Sipping at the wine with a healthy appreciation for its lack of delicacy, Ann answered in a more sincere, less aggressive mode of speech:

"It means I wonder what it's like to be black and trying to get a job; I know what it's like to be a Catholic and looking for work."

Sam snorted in disbelief. "How can they tell?"

"They can tell."

"Not like this!" he exclaimed, slapping his dark forearm for emphasis.

Ann accepted his response for what it was worth and sat silent, reflective for a moment. "No, not like that," she said in quiet song. "That's why I'm asking you, isn't it?"

"Asking me?..."

Sam leaned very far back in his chair at this, tilting it to a precarious two-legged balance. She needed *his* - what? Opinion? Experience? Repetition of stock phrases?

Then he began to speak.

Three things happened as he spoke, and each one was more surprising than the next. First, a group of students began sliding their chairs closer to Sam's table, listening in. This by itself was not unusual, Sam had a knack for drawing attention to himself. But he wasn't trying to be the center of attention this time - and even if he had, the simultaneous translation of what he said into French would have destroyed any of his usual stories and their timing.

And that was the second surprising occurrence, for Sam was not telling his usual stories. He was not telling any stories, in fact, he was telling his thoughts. He was not certain himself about what would come out until it did. Someone (and Sam thought it was the waiter, in fact) asked him why he let himself be drafted.

"Where'm I gonna go? Canada? Black boy in the snow!"

"You could have gone to Africa," Ann suggested eagerly.

"You got the money? I ain't no Panther, either!" And that was the first time Sam realized he was an American, too.

And that he did not mind Ann Shea's aggressive questioning - which was the third surprise. Sam found himself looking at a white girl as someone more than something either off-limits or the hourly wage-earner employed in bedtime pursuits just out-side base. He was looking at her and adding in all of the infor-mation he knew about Irish girls from the Catholic school in Detroit two blocks down from home. Ann Shea was older than Sam, but not by more than two - three years, with the pale skin and sharp features some Irish girls have, features not yet hardened by age into something unappealing. She did not come off too badly in the looks department either, Sam noted between pauses for translation or while waiting for another bottle of wine (the French students seemed to produce handfuls of francs at intervals enough to keep an inch of burgundy wine in the bottom of everyone's glass), although Ann Shea's style would be wiped off the streets if you stood her next to the typical Frenchwoman.

"You were really not so afraid of the police?" a wispily-bearded student asked in painfully slow English.

"I was scared of 'em," Sam admitted - then added a reali-zation: "They was scared of me."

"Because of the revolution, yes?"

"Yeah - No!"

Ann slid her hand over Sam's; it helped him to discover something, a thought, he'd never known he had before:

"They was scared because… they see me an'… who am I in *that* neighborhood? Am I a big ol' black kid wanting to play basketball - or a big ol' wild man high on horse an' about to go off any minute?" Ann's hand squeezed his and he understood his thought. "That's how *I* felt, too, even when I met some'a my friends - an' I wasn't no white pig target."

A jumble of faces and voices took over the conversation,

excitedly arguing the point among themselves. Ann's mouth whispered closely into Sam's ear, tickling with intimacy:

"It's not that different in Belfast, Sam."

He turned his hand over to grasp Ann's, palm-to-palm. Whether she squeezed again, or he did, the tightness of their touch was strong.

And when the question of where to find a cheap *pension* room at 2 A.M. was settled - there were none at 2 A.M. - then Sam had no hesitation in quietly, almost wordlessly, accompanying Ann Shea to her one-room hole. She was talked out. "You can pay me five francs tomorrow, Sam, if you've got it. Don't worry if you don't. I love you." She kissed his lips gently and slipped her tongue up between his teeth as if the erotic impulse it would give him was an everyday part of their lives. Sam slide down into the bed with her - a thick mattress laid out on the small floor, covered with scattered clothing and a heavy, worn comforter - and, even as his muscles fought a losing battle against weary fatigue, he was erect and hard, his abdomen quaking with anticipation. There weren't no sin this time, and no hurried glances at a bedroom door, listening to hear if parents coming home. Oh, God, she weren't no white girl and he weren't no black boy here in the pitch dark, her breath coming in short gasps into his face, his eyes tearing up in emotion. He just wanted to touch her face, touch her face, in the same instant that he could enter, come, stay, hold, as long as possible -

If only his arm would stop hurting. If only - one hour, two hours later - Sam could let the exhaustion close his eyes, instead of having to listen to these thoughts, the thoughts of a lonely, frightened nineteen year-old, whose mind could not clear itself of all that he said and heard that night, things *he* said that others listened to. Did it all make sense? And if it made sense, did he believe it?

Sam tightened his grip on Ann's hand - they had never let go of one another. It had to make sense, *she* listened. And it wasn't no stud talk or money girl that got her here.

Here...

"What the hell am I doing *here*?"

Ann, sleeping face-down on the mattress, looked up at Sam through a tangle of hair and half-closed eyes.

"You're with me, and we're both cold," she said groggily, sliding closer into Sam and pulling the comforter more thoroughly around their intertwined bodies. In the grey, pre-dawn light, Sam noticed for the first time that there was a small tattoo of a bluebird on her right shoulder blade. Ann pulled at Sam's arms.

"Put your arms under," she ordered, snuggling in even closer. "Sleep."

"I gotta do something," Sam sighed, without the slightest idea what he meant by the statement. He closed his eyes and, against all expectation, did not open them again until noon.

Cast

From one hilltop to another in the clear morning light of an autumn in southern Germany. Certainly, Jo thought, one could not dislike our country for its geography, especially here along the Rhine. It was the first day of *Fasching, Karneval* season, and even though the students would have no part in the city of Köln's festivities, Jo could not help but feel a nostalgic attraction to the notion. He sat in the front passenger seat - the plan involved having a different pair of front-seaters each time to discourage casual police identification along the road - and bounced along happily at Braun's side, looking out the front window with a cheery, insolent confidence. This would be a blast!

There was little traffic entering the outskirts of Köln: by 8 A.M. all commuters had left for work and the local shopkeepers (except the food vendors) were still inside their stores making preparations for the day's business. In the centrum traffic would be intense, of course; even crouched in the back Birgit could see clouds of diesel-colored smog rising around the immense flying buttresses of the cathedral. It was shameful, this corruption of the simple air. But the cathedral was on the other side of the Rhine, near the train station: they would not be driving any closer than the *Severinsbrücke* river crossing almost a kilometer away. Braun's plan was to stay in the noncommercial streets this morning, riding about the neighborhoods until 8:25 - five minutes before the start of the banking day.

The planned delay did nothing to steady Alex' and Wolf's

nerves. Alex was still not fully recovered from Karl's death; an anger seethed within him that made his actions unpredictably erratic. Some moments he would calmly set about performing whatever task was necessary - changing the van's license plates, telephoning his mother as if life was the same routine as before - and then he would simply forget: how to button a shirt, where to buy gasoline for the van, what he was saying in mid-sentence. This scared the shit out of the others. (Well, maybe not Braun: nobody knew what he actually felt.) Wolf was assigned the job of keeping an eye on Alex this morning. Which was why Wolf was nervous as Faustus at his last Sunday dinner.

8:20 A.M.

Braun steered the shining van (he had specifically ordered it washed and waxed yesterday) on a course directed at the small market square, within sight now and less than a hundred meters distant. Awnings were starting to be opened out over the sidewalks, sidewalks being swept and washed, fronting glass doors and display windows scraped clean and buffed only minutes earlier. Across the corner from the bank, in front of which Braun pulled his vehicle to a quiet stop, a sturdy *hausfrau* left the bakery carrying her day's bread in her arms.

There were glass entrance doors to this bank, as freshly shiny polished as the others facing the square. Although the entrance was still locked - it was, after all, only 8:25 A.M. - the clerks and tellers could be seen ritually preparing for opening. With a brief nod to those in the rear to brace themselves, Braun backed the van into the doors with a revved-up, violent crash.

Birgit reviewed the situation immediately: someone was

running towards the walk-in vault, pulling at the heavy iron door. She hurled a hand grenade over the tellers' counter in the general direction, stepping back to allow Alex and Wolf freedom to sweep the walls with automatic weapon fire at shoulder height. The explosion kept the vault open; the gunfire forced the bank employees onto the floor. A startled security guard ran for a side exit: Alex babbled Karl's name frantically but, fortunately, remembered to blast away with his Uzi at the exit - the security guard threw himself at the floor and crawled back to the center of the lobby, to join the other survivors at their exposed, apparently safe, refuge.

Oh, no, kinder: Do not run!

Whatever do you fear? These are our friends, these are your friends!

Who threw rocks today? Who shouted vile things? No one says these things to me, you are imagining things.

Oh, no, dzieci: Please do not run.

Silence.

With only the sound of his footsteps heard, Braun led Birgit and Jo through the smoke-filled lobby. As before, less than two weeks earlier, the administrative offices were just off the public space.

GESCHÄFTSFÜHRER
K. Sinder

"Telefonist, bitte besorgen Sie mir polizei! POLIZEI!" the manager's voice rang out loudly within the confines of the hard-surfaced bank walls.

Braun's voice interrupted his pleas: "Karl Sinder."

He fired a single shot from his automatic pistol, sending Karl Sinder sprawling away from the telephone, his shoulder taking the full impact of the bullet.

Without apparent command, Jo lifted the wounded man to his feet while Birgit proceeded to bind his hands and feet with heavy industrial tape. As she taped over his gaping mouth, a rope was slipped around his feet. A sudden tug on the rope pulled Karl Sinder's feet into the air and his head to the floor.

Jo slung the rope over the top of the door: through the opening he could see Wolf systematically ransacking the tellers' full cash boxes, Alex standing guard over the lobby. A momentary panic hit Jo's gut: *Alex has forgotten where we are!* He turned to Braun and Birgit to show them with a panicked gesture.

Braun was unconcerned. "They don't know," he said flatly, his thoughts in five worlds at once.

A quick glance back at the lobby convinced Jo of the accuracy of Braun's perception: the huddled bank employees were in a frozen panic, they did not notice that Alex was hardly looking at them, they saw only his gun. It was enough.

"Are you ready?!" Birgit hissed urgently in Jo's ear.

With a resentful nod, Jo hauled on the rope to pull the bound and wounded bank manager to an upside-down hanging position on the door. Birgit helped hold the man suspended while Jo looped the rope's end around a thick brass door handle.

The bullets from Braun's weapon that shattered Karl Sinder's body immediately thereafter caused the dead man to swing through the glass window cutting across the upper half of the door. Jo's loop held, though, and the body did not fall until the police cut him down.

* * * * * * * * *

"- They've done it for hundreds of years, even before your people's troubles started, -"

Ann rarely stopped talking when they went to the cafes, a fact that did not cause Sam to hesitate before joining her every afternoon.

"- they made it economic policy: almost a million people in one year, Sam! Can you understand that the Brits let so many people starve to death for reasons of economic policy?!"

She allowed Sam time to think about his answers, though, so she was really listening.

"That was a long time ago," he said after a moment's consideration. He was comfortable with Ann, if not with the topics she always chose. In her own way, she was not a lot different from McMasters, always expecting him to be on top of things.

"But it still happens!" she protested, not without a crack of emotion in her voice. "Five years ago the Prods blew up a school bus with my little sister in it. She walks on two half legs now. But do you see how many Prods the Brits put in jail?!"

"So that's why you join that IRA, yeah? Sounds like the tax man."

"It's not a joke, Sam. It's an army, a real army - for people! I'm not just talking about Prods: take away the Brits, take away their bloody *system* that makes people into machines in some capital enterprise-"

"And do what?" Sam cut in, annoyed at the reality of her frustration. "You sound like the Panthers, an' half the time they robbing banks!"

"Why not?!" Ann was unabashed by the comparison. "It's direct *action*, Sam. Someone has the power, they don't want to give it up. Here, let me show you -" she searched hurriedly through a pile of books heaped upon the small table next to them. Whatever she wanted was not there.

"Francoise," she called across the tiny cafe, and sped over to where a long-haired philosophy student was deeply immersed in another pile of books. The two began chattering in a low-voiced *patois* of English and French about probable locations of the obscure object of Ann's desire.

Sam leaned back onto two legs of his fragile chair and let escape a sigh of exhaustion. He let his eyes wander, too, looking around for orientation: there had been no chance to scout the place, Ann had leaped into her heavy rap the moment they arrived. The cafe owner flashed an expression of alarm at Sam's balancing act with the chair - unlike Sam, he *knew* how cheaply made his furniture was - Sam quickly brought all four legs back to earth: his Mom said not to do that, too. Which cafe was this?

Le Pendant - The Flag. Or was it *Les Pensées* - The Thoughts? Ann was never too clear on the distinctions. *Les Distinctions.* Sam found himself making-up fake Frenchy phrases all of the time now, his frustration at not being able to communicate with half the people in the cafes fighting with his natural inclination to make a joke out of the situation. *Le situation* - was that a real French word?

Real French or not, Sam felt comfortable enough with the situation, finding - with Ann at his side - an entrée into four or five cafes and the people inside that accepted him as one of their own. Give or take the fact they were French while he and Ann were not. (Sam dug the idea that the Frogs lumped him and Ann together like that.) They were all young, though, and that bond was something that seemed to beat out most other considerations. Even here, this afternoon, sitting in the comfortably stuffy Flag or Thoughts Cafe, loaded with dangerously sober students hyped-up on coffee (*strong* coffee!) and listening to mundane intellectual talk, i.e. solutions to certain course problems, and so forth. It even made *Sam* think attractive thoughts about college for a moment or two - before the idea of going back to school made him shudder with repulsion. He retreated to the security of a tourist mentality:

"Three days and not a one yet," Sam sighed, looking at the illustrations of famous Parisian attractions in the tour guide he carried religiously in his hip pocket. He did not take it out in front of Ann after their first morning together (afternoon, actually) when she had derisively dismissed the *Louvre*, *Montmartre* and the *Folies Bergère* with a disdainful, inclusive shrug.

"If you want," she smirked, then continued to lie beside him in catlike disarray for the next two hours. When finally they arose, Ann led Sam down to the first of many cafes, not-too-convincingly arguing that espresso with *tons* of sugar added made up for missed breakfast and lunch. By early evening they had come to the easily negotiated agreement that, since Sam would be saving money sleeping at Ann's, they could spend the profit margin on food - which Ann defined in terms of multiple versions of cheese and bread. After a day of gnawing hunger, Sam held out for some meat in the dietary plan, at which point Ann directed his attention to the deficiencies of her one-room flat. The bathroom was down the hall, shared: a weak-willed shower and a porcelain hole-in-the-floor for a toilet. Cooking facilities: non-existent. With an Irishly impish perversity, Ann introduced him to the subtleties of *pâté* (liverwurst, to Sam's mind) as a substitute for real meat. Sam broke down, upped the budget to seven dollars-a-day, and splurged on a daily hot meal for two. Ann did not object.

Sam enjoyed playing house.

"Fellas, I think we're gonna miss you this trip," he apologized to the assembled attractions of Paris in his guide, dropping it on the table and turning to the *Herald American* for the comics, page A-15.

A blurred photograph of Braun dominated the top half of the front page.

"I know them, you know."

Ann was leaning over Sam's shoulder, reading the newspaper; she could not see the glazed expression cross his face as he recognized the man in the bank fuzzily defined by a surveillance camera photograph transferred to newsprint.

"Um-hmm," she nodded with matter-of-fact confirmation before sliding back into her former seat and proceeding to open the textbook she had borrowed from Francoise to illustrate her earlier point of conversation. "I think I met one or two of them, even; I definitely know who they are," she whispered confidentially as she leafed through the pages looking for her specific reference.

"Can you help me find them?"

The words were out before Sam had thought of their meaning.

Ann looked up from the textbook; she saw now the impossible-to-read expression in his eyes. Sam felt a desire to look away, but his interest would not let him. He had not discussed with Ann, or anyone, his reason for having thirty days leave: for all his talking, he could not bare his emotions on the subject. Until seeing the photograph, he had almost convinced himself that he'd forgotten the incident; it wasn't anything worse than what happened in Detroit - or 'Nam.

"Can I help you find him?" Ann repeated Sam's words. Then: "Not for free," she answered, almost coldly.

In an instant they both shared the moment of astonished loneliness at the pain they were trying to hide from one another. Sam suddenly folded the newspaper back up and dropped it down on the table. Pawn to King-four.

"What's his name?"

"Braun."

"And the others?"

"Jo, Birgit, Alex - it's all in the newspapers."

"Is it? I..." Two moves before getting lost: McMasters would have been unimpressed. "I didn't see it."

"No. It's not in there, Sam. The papers don't know who they are," Ann's singing Irish accent sighed through the words with an intimacy that was at once harsh and confiding. "I know, and half a hundred others in Europe know... It's not a secret, but it's not for informers."

"You know..." the information continued to dull Sam's perceptions.

"And *you* want to know," Ann continued the phrase, bringing the conversation back to the subject of Sam's original query. She let the phrase linger, though, because neither she nor Sam was able to look at one another anymore.

Instead, she picked up Sam's tourist guide and idly o-pened it. "I'm not supposed to trust you..." She let the words fall, perusing the map on Metro connections, "but for the life of me I can't imagine you to be an informer."

"I got nothing I'd tell the Man, if that's what you mean." Captains and majors and lieutenants didn't listen anyway. "What do you mean, 'not for free'?"

Ann could look up now, and tell Sam her heart: "Sam, you can help the people. You have access to weapons that can be used to strike against the oppressors."

"And you want me to take...?"

"No, you want me to lead," Ann's voice was strong with-out harshness; she did not try to persuade because she believed both in what she was saying - and who she was saying it to:

"And I have to believe in you, Sam. To believe in you be-cause, if you want to meet Braun, I am going to have to introduce you to many people who operate only on trust and belief."

Not entirely sure of why, Sam nodded, "I have to see this man."

Ann gently touched his hand. "I've known you for three days," she smiled, very much appreciating the deepness in his eyes. "You are much more intelligent than I am, and have the potential to be very powerful -" The intimacy was growing too great, and she forced herself to add: "- when you make the break."

Quick thoughts and plans jogged her brain. "We'd have to go to Amsterdam..." she said quickly, voicing her first steps. Suddenly Ann pulled tightly on Sam's hand, exposing some of the pain that made her want to trust him and fear him:

"It's hard, Sam, hard: I miss Ireland like a dog! But at least I know I'm trying! You were right about Canada, about not going there. They play neutrality games, but they'd put you in a political straightjacket... Do you really want to do it and all?"

"Yeah," Sam answered at once, even if he did not know why he was so certain.

"How soon could you have weapons?"

This was another problem, from every angle. "I can't go back to base for another two weeks. I'd need another month."

"The guns are needed, Sam."

"Nothing I can do about that!" That was fact, pure and sim-ple, no talking. Sam's resolve hardened into part of an alternative plan. "Anyway, I'm not giving anything until I meet the guy."

Ann's twenty-three year-old pride was offended by the implication. At the same time, she respected caution. "You don't trust my credentials, Sam?"

"I don't know. I know you, and I know you talk a lot-"

"It's an Irish thing," she smiled sweetly.

"Yeah, Irish thing," Sam nodded dismissively, "but I'm not going to go over the hill just to find out you got a fantasy thing about guns, is all. And what's this about A-dam?"

"Amsterdam is where people I know are. That's all. And I guess the guns can wait - since it's *you* that counts. You're a soldier, you know their tactics, and we can learn from you. We'll set up a drop point for the weapons once we're in Amsterdam."

Ann was not displeased with Sam's assertive inquiries. It was *action*, not words. "You've given me quite a job to set up things," she explained eagerly, scribbling an address on a corner of the *Herald American*. She shoved the newspaper across to Sam: "Meet me there tomorrow night. It's on the *Liedseplein*."

Ann was halfway out of the cafe before Sam could ask, "Where's the *Liedseplein*?"

She did not bother to slow her exit, calling out for the world to hear:

"Everybody knows, just ask - they all speak English!"

And then Stevie Wonder started singing. *Ma Cherie Amour*. On the radio. Sam turned his attention back to the cafe to discover three other black G.I.s (in civvies, but obviously Army) dancing very well with French girls. It was time to leave the cafe at once if he did not want to become the Flavor Of The Month. Sam wondered if that's what he was to Ann: the exotic black fantasy, *à la môde* for the month of November. He knew he wasn't, but caring about her in return did not make him feel any calmer.

* * * * * * * * *

The man was not distinguished looking. Not today. An aura of command stayed with him, naturally, but that may have been simply a matter of position, the deference paid him by others, not an element of his personality.

"...were here less than five minutes," Köln's Chief of *Polizei* explained to the man, "so we were not able to blockade the streets adequately to stop their getaway. Using explosives they were able to disable the two police vehicles already in position, they..."

Yet, even to those who deferred to him, the man being addressed did not appear distinguished today. His facial expression was not one easily read; his emotions, either way, were not betrayed. Tastefully well-dressed, observant, he stepped through the rubble of the bank. It had been largely cleaned-up since yesterday, but there was still considerable evidence of the havoc wreaked, if only by the insinuation of the massive repairs being undertaken at the moment.

"This was destroyed by explosives," a bank official interrupted the Police Chief to point out the tellers' counter.

"They use a nondescript van," the Chief resumed, refusing to let the civilian's observation interrupt the flow of his technical narrative, "apparently altering or removing the license numbers, since no witness reports have led to a positive identification..."

They had crossed the lobby and were almost to the *Geschäftsführer*'s administrative office.

"...pursuit was suspended in light of the firepower they had previously exhibited and the known injured here on the scene." So concluded the official *Polizei* account.

As if by mutual agreement, they did not cross through the shattered door, turning instead back towards the entrance.

A second bank official felt it necessary to add: "They didn't enter the vault. They couldn't: they started a fire with the explosives they threw. Everything inside was destroyed."

The man they reported to, having reached the entrance door, surveyed the bank lobby and asked the Chief:

"How many *were* injured? Seriously."

"Three, seriously."

"How many died?"

"One here, Herr Sinder." The Chief looked at the bank's owner with a mixture of pity and awe: he did not know how he would react under these circumstances.

"They are killing my sons," Josef Sinder said simply, looking intently at the *Geschäftsführer*'s office, where the broken glass top half of the door was in the process of being replaced.

A'dam

Amsterdam.

Don't even bother to look at a canal as a first impression, look instead at Dutch boys and girls walking about in henna-purple hair, turtleneck sweaters and "fashion" clog shoes. Heelless. Sam could not figure how anyone - male or female - managed to shuffled across the cobblestone-and-brick streets on top of the open-heeled, thick-soled clogs. The old-timers' wooden shoes (and there were still enough of them around for a newcomer like Sam to gawk at) made more sense, even if they did clunk around on the wet stones.

It never seemed to stop drizzling. From the moment Sam arrived at the Central Station, leaving behind a sun-shining morning only fifty klicks south, a grey dampness sprinkled down on his clothing from everywhere. His cheeks were constantly wet from the drizzle and, even though his scalp did not feel wet, a reflection in a display window showed Sam that his hair wore a frosting of droplets. It seeped into him, making him feel more depressed than the empty stomach of an overnight train trip could account for. He was twelve hours early: there had been no reason to stay in Paris after Ann left, even with the security of a key to her flat. He waited now at some sort of public transport stop, nearly lost his left foot at the passing of a quietly running tramcar; only at the last moment did Sam remember that he was resting it on a recessed rail. Better to walk anyway.

And get run down in the narrow narrow streets with their hundreds of people on motorcycles, bicycles and *bromfietsen* - bicycles with mosquito-sized motors, noisy and foul-smelling (not to mention slow), ridden almost exclusively by high schoolers. It impressed Sam, though, that *everybody* rode a two-wheeler of some sort, even the elderly: it was a kick seeing ancient farts in business suits pedaling next to six year-olds. An older lady of uncertain age (but certainly over forty, Sam was sure), kicked back on her motor scooter, letting the wind grab at her basket of eggs and fresh bread purchased at the small shops lining the multitude of canals. They held their own with the cars, that was for sure, often passing the ungainly larger vehicles, which seemed to circle endlessly looking for parking spaces. Parking was accomplished by jamming any combination of two wheels onto the sidewalk. The nose of the car could practically sever the foot traffic route, but as long as the auto was roughly in line with the other parkees on the street side all systems were apparently Go. Sam wondered how such a practice would fare in Detroit. Probably wouldn't change much from the current mess, no matter what.

The two-wheelers even had their own roads in some places - La, De, Da! 'Didn't make it any less damp an' miserable. Sam was starved as sin and didn't know what to ask for in A'dam, a replay of his first day's shyness in Paris. He latched onto the rear end of a walking tour group made up of Midwestern middle-agers following in ragged procession behind a Dutchman in his late twenties speaking down to them with lofty condescension. The Hollander smelled badly of cigarettes and body odor.

"- They come here because Holland has a tradition of

tolerance, dating back several hundred years when -"

The Dutchman pointed at the half-hundred foreign hippies seated around the central monument dominating *Dom* Square. By his manner the tour was led to understand that such beings were of less-than-human status: Dutch "tolerance", well-renowned, did not have to include compassion. Place the foreign freeloaders on a par with the architecture: Come to Holland! See the Sights!

The hippies, for their part, played the role extremely well, ignoring the hovering tourists in general, posing for pictures with a brave housewife on request - oh, of course, a dozen guitar players - gently panhandling. As fate had it, none were from the U.S. of A. this particular day, so there were no unseemly confront-ations between the solid-citizen Midwestern tourists and any sus-pected, long-haired draft dodgers.

Nor was there anyone for Sam to ask where and how to get a decent bite to eat; he did not feel comfortable talking to the Swedish and German and anything-else-but-American youths. Nobody black there, either, although Sam thought of that later, after the tour group had passed out of the Dom Square.

It was so *small* there!, everything so crammed together, tall and thin, no room for Sam to spread his arms wide and holler. He had a perverse desire to holler, to make noise, be large, wild, AMERI-CAN! It was not a normal "Sam" feeling, this delib-erate need to express loud emotions. The closeness of Amsterdam was making him feel this way. It was cramped in places in Detroit, too, but not the same, not everywhere, like in A'dam. Everyone on the streets - the purple hairs and the grey-hairs - a lot of Asian faces (Indonesians, he later learned, looking sort of like the way

Sam heard that the Vietnamese looked) - they all kept themselves so, so *middle*.

Sam started thinking McMasters-style, comparing Europe on its own standards instead of against Detroit parochialism. Frankfurt didn't fit in to the equation: Sam had never been there alone, was always aware of his military status inside the West German metropolis. Paris was different. Paris was where Sam had been alone. He put Amsterdam up against Paris.

Paris was the opposite of A'dam: so grand - and always, always noisy - that Sam had begun to sink into himself, trying to find quiet and solitude. Escaping from Ann one morning while she slept her usual lateness, he had returned to Notre Dame. The cathedral was crowded, as always. Sam searched for a place to be alone, and found an empty corner to himself up on an exterior *balcon* (prix d'entrée: 2 francs) shared with a gargoyle. The gargoyle had his own ideas about Parisian life, sticking his tongue out insolently. It made Sam feel calmer.

There were no snotty-faced gargoyles in A'dam to do the same.

Amsterdam. Sam began to appreciate the grey sky overhead in a twisted way: at least the drizzle gave horizons a hazy infinity. He could imagine each narrow-banded street stretching off into emptiness, even if he knew there was a dead-end building just beyond the mist.

It was not unattractive, though. Sam found himself more instantly warming to the small-scale architecture the guide was rushing them through than he ever had felt towards the Parisian grandeur. He had no trouble imagining people living inside the centuries-old houses that bordered the canals ringing the *Centrum*, fanning out from the train station where his day had begun and back to which all roads seemed to lead.

"- there are a dozen such 'hidden churches'- or *kirk*s - here in the Old Town," the tour guide intoned, impressing even himself with his erudition, "places where religious freedom was permitted in Holland while the Inquisition was pursued vigorously in the south -"

Sam stepped backward to get a better look at the sight, nearly falling into a *gracht* - canal - as he did so. He let out a small cry of anxiety at the near miss. The tour guide fixed a cold-fish stare on Sam, letting the intruder know by his manner that this "hitchhiking" with the paying customers was at an end. Sam pretended he did not notice the man, turning with elaborate care to look down into the *gracht* as if that had been his original intention all along - an intention interrupted by the arrival of these Midwestern tourists. A barge sat in the water, dark, metallic.

The ruse didn't work. "*Niet zo leuk*," the smelly tour guide whispered under his breath to Sam as he led his prepaid clientele on to the next sight, "not so good. *Kijk uit, jonger, dat mag niet*: we accept everything you do here as long as you pay. Don't cheat here." He was gone a minute later, steering his damp Midwesterners into the drizzle cloud on the opposite side of the footbridge crossing the canal.

It was only eleven o'clock in the morning - and Ann had made arrangements to rendezvous an hour after darkness.

An entire day still to kill

Which did not take an entire day.

Sam had not realized how early darkness fell on a northern European city in mid-November. He had found a movie theater playing a Charles Bronson western - or a sort of western: there was a Japanese samurai, a French gunslinger and Ursula Andress (what she was doing there Sam never quite figured out, but she looked good). *Red Sun*. It didn't make much sense. But it was a lot of fun to listen to English (even dubbed in), ignore the Dutch subtitles, and pretend he was home. Sam stayed for two showings, falling asleep in the warm, dry seat sometime before the end of the first screening, waking up when a bunch of Comanches (Indians suddenly!) surrounded the samurai and kept getting close enough to be whacked by his sword. Didn't they believe in arrows? Didn't anybody use *guns*? (They did, finally: after the Indians were all killed off, belatedly the gunslinger got smart and shot the samurai, then got blasted himself by cowboy Charlie Bronson - Sam was still half-asleep, but he figured the movie was about to end.)

It was a surprise, then, to walk out of the theater into darkness. Suddenly Sam was afraid: how long had it been dark? He had to look at his wristwatch three times to reassure himself that, no matter what, at four o'clock it could not have been dark more than a few minutes. If he made it to where Ann said to go - a discotheque called "The Table" - made it by five, he would be all right. According to the (minimal) directions Ann wrote in the front page margins of the *Herald American*, it was supposed to be on the *Liedseplein*.

What was a "*Liedseplein*"?

Where was a *Liedseplein*? Sam had no trouble finding the

coordinates on a map, but the crooked, circular streets left him slightly disoriented; there was no sun, visible horizon or familiar landmark on which to fix his bearings. Rather than stumble in a random direction until he located his present position on the map, Sam decided to return to the central train station - he knew where the movie theater was in relation to that - then tromp down to the *Liedseplein* from there: A'dam was small, the *Centrum* compact - nothing would be more than a fifteen minutes' walk distant.

"I don't believe this, isn't this the church?"

The speaker was one of the morning's Midwesterners, peeled off from the tour group for an evening stroll through the Old Town with two of her girlfriends. Sam was passing them briskly when he realized that the woman was asking the question out loud in the hope that he would overhear and confirm her opinion. With the casual presumption of intimacy common among Americans abroad, he nodded familiarly, "Yes, ma'am, I think it was," and stopped to inspect the object of inquiry. Without a doubt, it was the same homely facade behind which the famous "hidden *kirk*" was disguised.

It was also, now that daylight had ended, fronting a sex shop display window. Sam swallowed the same question his Midwestern countrywomen had asked and stared.

Red lights and glowing neons alternated with the very tasteful building facades up and down the winding block, sometimes encasing one another. Picture windows shuttered in the morning were now flung open to display whores on sale to the tourist trade.

Sam gradually realized, after looking at the brazen selections for several astonished minutes, that the Old Town was refilling with tourists by the minute. A different kind of tourist from those in the daytime. A type familiar to Sam: small groups of young sailors on leave from the ships crowding Amsterdam harbor roamed its cobbled sidewalks, drinking in the shop window wares.

The Midwestern ladies, like Sam, remained staring at the window: a new sideshow was premiering. A group of Norwegian sailors in thick wool regalia jostled to a stop in front of the display, where a hefty woman of indeterminate age and attraction reclined on a couch in her "night" clothes. Without comprehending a word of Norwegian (and he only knew they were speaking Norwegian because Lucy, the lady who had stopped him in the first place, said she was part Norwegian and that's what the sailors were talking in), Sam understood their conversation completely. First, each sailor made an admiring comment about the display woman's specific physical attributes, "ripe" being one such adjective, emphasized by the Universal Hand Gesture Code for the word. Then each sailor described his *own* attribute - and how to employ it; again, the hand gestures fit into the international coding.

And then there was the set-up.

Someone spoke louder than the rest, a curly-haired redhead with freckles and a dopey grin. Immediately three other sailors clapped him on the back, releasing a small cheer: the display window woman looked through the glass at the redhead, "swooned" impressively, and beckoned with her left hand for him to enter (her right hand pointed to a small printed sign indicating "ƒ40.00").

"That's forty guilders!," Lucy's friend exclaimed, "almost fifteen dollars!"

"H-it is-s goot price," a Norwegian winked, "t-hey give t-hem inyections in Nederlandts."

Lucy's friend did not understand.

"No syphilis," the sailor winked again, then joined his friend in chanting "Lars - HA! - Lars - HA!" at the embarrassed redhead, who was carefully counting a wad of Dutch money pulled from his pocket. Apparently coming up with the scratch, Lars boldly held up a handful of guilders and strode through the same door that led to the hidden church. Taking a left for sin instead of the stairway to heaven, he emerged a second later to join the woman inside the display window. To his friends' vocal disappointment, she drew a thick curtain across the plate glass.

Curiosity knows no cultural distinction: Sam was a little surprised to find himself remaining by the Norwegian sailors in front of the display window - with Lucy, her friend and the third Midwestern lady still beside him. All eyes were riveted upon the window but, since nothing could be seen, small comments began to pass back and forth among the various spectators. Sam discovered that Lucy & Co. were from Lansing, Omaha and Fort Dodge, respectively, acquaintances only for the past three days. He told them about the best place to get a cheap but decent hot lunch in Paris (they were on a budget, too) when the tour headed down there (after a stop in Brussels - Sam didn't know a thing about Brussels).

"She's not very attractive," the heretofore-silent Omaha *dama* commented, nodding towards the curtain behind which the prostitute was plying her trade.

"No," Lucy agreed, "those stretch marks are horrid: she got too fat when she was pregnant."

"She was pregnant?" Sam asked, mystified by the ladies' perceptiveness.

"Baby, several times," Lucy cooed. She then told him about *Rijsttafel*, Indonesian food with a lot of dishes, which sounded great to Sam's empty stomach, and gave him specific directions on how to order it. A cheer from the Norwegian contingent interrupted her in mid-directions to a place.

Lars The Redhead burst through the door triumphantly. To the casual observer his broad smile clearly announced that he had just conquered Brigitte Bardot.

Behind him in the display window, however, the curtain slowly opened: the prostitute looked through the plate glass at Lars and gave her head a mock-tragic shake: "No."

"Oh, man, I couldn't do that!" Sam said to himself as he watched the humiliated Lars slink away from the display window surrounded by his derisively hooting compatriots.

The several-times-pregnant display woman settled once more into her "boudoir" in anticipation of the evening's next customer.

"They're all churches here," Lucy giggled to her two friends, drifting away from the window as well. "Temples of Love!"

Sam laughed and groaned all the way to the train station; he passed Lucy and her gang twice on his trek back to finding the *Liedseplein*. It didn't hit him that they probably never would have spoken to one another if they met on the streets of Detroit.

The *Liedseplein* was outside the concentric canal rings of the *Centrum*. It was still an easy walk, though transportation was primarily by tram and auto - very few bicycles around - and still no places to park. Drizzle was replaced by a curling, wispy fog. The reds and neons of the Old Town were not dominant here; instead, orange-pink streetlights stood like clouds of drifting color above the streets and omni-present canals.

"*Sprecken zie Englische?*" Sam stopped a passerby, still uncertain where the *Liedseplein* proper began.

"Better than you speak German," was the perfunctory reply.

"*Liedseplein?*" Sam resorted to pidgin language.

"Yes?"

"Where?"

"Oh - ? Here!"

Geography established, Sam had the leisure to reconnoiter the locale. An open space, crisscrossed by tram tracks and (it followed logically) trams that whirled in from the fog and bore down on passersby foolish enough to stand between the parallel rails. Sam felt foolish enough three times.

It was not a tourist area, not neon-lit nor gaudy - nor particularly attractive architecturally. It *was* crowded, though, with cafes and discotheques lining the block, basking in the orange glow cast by the rolling fog and streetlights. Sam retrieved the address for The Table that Ann had scribbled for him.

"American?" the British-accented voice inquired; it accompanied a blondish man of twenty-five or so, wearing a Dutch-style suit over a heavy white turtleneck sweater, a roundish face, relatively short hair accented by long sideburns. He very much was sure of himself. As was the girlfriend holding onto his arm: she was dressed almost the same, but with shoulder-length, henna-dyed hair.

"Uh-huh," Sam acknowledged the identification. "You English?" He knew the guy wasn't, but it would please the shit out of him to be asked. It never hurt to be friendly.

"Dutch," a smile of satisfaction. "I visit England a lot. Do you want to buy some hash?"

Sam was taken aback by the openness. "What!?"

"Do you want to buy some hash? *Hashish*?" He turned to his girlfriend and muttered, "*Mag ich -*", and as she started to reach into her shoulder bag he continued his sales pitch:

"I have some very good Moroccan-"

"Hey, look!" Sam forced the girl's hand to stay inside her shoulder bag. "I don't know if you're narcs or what - but you're not bustin' me like this!"

"But we-" the man protested.

Sam walked away.

"I heard about this shit in Turkey, but nobody does it wide-open on the streets without a bust!"

He was already a good ten yards away when he heard the man laughing behind his back. Then the woman. There was nothing vaguely sarcastic about their laughter: it was genuinely good-humored. Intrigued, Sam stopped walking away and turned to face them.

"You are right, of course!" the man laughed across the dew-glistening cobblestones for any and all to hear.

"You're a narc, right?"

"No!" the girlfriend cried, "*I* am a nar-C!" Her heavy accent came down on the final *c* with a throat-scratching crash. Sam started to back away from them. The man stopped laughing and held up his hands in innocent denial.

"No, we are not police." Once again, Sam stopped moving. "But you are right," the man agreed, "it is not legal."

"Yeah! So what *you* doing setting me up?"

"It is only hash. Who cares?!"

"Polices, that's who."

The man and his girlfriend had had their laugh, now it was time to go back to business. They displayed no resentment towards Sam as they re-linked arms and walked past him. "Nobody cares on *Liedseplein*. Go to *Den Taffel* - it's licensed by the government. They sell hash there for the open." The henna-haired girlfriend whispered into his ear. "*In* the open," he corrected himself.

A sick sense of inevitability scratched at Sam's stomach. "*Den Taffel* - 'The Table'?" he asked.

"In English, yes: The Table. 'You know it?"

* * * * * * * * *

"Ah, it's probably true here: they even license the bordellos and provide child care for the 'working' mothers," Ann's Gaelic accents rang sarcastic as she bit into the words, clutching Sam's hand tightly, warmly, between her thighs as they sat crowded together at one of *Den Taffel*'s (larger-than-Parisian) tables.

"You have to understand that they're very tolerant here. They may hate your guts, but if it's good business the Dutch will let you do anything. Sort of like a Switzerland without the mountains. Not quite so holier-than-thou, either, I think. Probably because the Nazis wiped out their mercantile neutrality and they had a rude education in the politics of imperialism from the bottom side. The Swiss need a good kick like that. But, then, where would the Mafia bank?"

"Excuse me," three others were squeezed around the table, the one speaking miraculously juggling five heavy glasses of beer, "but if you are completed insulting our country would you let us discuss mutual friends now?" He distributed the quart-sized containers of Amstel beer Ann had earlier sent him to purchase.

"Certainly, Jurgen," Ann graciously agreed, finally turning her attention to her duties as mistress of ceremonies: "This is Jurgen, Sam. Next to him is Dineka -," an interesting if unattractive woman in her early twenties nodded her head at Sam, "and the gentleman down there has refused to tell anyone here his name, but comes highly recommended." Sam's attention lingered on Dineka, who smiled shyly, revealing a gold-capped bicuspid and a self-consciousness about its prominence. Her eyes were slate grey, focused directly on whomever she spoke to.

Sam attempted to shake hands with each one in turn, drawing an awkward blank when he came to the Nameless One. This person, somewhat decadent looking, a decade older than the oldest at the table, stood up instead. His attention was on everything in the room except the people at the table in front of him.

"You don't want me here right now -" There was a British sneer to his voice, "- and I don't particularly want to 'hear' you." He finally looked at them, wearing a smile appreciative of his own poor wordplay. "Call me when you're ready."

He deserted their table to seat himself at another, talking with its occupants in the same desultory manner.

"Why's everyone here talk like a Brit?" Sam leaned into Ann's ear to whisper.

"Because it's a lot closer than New York: if they're going to learn English, who do you think they'll sound like?" Ann smiled with gracious sarcasm.

Dineka, meanwhile, picked up on Sam's reservations about the Nameless One. "Don't worry about him," she said, her own British-tinged accents muted, thought out. "They say he's quite good."

"Yeah. What's he good at?"

"Hash. It's very good stuff he sells," Jurgen explained, wiping a thin line of foam from an impressive handlebar moustache.

"I thought it was legal in this place? He's a private dealer."

Ann shrugged. "Well, it is, almost. But he's a lot cheaper and a lot better."

"He just came up from Rotterdam," Dineka added. "He has to make his own place here. He will be good and cheap."

To which Jurgen cautiously added: "Or violent."

Sam allowed only his eyes to jerk askance, which took an effort of self-control. Jurgen noticed anyway. "Well, it happens," he admitted, "just not usually in Amsterdam."

Ann did not like the direction the conversation was taking. "Good, now let's-"

"Of course," Jurgen rambled on, almost as an aside, "he could be from Belgium, it's -"

Ann's glare caught him squarely.

"- a lot rougher… there…"

With motherly finality, Ann flashed an "Are we finished?" smile at Jurgen, Dineka and Sam, then pulled out a tattered map and laid it across the table.

"All right, Sam -", she began. He was acutely aware that Derek and the Dominoes' *Layla* had started its fourth repetition over *Den Taffel*'s sound system; Eric Clapton's pulling guitar ran through Sam's pulse. "- they're already working on a drop point for your guns…"

"When?" Sam asked professionally; Ann had coached him on the proper attitude to take with her A'dam contacts. She was ready with the rehearsed answer:

"*When* I've delivered the goods, Sam: you'll see our organizations are well-organized." She turned to Jurgen and Dineka with a proud smile: Sam's apparent eagerness had been her trump card.

"Do you have any questions now?"

Neither one did. Ann returned to an inspection of her map.

And Sam wondered if he was half as eager as Ann presumed him to be. Eager for what? It was easy to pretend anything for Ann, because he was not certain how much was pretend. He needed to see the man who killed McMasters. The man Ann admired. He could not put a *why* to any of it. Ann knew her own reasons; she had not asked his. Her attention was on the East-West German border at the moment.

"The thing is, Sam, it's got to be a splinter group, a new K-Group from Berlin most likely."

"What's a 'K-Group'?"

"They're the violent ones in Germany, the ones who *do*, instead of talk."

"But everybody says the dudes who hit the bank are from France," Sam objected, "the newspaper-"

"*Everybody* is wrong," Ann said fiercely, not to be contradicted, "which is the beauty of organization and tactics. Anyway, Jurgen knows more."

Jurgen lowered his eyes to the map and aimed them at a point within East Germany. "I know two of them. Jo and Birgit are from Berlin. That means they have eastern access."

"There are three regular crossings for liberation patrols," Dineka took over, pointing to a place along the two Germanys' border where no road crossed, "but only one of them - here - is close to the robberies that have already taken place."

"So how do I meet 'em?" Sam asked, taking the plunge.

Ann had the answer ready.

"We'll go there, just us two. Dineka has gotten us a van for $25.00 - it drives, that's all you need to know - and, uh," she rushed over the next part, "we'll be needing one more gun, Sam, and they've probably got a safe house there. We'll try to find it."

Sam leaned back from the map in disbelief.

"I don't - ? - y'know - How come if it's so open the police don't do this?"

A fifth repetition of *Layla*; Sam began to love it and hate it. Even Ann felt it; the music made her happy to tell her tale.

"Well, there's two reasons for that, Sam: political and practical. Politically, they're the oppressors - they don't listen to the people, so a lot of things go right on in front of their noses."

Layla, you got me on my knees!

"Practically speaking, they're looking south, and they don't know *who* to ask - and even if they did, the who's wouldn't tell 'em."

Layla, I beg you darlin', please!

Ann began to move to the music. "And I won't be lying to you, Sam: I'm not telling *you*, either. I'm *taking* you."

The Nameless One reappeared at the table.

"*Mag ich ein moment?*" he said to Jurgen and Dineka.

"*Ja,*" Jurgen reluctantly nodded, rising to join Dineka, who had already stepped behind her chair. "We are finished here anyway. See us tonight for the van," he directed the words at Ann.

"*Tot sens.*"

"*Kijk uit, jongen!*" she burbled magnanimously, adding for Sam's benefit (and a quick, open-lipped kiss), "That means 'Look out, kid!'"

The Nameless One slid into his former chair, across from Sam. He waited for Ann to remove her tongue from Sam's mouth before scraping his fingernail along the tabletop to remind her of his presence. Sam grew a tremendous hard-on and had a difficult time noticing the man. Ann, however, pulled herself together and addressed the Nameless One seriously, albeit with a hardly suppressed undertone of giggling.

"We want to do business with you," she said. "I think

we'll be good customers." Sam felt the same sinking sensation he did back in high school whenever trying to buy wine on a fake I.D. Like the store owners, the Nameless One was unimpressed by Ann's type of confidence.

"Really?" he smiled flatly. "How much money do you have?"

Nothing fazes a self-possessed Irishwoman. "Sam, how much is the operating capital?" she shrugged breezily.

Sam looked into his wallet: three traveler's checks for one hundred dollars each.

"Two, three-" he began to answer.

"Three thousand dollars!" Ann quickly interrupted, adding even more quickly: "Or do you want it in Dutchy guilders?"

"I want it in my pocket," the Nameless One smiled once more, pleased again at his own sense of humor. Back to business:

"Three thousand: 'you want heroin, then?"

"No, man," Sam asserted before Ann could get ideas. "Just hash. You keep the horse for the lost ones."

The Nameless One laughed to himself at this lack of ambition. "Very well. They," he started to rise, "don't appreciate my stealing their business in here. Come with me to my car."

Without waiting to see how closely they followed, he went out to the sidewalk.

Sam and Ann hesitated at the table. Ann misread the doubts crossing Sam's face:

"Well... You don't mind getting high, do you?"

"Let's go, lady!" He grabbed her hand and plowed through the crowd.

"Y'know, I only got three *hundred* dollars!" Sam hollered over his shoulder, almost overpowering the volume of the music as they crossed in front of the speakers. Ann seemingly read lips:

"Good! I thought it was guilders you had, that would have been even less. We'll spend twenty dollars and tell him we'll think it over."

They had reached the sidewalk and could talk without shouting. The Nameless One was already half a block down the street; seeing them, he continued walking away from the vicinity of *Den Taffel*.

"It's in traveler's checks," Sam confessed, "*hundred* dollar traveler's checks."

"Oh…" Ann's thoughts lingered on the joint awkwardnesses of monetary tender and denomination. "Let's hope he takes one and we'll have a better time than we planned. Volume versus Quality: never had that choice before."

The Nameless One waited by a narrow side street deadending in a canal a half block away. "I am down here. Parking is a bastard, right?"

"'Bitch'," Sam corrected.

"Oh, right," the Nameless One shrugged off the vocabulary lesson, passing a small bag from his coat pocket into Ann's. "Here, check out if this is good enough for you."

As soon as the bag was in Ann's possession, the Nameless One stepped up his pace, quickly leaving them behind to wind their way between a wall of windowless brick buildings and the row of small automobiles parked along the sidewalk.

And then, although the Nameless One spoke Dutch,

Sam very clearly understood the man say to the shadows: "They are yours now."

He spun around and walked one step aggressively back towards Sam and Ann. An Indonesian appeared from between two parked cars and stood next to the Nameless One, whose outstretched hand needed no translation.

"All right now, the money, give it to me and go."

An arm reached around from behind and grabbed at Sam's belt.

"Hey!"

"What the bloody hell!" Ann barked. Almost as one, she and Sam jumped across the street: it was no great accomplishment - there were only six feet of road space to the next row of sardine-parked vehicles. The two Indonesians who had come up behind them stepped out into the narrow street to dispel any thoughts of running away. The Nameless One and his partner closed in on the other side.

"I'll tell you 'what the hell!" the Nameless One punched the words in angry threat. "I'll tell you I want money!"

"You're dead around here if you do this!" Ann panted, crowding back into Sam. As before, the Nameless One was unimpressed by her words:

"The Dutch don't kill, they talk. And anyway, you're foreigners, who cares!? We're all foreigners! Who cares!?" He *still* appreciated his own sense of humor, even under pressure. In Dutch business tones he said to the Indonesians: "The American has three thousand dollars, take it."

His shoulder partner reached forward and shoved Ann

back towards the canal. The other two pushed in on Sam - who blindly pushed them back: it bought him about a yard of room, one moment's breathing space.

Enough time for Sam to unfasten his wide-buckled leather belt. He pulled the heavy-ended thick piece of cowhide out of his pants with a jerk.

"Get back, you mothers!"

The two men closest to Sam saw why he was suddenly so aggressive and stepped back instinctively.

Knight jumps two spaces, over one: unpredictable in any direction. Despite his rage, Sam saw the movements in sharp focus.

The Nameless One's partner was still attending to disposing of Ann, unaware of what had just happened. He turned back towards the black man just in time to have Sam swing the belt and heavy buckle across his face, gashing him only superficially, but knocking him down.

"YOU MOTHER FUCKER I SAID GET BACK!"

Defense moves.

Sam swung the belt back and forth in front of his body, lunging first at the Nameless One, then at the two Indonesians originally pressing in on him.

"Mother fuckers, get outta my way!"

They opened wide for him as he swung his way through.

"Mother fuckers," Sam yelled. "Mother-"

He grabbed Ann's arm - "GET OUTTA HERE!!!" - and started running with her towards the *Liedseplein*.

The Nameless One and the Indonesians watched Sam

and Ann escape without making a move to stop them. Finally, in fact, the Nameless One shrugged the thought of them off as he turned his attention to his hurt partner.

The wound was not very deep. The injured man was more annoyed than anything, muttering over and over again in Indonesian, "Crazy mother fucker." Or words to that equivalent effect. His was a rich language, given to colorful expressions not limited to Oedipal scatologies.

Borders

It did not make overnight driving any more difficult, then, for Sam to have a bloodstream full of adrenaline. It was almost ten o'clock before Jurgen and Dineka reappeared outside *Den Taffel*, circling the *Liedseplein* in a battered yellow van that gave new meaning to the word "old". Ann had still not talked down Sam from his anger-filled high (fortunately, the Nameless One decided not to push his luck by returning to the discotheque in search of new customers and/or victims) and when Dineka appeared in the doorway motioning Sam and Ann to follow her out to Jurgen, Ann was hard-pressed to keep Sam from yelling at them.

She shouted at them instead.

Hours of bottled-up nerves burst forth in a stream of angry accusation the moment Ann saw the crappy van.

"I - told - it was not so good," Jurgen tried to cock his head deprecatingly, "but it drives."

"Oh, but certainly!" Ann hooted. "Probably about as far out of Amsterdam as The Hague before breaking down. Thank you very much!"

"It is for only twenty-five dollars," Dineka offered quietly, trying to placate.

"And the guns!" Ann shot back, *not* quietly. Sam sided with the Dutch contingent in casting anxious glances around the *Liedseplein*'s near-silent square.

"We do not have the guns yet. This is on trust."

"And I *trust* we are on the same side! Given the looks of this deathtrap you're sending us off in, I wouldn't be surprised to learn you were a coupla Prods tryin' to do in this little Catholic girl and her nigger boyfriend!"

At that point even Sam drew back from the vehemence of Ann's attack. Jurgen literally stepped away from the group, as if he was not a part of their society.

Ann ranted on viciously about trust and betrayal - including a sexually-castrating description of the Nameless One punctuated by a barrage of expletives - all the while stared at squarely by grey-eyed, silent Dineka. After a few moments of listening, the Dutchwoman let her eyes shift from Ann to Sam: there was a signal of release in her gesture, and Sam understood that he was to leave the women alone. Already Ann's voice was lower and more controlled as he joined Jurgen.

"She is very - committed - I heard," Jurgen exhaled deeply, bringing a crooked, hand-rolled cigarette to his lips on the rebound.

"You didn't work with her before?" Sam asked, more out of need to make polite conversation than from interest: Dineka was saying something in her low, calm voice that shut Ann up for a few seconds; Sam, who understood *exactly* how Ann felt after their betrayal by the Nameless One, wondered what words could possibly have that effect.

"No. We met only this morning."

Wait a minute...

Sam's attention was captured. "You guys just *met?*"

Jurgen was in the midst of explaining how actually roadworthy the yellow van was, appearances aside: "- the tires are not new, but very little used -" It took him a second to realize that Sam had not paid attention to his last minute's monologue. Then he smiled proudly.

"We know *of* her, she of us: we are in trust - against the oppressors." Jurgen looked over at Dineka, patiently reassuring a still-passionate (if coldly calm) Ann that the yellow van was (a) drivable, (b) untraceable, (c) papers in order, (d) not going to attract Official Attention. The young Dutchman caught Dineka's eye, received a quiet smile in response, then turned his attention back to Sam. Jurgen understood that he needed to lend some moral support to the American, just as Dineka was doing for the Irish woman: those two were on the front lines, keyed-up for action. But it was the cool, logical support of *Nederlanders* and other like-enlightened societies that kept the fighters in action - and directed against the oppressors instead of at one another. He was content with - and proud of - the part he played in the process.

"Ann says you may distrust us, may distrust her: Do not. If I cannot vouch for myself (which would be egotistical, would it not?), I can tell you that the Irish Republican Army valued her enough to help Ann leave her country. She cannot go back, because British imperialism still reigns there, but she is not only 'talk', as you may fear."

Sam observed Ann and Dineka carefully: the two women were hugging now, still talking, clutching one another. "What'd she do?"

"I do not know," Jurgen acknowledged the defenselessness of his testimonial. "We do not ask for details, it would be - unwise."

"Unwise?"

"Unsafe."

Sam understood: he had never asked a lot of the people he knew in Detroit any details about their lives. "Unsafe." Righteously unsafe. It made Sam feel more alone than ever to know that, however much he was holding back from Ann about McMasters and the Frankfurt bank, she was not telling him equally important moments in her life.

They were driving out of A-dam now, leaving the cramped, storybook city behind – to be replaced by a flat countryside with a straight highway that left Sam time to think. He was aiming for the German border, getting what he wanted. He could not get songs out of his head.

> *Ohhh, la, la, la*
> *La.*
> *I - didn't - run*
> *My heart*
> > *went out*
> > > *to play*
> *But in the game I lost you*
> *What – a – price – to – pay*

Ann fell asleep almost immediately, curled up on the van's long bench seat, head pillowed in the large shoulder bag she carried everywhere, her red hair spilling over her face in one direction, across Sam's right thigh where the top of her head touched his leg. Jurgen had crouched behind Sam (there was only a rusty-smelling metal floor behind the bench seat, empty save for a rattling gas can, two spare tires and an inadequate-looking hand jack); he guided them through Amsterdam to a traffic circle on the edge of the city, where a highway entrance sign announced West Germany's border to be indecently close.

"We are a small country," Jurgen apologized, exiting the van to run towards an approaching tram. "The last one tonight," he called over his shoulder. "I must catch it. *Tot sens!*"

The adrenaline in Sam's veins would not dilute: he was wide awake, singing song after song in his head, sometimes under his breath, lost in a midnight melancholia that was beautifully sad to a nineteen year-old sensitivity. For long minutes at a stretch Sam forgot where he was going, cocooned deeply inside the combined rhythms of Motown balladry and moonlit, unreal landscape.

Ooh, ooh, ooooh -
Ba-by, ba-by!

Oh, yeah, the music of Smokey was everywhere, skimmin' along the top of this highway dike. (*Dike?* They really have dikes!) Sam saw the shadow of his own van silhouetted clearly on the two-lane highway in front of him: only a dozen kilometers outside of A'dam and already the weather was clear. You could read by the moon, hanging there behind your shoulder, ex-hippie van heading east. (Was it an ex-*hippie* van? Sam thought he could detect the sweet undertow smell of marijuana beneath the metallic rustiness of the cargo area. Either that, or his clothes still reeked from the "atmosphere" in *Den Taffel*. If ever he did *not* want to get high and chilled, it was after going back into *Den Taffel* after the biz with the Nameless One. Damn three hours of waiting and thinking every other minute of bolting the entire situation. Except that he had created the situation. For himself... And was now chickening out - or too afraid of chickening out to be smart and step away while still relatively clean. How much was Ann a part of that decision? She didn't try to talk him into anything, just listened to him motormouth through his delayed motherfucking ANGER! at the Nameless One! What the fuck was the guy's *name?*, anyway, the fuck, motherfucker!, tryin' to shake us down like a coupla ofay chumps! Malcolm be right, Panthers be right, Huey be right! Violence is as American as cherry pie! And Sammy T. Williams' gonna the fuck show those motherfuckers shitass kickin' violence!

Which he knew from the start he wouldn't do.

It was too easy.

The dike highway looked like a straight line ahead drawn by the hand of God in superhuman perfection. A cartoon vista, unreal. Sam drove down it flat out, topping one-twenty klicks to the hour without noticing.

Something seemed wrong about even *wanting* to go back and waste the Nameless One, though Sam knew that with surprise, size and military training on his side if he suddenly reappeared and attacked the drug dealer he could pound the guy down in five seconds, be gone back to safety before the Indonesians had time to catch their breath. Don't waste time, that was the key: not like McMasters done in the bank, hesitating. The German guy, Braun, didn't hesitate - and he won: the whole point was to beat the other guy, right? Damn McMasters, always so smartass smart in chess, screwing up on a basic tactics move.

"Why're you not a officer?" Sam asked once. "You smart enough in strategy."

"Strategy isn't very human," the career soldier replied, not bothering to elaborate on his answer beyond a cryptic, "It's a whole different league from playing with wooden pawns."

Whatever.

Sam did not share McMasters' perceptions, still... His own bit of church-going savvy told him that justice was just a little more complicated than simply going out and pounding down the other guy - not a very military concept - but sitting in Sunday schools and (duuullll) church services every week for eighteen some years pounded something into his brain. He wasn't going back after the Nameless One. In fact, his rage was as much self-directed at knowing that he wasn't going to out-animal the animals as it was anything else.

He let his right hand drop from the steering wheel and felt the smooth silkiness of Ann's hair across his jeans. He let his fingers drift to her jaw and rest there.

"Ohh, yesss," she moaned, waking just enough to command "Rub there..." before drifting off to sleep again. Sam obeyed, rotating his thumb in a tiny circle just below her earlobe. He could feel tight muscles relax. How had she slept with a neck so tense?

The landscape below the dike highway was flat. Sam had never imagined anything so resembling a tabletop. Or a game board. The alternating fields of whatever reflected the moonlight in huge squares. A town of thirty houses stood out to the north, so poorly in his chess matches against McMasters.

McMasters is the happy one, the German doctor said. Braun really did crucify that German in the bank. Why?

The highway surprised Sam by curving - into the town. It was necessary to decelerate.

"We'll be reaching the German border in a few minutes, Sam." Ann pulled herself up to a sitting position, sleep still half in control of her body, despite the alertness in her eyes. "I want you to stop before then."

"Here," she said two kilometers later, then gave a shudder at the cold. "This will be fine," she added in her familiar, don't-contradict-me-please tone when Sam did not slow the van down sufficiently fast enough to her liking. "I don't want to be in sight of the border - or under a streetlight."

Sam stopped the van next to a sign indicating that the border was only one kilometer distant. Ann opened her door and started to leave.

"Where you going?" Sam asked, stopping Ann in the doorway with a simple touch on her hand.

She shivered again, this time at the fresh air invading the van. "Oh, it's chock full of winter now - and six weeks still to go!" Ann slid out of the van, pulling her large shoulder bag along behind. "Just go on through the border, Sam. If they ask you anything, tell them you borrowed this beautiful piece of crap. Stop and wait for me about a kilometer past." She shut the door between them to discourage further conversation.

Sam obeyed. He knew little enough about border crossings

- and a lot about Ann's pigheadedness - not to consider doing anything else but what she said. And, as it happened, the passage from Holland into Germany was hardly more than a sleepy formality; a Stop sign, actually, where a guard stepped out of a boxlike house (Sam did not know if he was Dutch or German, the door straddled the borderline), favored Sam's military travel documents with an obligatory glance, and limited conversation to a yawned "*Danke*" as he handed the papers back while waving the van through without further interest.

There was only a single main street through the remainder of the town. (Was it still the same town, or was it dif-ferent now because this was Germany?), stringing out in scattered store fronts interspersed between residences and wide garden plots. Ann had instructed Sam to wait a kilometer beyond the border, but the town ran out of steam before then - though streetlights extended another two hundred meters into the fields, where the smooth asphalt of the highway reasserted itself on the brick-paved town road the route had temporarily become. Sam stopped the van along the shoulder, resting in the grey shadow between two street lights, just beyond the fence of the last house.

"Jesus, it's cold!" Ann shivered, opening the driver's door as she said: "D'you want me to drive for a while, Sam?"

In spite of his acquiescence, Sam was a bit ticked off by the past fifteen minutes' secrecy. "What was that all about?!" he asked sharply.

Ann ignored the tone of his voice. "Sleep," she advised, sliding next to Sam and gently forcing him to let her take over the steering wheel, "I'm only good for about an hour before I crash again." It was a sweet smile she flashed at him now, Celtic charm in dangerous abundance. "These walk-across borders were made exactly for my passport."

She started the engine with a smooth crunch of gears so that Sam would have other things on his mind.

And she did not lie about how long she would be driving: Sam's uncomfortable sitting sleep was interrupted less than fifty minutes later by Ann's steady, prodding touch.

"I'm falling asleep, Sam. Can you take over?"

He could, reluctantly, for the alternative involved lying down on the cold back floor while Ann stretched out on the bench seat. (She fit, Sam didn't - why shouldn't *one* of them be comfortable?) Driving was at least warmer, the engine running and a thin stream of warm air (probably exhaust fumes) tickling at his ankles.

The flat, flat, flatness of Holland was behind them now, as was the brightness of the moon, descended in the pre-dawn hours to a dull spot on the low-lying hills. Sam began to look forward to seeing the small mountains he knew surrounded Frankfurt. That was the direction they were headed, east-southeast, before angling northeast from there. It wasn't home, but it was familiar territory. The German highway - *autobahn* - widened out to two lanes in each direction, then three; speeds of one-fifty to one-seventy-five kilometers per hour were the norm here. The yellow van was passed frequently as it struggled to maintain a one hundred klick average up the steeper inclines. When, finally, the sky ahead turned crimson, then orange, and - into Sam's squinting eyes - daylight, Frankfurt was not far away.

A city glistening in the early morning light.

"Do you want to rest here for a few hours?" Ann asked, half-awakening as she did every fifteen minutes (the bench seat was more comfortable than the van floor, but not *that* sleep-supportive).

"No... it's too close to base... 'Don't want to see anybody I know."

"Why?" The question was obligatory; Ann was already dozing again.

Sam looked down at her jealously. He had reached the too-tired-to-sleep state: once he closed his eyes, it was over for the next twelve hours. *Wherever* he fell asleep.

They passed Frankfurt - and the base - at a safe distance, then altered course for the spot on the map where Ann had placed her fingertip back at *Den Taffel*: an empty thrust of East German territory into West Germany, in the fields north of a burg called Fladungen. There was no highway there, at that spot on the border. No town. No official checkpoint.

Only a place were people safely crossed the barbed-wire fenced, minefield-strewn border from east to west - with the cooperation of the East German government.

Only select people, at certain places, under specific time designations. Only a hundred people in the world knew the certain places, fewer than half that knew the select people, only the people involved knew the times. But you could guess.

"This is where crossings are made -" Ann explained, stopping her arm in mid-sweeping panoramic embrace of the border. "It took me awhile to link up with Dineka, then convince her of my sincerity, but it was worth it, don't you think?"

Sam was too tired to think, period. His brain worked anyway. "Dineka knew about this crossing point?"

"Nopey dopey, that *I* knew," Ann nodded proudly, looking out through the front windshield at the autumnal fields. "But I didn't know if Braun was K-Group associated - Mother Jesus, maybe he *was* holing up somewhere in France like the newsies think! - so knowing this is here and knowing Braun is using it are different things entirely."

Sam vaguely resented the thought of Ann's intriguing him up to Amsterdam for no reason. "But you knew enough: why'd we have to bring anybody else in?"

"Maybe I didn't know enough." Ann's enigmatic smile annoyed Sam like hell - or maybe his skin was just aching from exhaustion. "I told you I'm not telling you everything, Sam... otherwise you wouldn't need me. I want to meet Braun, too." She said this last with the sincere awe of a fan, an emotion she quickly disguised under a bluster of practical consideration:

"Besides, do you know how *disorganized* the Germans are? Just knowing Braun doesn't tell me who he's allied with: Jo was with *L'Armée Rouge* up until a year ago, Birgit writing for - I don't know - some sexual exploitation rag that occasionally put out a good exposé of the Nazi politicians still creeping around power in dear old Deutschland, Deutschland, Deutschland uber alles. Germans love that sort of thing: kinky sex and politics. So do the Brits, for that matter."

Sam had long since lost track of what she was saying, staring as he was at the border itself. It was not the famed Iron

Curtain as he had imagined it, not the border of newspaper front pages, full of armed guards and military face-offs. Instead, there was here the almost natural looking separation of a land: a barbed wire fence cutting across farm fields. That was the first impression.

After looking at the area for a few minutes, Sam began to see the differences. On the near side, West Germany, where the Dutch van was parked on an unpaved road, occasional farm buildings and trees stood out from the fields, some relatively close to the border fence. A packed-dirt road ran alongside the barbed wire on the East German side - beyond that only empty fields: no crops, no fallow/fertile alternation of plots. Only plowed-up earth stretching to the first hilly horizon.

One exception: a single tree, standing in the middle of the torn-up field. It stood out starkly, its orange-red leaves the only splotch of color across the border. It struck Sam suddenly that very few of the trees on his side of the border were also brilliant-hued - autumn had seized full hold on Germany since he had left it only a few weeks ago, stripping the tree limbs almost barren.

"- They make the crossings at night, of course -" Ann continued to explain.

"What stops anybody else from cutting across?" Sam asked, guessing the answer.

"Mine fields, patrols." The expected response. "They even plant some machine guns activated by-"

"So how do Braun's people get over?"

"Where there's a will there's a way, especially with help." Ann answered curtly: she was tired, too, even with her fitful night's sleep. "They probably know the patrol schedules, the lo-

cations of the mines - I don't know, they do it enough. It works."
She lost interest in the border in favor of a small farm village five
kilometers down the horizon on the West German side. "Let's
find a place to stay."

It was not a suggestion to be argued with. Dragging himself back behind the wheel, Sam guided the van towards the village, a crooked journey. There was no direct route, only inter-
linking small roads between farm houses, storage buildings and
grouped processing complexes - granaries, mills - that probably
covered more land area than the village whose church tower Sam
struggled to keep in sight as his beacon. For a brief moment Sam
thought he was back in the States, in Indiana, wandering around
in one of those hick backroad farmer places on the way down to
Chicago. He'd done that once, with a buncha the brothers -
"junior class trip" they called it (which meant that Sly and the
Family Stone was doing a concert in Chi-town on a Friday night
and you had to leave by noon to get there) - and Cousin Rip kept
going south on 69 ("Sixty-nine, yo!") instead of catching the turnoff
to 80 straight into Chi. Wandering around in the cornfields, trying to
find Chicago. Buncha black asses. Fun, though.

Thoughts of the present, too:

"How long do you think we'll be here?" Sam asked, keying
in on the fact that Ann mentioned knowledge of people and place -
but not time. "I've only got a week left."

Ann was too tired to snort, although she attempted to.
"You're in no hurry now, Sam, not if you're coming with us."

"You want the guns, I better be back on time."

"…Yeah." The thought of giving Sam back to the American army, even for a short while, hurt Ann in an unexpected way. The emotional stitch had cramped her style on the way to Amsterdam, too: she was suddenly hurrying through things, then waiting impatiently, all because Sam wasn't with her. Stupid - damn him to bloody hell!

"Tonight or tomorrow night," she replied through a stifled sniff, "that's when they'll be coming. Nobody likes to stay in the East too long - it's a grim place."

"Then why do you deal with them?" Sam made his final turn; the village was only an easy hundred meter cruise away.

"Y'know... any port in a storm sort of thing." Talking politics helped Ann forget Sam, remember why she existed. "When the oppressors break all rules of morality, you have to use their own weapons sometimes just to survive. 'Doesn't mean you endorse the reality, only recognize it. Here's a place to eat. Maybe they have rooms above."

Minus the specific German touches, the place could have been in the south of France, the seacoast of Maine, or the heart of Kansas. A farm country eating place, and most of the people inside were the townspeople who serviced those farmers: an equipment salesman taking a break with an equipment repairman; at a prominent table sat a balding man who was probably the village clerk - visiting with the very obvious local police constable; three farmers had stopped in the village for some quick late-morning business, deciding to eat a second breakfast; the owner of the place, of course, his wife hovering behind, watching a woman in her early twenties servicing the customers, who may or may not be their daughter but most assuredly was from the village. A rather comfortable scene since, unlike its larger-town fast-food counterparts, the meals prepared here were homemade and filling - and the people here not so far away from large cities that they harbored (too many) restless feelings.

All the same, the sight of a white woman and a black man walking in together was not an everyday occurrence.

"- they probably won't have a hotel here," Ann was busily explaining to Sam as they approached the counter. Without missing a beat she addressed the young serving woman: "Do you speak English?"

"*Nein.*"

Sam darted a tiny grimace/smile at Ann and held up two fingers to the serving woman. "*Zwei bier*s."

A little chagrined, Ann said defensively, "I can speak German, don't worry about it. Better than you."

"You just heard *my* vocabulary," Sam replied, accepting the two draft beers from the serving woman, adding, "*Danke schön.*" He grinned to Ann: "I also know 'please'."

"You just go sit down, why don't you? I'll do better without the pressure of your critical ear."

A bantering smile illuminated Sam's tired facial muscles. "I didn't say anyth-"

"*Alone*, please?" Ann insisted.

With a tired chuckle, Sam carefully transported himself and his filled-to-the-brim glass over to an open table, listening to Ann flay the German language behind his back - without success.

"*Ist ein* hotel *hier*?"

"*Nein.*"

"*Ist ein* roomen *vermieten, für* rent - *ein fremdenheime* pension?"

"*Nein.*"

Ann turned away from the serving woman, raising her eyes up towards the ceiling. Sam leaned back in his chair, tilting the front legs off the floor as he always did, and called across:

"What's the matter?"

"I'm trying to remember the words in German," she answered, not bothering to look at Sam, "I don't think I said it right."

"Are you married?"

The German serving woman said the words clearly, if without confidence, in English.

Ann's response was a profound "Huh?"

"Hus - band?" the woman nodded her head towards Sam. Ann stared at her, blank-eyed, in response. The serving woman held up her own hand and pointed to a narrow gold band: a wedding ring.

"Married?" Ann laughed, understanding at last that the topic was no longer hotel rooms. "Oh, no-no-no! *Nein!*"

"Oh."

The look of disapproval that fell across the serving woman's face did not go unnoticed by Sam; his back visibly stiffened. Ann was unaware of either response. "We need a place to stay tonight," she explained in rushed English to the woman who had to be her same age across the serving counter. "Where? *Wo?*"

"You're missing the point."

Sam could not let Ann continue stepping deeper into her mistake. He finished off his beer and rejoined her at the counter, quietly explaining:

"I think you've been selling us together. A pair. This don't look like Paris to me."

"Paris? - Uuuuh!" the realization hit Ann finally. "I thought I'd left this kind of bigotry shit back in Ireland."

"Yeah. I miss it, too," Sam growled, stalking across to the entrance. Disappointment displayed itself as a scowl across his face as he waited there for Ann to break away from the serving woman. All those German-white faces looking at him.

Which Ann saw, too -

- and decided to turn to her advantage.

"Look," she said in a low voice, hurriedly turning back to the serving woman, "you didn't think I'd be *with* him, did you?"

The young woman answered with an embarrassed downward cast to her eyes at this openness. Ann raised her voice to bring the owner and his wife into her confidence:

"Well, of course not! Come on, look at him!" She discreetly (but not too) pointed at Sam hulking in the doorway. "The man's strong! I'm a woman travelling alone…" She paused to let the import of her words sink in.

And Sam, like everyone else in the room unable *not* to miss understanding the gist of the conversation, began to frown in a truly overplayed parody of a "mean mother."

Ann appreciated his thespian contribution to the cause.

"I need muscle!" she whispered to the serving woman in confidential tones for the room to hear. "I mean, have you ever *been* to Berlin? To *Berlin!?*"

"*Ja,*" the serving woman nodded in fearful understanding; she had never been to Berlin, but she *knew* all about it.

"A woman needs protection there, yes?"

Sam stood, large and menacing, in the doorway. The beer hitting his blood stream on an empty stomach and sleepless night made it difficult not to wobble, but he managed it.

The serving woman looked at Sam, at the owner and his wife, at the young Irish girl who was her own age - then grabbed a scrap of paper and scribbled something down on it.

"Here -" she said, sliding the paper across the counter to Ann. "Tey vant deutschmarks more tsan anytsing else."

"*Danke*," Ann smiled gratefully, taking the directions and turning to join Sam at the door. The meaning of the phrase "more than anything else" hit her then. She stopped in mid-step, turning back to the serving woman with the grateful smile now frozen on her face. That was all. Just the smile. Held a moment too long. Then dropped a second too abruptly. She stepped over to Sam, who held open the door, noting the previous exchange.

"Yes, massa?" he asked in dripping accents.

"Not bad, Sam. You can kick over a chair for effect if you want." He declined the suggestion, but left the door hanging open behind them as they returned to the van. The owner was forced to scurry from behind the counter and cross the room to close it, explaining to his regular patrons as he did so:

"She told them about the crazy Pollack."

The serving woman smiled, naively embarrassed, which caused the others to burst out in good-humored laughter, both at her and the concept of the two foreigners meeting up with the "crazy Pollack."

"- 'reminds me that we'll have the same problem if we

ever get into the small towns of Italy together, Sam."

The serving woman's directions led them back along farm roads they were vaguely familiar with.

"Yeah, well, color-"

"No! It's because you're under twenty-one, Sam. You're a minor, there, and they take it very seriously. I could be corrupting you."

Disbelief crossed Sam's face as he turned his attention from the road to Ann.

"Bull-shit!" he laughed.

"It's true!" Ann chortled back in relaxed defense of her position. "It's a Catholic country, Sam: Mafia and old lady morality!"

They had arrived. Neither one could stop laughing hysterically, even as they descended from the van.

"I be tired, lady," Sam wheezed, "'cause this whole situation is stupid and I'm laughin'."

"Put on a straight face, Sam."

"I try."

They stood at the front door of the tiny, two-storied farm house and attempted to knock on the front door without breaking into giggles. Small farm animal sounds emanated from behind the house - which sent them into another fit.

"Hoink, hoink!" Ann cried.

"What's that?!" Sam cried back.

"A pig, Sam, a pig!"

"Pigs don't got no Irish accents! It's 'Oink, oink! 'Do it right!"

"Hoink-"

"*O*ink!"

"OINK! You bloody American bastard!"

"Irish bitch!"

"OINK! OINK!" they screamed together.

"Moo?" a quiet voice said tentatively.

An old man was standing by the side of the house, smiling lazily at them. "Moo-ooo," he lowed again, much more confidently than the first time. Ann and Sam stopped laughing immediately.

"Uh -" Ann stepped demurely over to the old man, stumbling through words in her mind, "*Ist ein* room - uh, they - we were told that rooms were for rent."

"*Ja?*" the old man did not move anything but his head, which bobbed up-and-down on his shoulders in clear indication of a total lack of understanding.

"They told us in town that this was a pension - *ein fremdenheime...* that we could rent a room here?"

The old man stepped past Ann to stand at a point mid-way between her and Sam. He stared at Sam's kinky hair in amazement, Not aggressive, just - in wonder. Then he began to speak in labored German, rotating his head back-and-forth in 180-degree swivels between the two visitors.

"*Es tut mir sehr leid... wie sagt man auf Deutsch?...*" He pointed at himself: "*Polen - Jüden einwanderer. Mein córka, nein!, mein tochter - München.*" He smiled helplessly.

Ann talked across the old man to Sam, an air of exasperation wearing at her patience. "I don't know the whole bit of it, Sam, but he doesn't speak German. He's Polish!"

She stepped next to the old man and began trying to converse in a combination of pidgin German and pantomime. "*Wir -*" Ann pointed at herself and Sam, "*schlafen -*" Face tilted on folded "pillow" hands, eyes closed.

"*Mein tochter-*" the old Pollack explained.

"- yes, your daughter - WE, no, *wir SCHLAFEN-*"

Sam's interruption was rude, crude and in Polish:

"*Prosze, pan! Pokoj -*" He held up a handful of marks. "*Dla pieniadze?*"

"*TAK!*" the old Pollack grabbed happily at the wad of money, chattering gaily in Polish: "Yes, sir, we are very happy to have guests here!" He counted out twenty, then twenty-five, marks from the handful, returned the rest to Sam. "Breakfast is included, of course. Wait here while I open the door from inside! Wait!"

"*Czekaj!*" he called again as he rounded the corner of the house on his way to the back door.

Ann looked at Sam with the same wonder the old Pollack had displayed about the black man's hair: a canary-filled cat could not have grinned back at her so sublimely pleased with himself.

"They was always a few Polacks in Detroit. You just say 'please' and 'thank you' and pay your bills and they polite as hell."

The old man opened the front door to his daughter's farm house, revealing a very comfortable home within.

"*Dzien-ku-je,*" Sam drawled his thanks in drawn-out, appreciative Polish. Dee-troit Polish.

* * * * * * * * *

The interior of an office. A very rich office with plate glass windows expanding two walls.

"This will be the future of design," the architects had explained. "By the '80s all contemporary buildings will use glass exterior walls, opening the interior to the space of the wide open, yet providing a barrier, a border of security, from the vagaries of the weather."

Josef Sinder accepted their advice. "You are professionals in your field, I am in mine."

His business smile had spoken the unvoiced, clearly heard, coda: "Besides, if you botch the job, how *will* you obtain financing for future projects in Frankfurt, Köln or Aachen?" The banking firm of *Sinder & Sons* was not large, but it had enough influence to cow any builders who tried to unload a white elephant on Josef Sinder.

They had not tried: the two-story living/office compound constructed midway between the three cities of *Sinder & Sons'* operations was pleasing to the eye from outside, pleasant enough within. Matters of furniture, art and room arrangement were always a question of individual taste anyway. Josef Sinder's ground floor office reflected his taste; he liked it. Until this autumn he had enjoyed looking out the wall-wide picture window onto the back courtyard -

Where weapon-toting security guards now nervously patrolled.

Where the foliage-covered wall showed recent damage from the hastily-installed electronic alarm system.

Josef Sinder did not like looking out on this newly-arranged protective border between himself and danger, but he appreciated it.

When he thought about it.

And he thought about it often these past three weeks.

He thought about it as he stared at the morning's mail stacked in a neat pile at the edge of the large desk dominating his office. There was nothing in that pile to disturb him. The piece of paper shattering his already-fragile life had arrived a week earlier, after the second bank robbery. The same two words were written on the paper, three times: in German, in Polish - in Yiddish.

"Your children."

"I came - as you asked," Josef said, and once again he wondered at his own courage in playing this game the Gestapo did not take kindly to night visits on darkened landings.

"I - appreciate - your taking the risk," the clerk answered, his Silesian accent tempering the German fluidity of his speech. Josef knew that the young man - a stranger, really, how could this Braun think that a word said here and there at the office was intimacy? - spoke Polish and Yiddish as well as his own dialect. A dangerous accomplishment in 1943 Breslau. "I don't want to take risks," Josef shrugged, trying to act as if he didn't care, "but..." He could not maintain the pretense. "Is it true?" he demanded nervously.

"You know it as well as I do: next week, the week after - they will take my apartment building." A shaft of muted light caught Braun's shoulder then, penetrating even the dark landing between floors to make the yellow Star of David sewn on the man's coat reflect its ominous six-pointed glory.

"Why do you wear the Jüden *Star?" Josef demanded in quiet fury.*

"You are not a Jew, Braun! You can be free!"

"My wife is. It is enough to make my children Jews..."He held out the bulging purse filled with gold rings and other jewelry, the agreed-upon amount. "Life, money, is worth nothing when your family are dead."

Josef saw the young man, only a few years past his teens, look up at him with ancient eyes. "You have contacts, Josef. I trust you; you know that you can trust me - after so many years of working for you, of our children playing together. Take my children, bribe the guards at the Swiss border - they will take the money from you - "

Josef accepted the purse carefully, with respect for the Silesian's dilemma. "Your kinder will have the money, Braun - whatever is left after the bribes."

Rumors

"The story goes like this: Back in the war -"

Ann's hushed tones reflected the quiet anticipation they both felt, waiting the past two hours since midnight on the low hill overlooking the border, staring through a dust-splotched wind-shield at the empty stretch of barbed wire fencing.

"- there was a nifty little business or two going on 'helping' Jewish children escape from the Bosch." The sound of her own voice comforted Ann, rhythmic waves of rolling syllables; there was no such thing as a Celtic silence.

"Hearsay has it that several families paid good gold to non-Jews who somehow got into and out of the ghetto. When they knew that their number was coming up - and somehow every-body knew, no matter how much they protested their surprise - they would pay to have one or two of the younger ones taken 'somewhere'. There were even rumors that, if you could get your kinder into Switzerland, they would be adopted and spirited off to the safety of America."

The story was not comforting, though, and Ann's voice grew cold in the telling. "'Problem was, it seems Mr. Sinder was holding onto the kids until he knew the families were safely tucked away in Auschwitz or Birkenau or wherever they ended up dying, then he would turn them over for a reward to the Germans…

"… Only one problem. *Two*, really - no, *one*: you can call the whole thing hearsay, but I know it's true. No, *the* problem is that that bastard Sinder went on to take his gold and come to Köln and make a fortune."

Sam turned on a flashlight and looked at his watch.

"Three o'clock almost."

"Tonight or tomorrow night."

A spotlight suddenly flashed across the plowed-up field on the East German side of the border. Sam and Ann did not jump inside their skins this time; the periodic illumination had developed a pattern - random, yes, but not unexpected. A quick sweep of the raw, frozen earth, then darkness again. The spotlight never crossed into the West.

"It makes sense," Sam said, nodding in agreement with his own thoughts.

"What?"

"What Braun's doing."

Ann had no response to that: she had never considered questioning the validity of Braun's actions to begin with.

Sam's next thought imposed itself on the silence as well.

"McMasters..."

"Hmm?" Ann had heard the word too many times

"Nothing. 'Guy I knew. He made sense, too."

The quiet had gone on too long. Ann picked up on a different thread of Sam's thought, just to hear the music of words again:

"You have to, Sam! You make sense of it all and you begin to see that individuals have to do something. Braun is attacking a symbol of oppression: Destroying banks! - which are part of the real government of the world. Tell the Brits about *that* and their damned economic theories!"

Sam was still with his own thoughts. "Yeah," he answered vaguely – but Ann was into her own circle of thinking, too. "You never heard of the Great Famine of Ireland, Sam, but it's where the true nature of their system showed its colors. Y'see, the Brits controlled Ireland and said that the only food we could eat was the potatoes we grew in our own rock-poor piece of soil - whilst the grains, cattle and other foods were for export only. Oh, a fine 'n dandy economic theory it was: the people feed themselves and Ireland feeds the rest of the British Empire...

"Except when a blight hits the potato crop - and the British authorities refuse to let Irish mothers feed their children from the export larder. 'Twould *not* be in the overall economic interest to divert food for Britain to the *Irish*."

Ann paused to catch her breath and let Sam utter an appropriate "fuck" at the obscenity of the British mercantile policy. He didn't answer, though, didn't even hear her words, actually. He was thinking of Sly Stone's singing and surprising his own thoughts that it made sense here. *Here!*

> *One child*
> *Grows up to be*
> *Somebody who loves to learn*
> *One child*
> *Grows up to be*
> *Somebody who just loves to burn*
> *Mom loves*
> *Both of them*

You see it's in the blood
Both childs
Love their Mom
Blood is thicker than the mud

He let the music and the song in his head move his body in slight, swaying circles. Too small, almost, for Ann to notice: they were sitting apart, each burrowed deeply inside their own coats, fighting off the shivering cold that invaded the van once the engine was switched off. They could not chance running a motor so near the border; whatever Braun's arrangements with the East Germans for crossing were, they did not include Sam and Ann.

It's a fam'ly affair
It's a fam'ly af-fa-air
A-air
Air

Besides, if they touched they would be in one another's arms again in a minute: it had taken an effort to leave the old Pollack's farmhouse at midnight. Maybe if he had just let them crash, left them alone in the dead man's sleep they had sunk into as soon as their heads touched pillow minutes after arriving.

But, no. The old man had pounded on their door at six o'clock, forcing them to wake and join his daughter "from Munich, she is from Munich" and himself for dinner. Maybe it was a good dinner; neither Sam nor Ann had an appetite. After an hour of polite attempts at pidgin Polish-German conversation, they were allowed to return to their room.

Where they could not sleep.

Sam's eyes were closed for a solid hour, maybe more - he assumed Ann's were, too - when he heard her ask:

"You asleep?"

"Not yet."

"Me, too."

He opened his eyes; there was no difference in degrees of darkness. Small fireworks of color exploded lazily in the empty void. From somewhere in the kitchen down below there echoed the familiar clink of china being stacked.

Ann turned on her side and slid next to him under the thick, warm comforter. "We'll have to leave in a couple of hours," she said quietly, not a whisper, perching her chin on his right shoulder. "They'll come sometime between midnight and dawn, if they come at all tonight."

"Or tomorrow night."

"Right. Do you think we can sneak right back in?"

"I don't know if we can sneak right *out*."

"Oh, c'mon!" she chided. "Didn't you ever sneak out after your mother and father said 'no'?"

"I-"

"C'mon, c'mon - I'll bet you did!"

"Sure, I-"

They laid there in the dark, curled up together, swapping high school adventure stories, stories that sounded amazingly alike despite a distance of six thousand miles and an Atlantic Ocean and a few shades of color, religion, politics and family composition. Or maybe they made things up just to be amenable: Sam knew that *he* wasn't telling the whole story, just remembering the parts that fit into the moment, a moment where - at some point - Ann burrowed under the covers and rested her head on Sam's belly, gently licking his skin there in small, ticklish circles. He stifled a giggle. He ducked his head down under the comforter to whisper something to her - they clunked heads instead - then they both started giggling, trying to muffle their voices in the blankets. Almost as one they both emerged for air, pulling the cold oxygen deep into their lungs before feeling their faces bend wide in silly grins again.

Whether Ann started to giggle again first, or Sam, neither one could tell - just as neither one could really tell afterwards who came up with the sudden inspiration to enforce silence by crashing into the other's lips in an open-mouthed kiss, tongues thrusting strongly around one another. Ann had worn only a T-shirt and panties to bed: they were off in a flash as she arched her back in response to the cold air outside the blankets, sitting astride Sam, dropping onto his penis and riding him in furious, wordless gasps until she came, then he came, then they both collapsed on one another, still joined. Even with Ann's entire body on top of him, Sam felt no discomfort; she was scarcely half his weight. A human blanket. But, as his muscle tension dissolved into beautiful jelly, his fingers noticed the gooseflesh prickling her back: he carefully drew up the comforter to her shoulders. In a moment they would both be able to sleep.

Or not. Against all better judgment - or control - Sam felt his member begin to expand again. "Oh, shit!" he thought. Or thought he thought. "That's not shit, that's the power of the oppressed, rising up from the ashes of honest labor to strike another blow!" Ann giggled, giggle turning to purr as she slid over to the side - still locked with Sam - and murmured: "My shift is over, your turn now, Mister Sam." The bedstead creaked slightly as Sam slowly began rotating his pelvis, thinking all the while how embarrassed he would be if getting it up was only as far as he could go this second time around.

He got a little farther - though it took a lot longer. By the end of the second round both Sam and Ann were thoroughly exhausted, deeply in love, and feeling like total shitheads: they knew if they fell asleep now they would *never* wake up in time to go out and wait for Braun.

There was no sound from downstairs, none from the room next door on the second floor: it was probable (although neither Sam nor Ann had any way of being certain) that the old Pollack and his daughter had gone to bed. It was only 10:30. They forced themselves to sit up in the dark, naked shoulders exposed to the cold to keep themselves awake, and waited forty-five minutes before daring to creep around the room, dressing and assembling their things. A clucking chicken wandering outside by the front door was the only sentinel challenging their exit.

"Zero hour."

Ann was dozing; Sam had to nudge her gently.

"What?" she asked, blinking her eyes rapidly in surprise at her own unconsciousness.

"They're here... I hope."

Ann turned to see the same change in the border that had caught Sam's eye.

A small change, actually, nothing specific: the faint glow of a light on the horizon, too bright and too quickly rising to be the sun, even though coming from the east. Sam and Ann stared fixedly at the opposite hills, trying to will meaning into the changing reflections of headlight beam dancing along a road cut just beyond the range of their sight. It might only be the East German border patrol...

A private vehicle crested the ridge.

"It's them," Ann whispered.

It was a van, a vehicle like theirs. That was all they had time to establish, however: driving a few yards down the hill, towards the border, the van doused its headlights. The sudden change made a glowing blank in Sam's retina. He squeezed his eyelids closed in an attempt to accelerate an improvement in his night vision.

Ann located Braun's van first - by sound: she rolled down her window and listened for the motor. The sound was erratic, shifting gears, but combined with her own improving night sight to aid her in homing in on the general location.

"Over there," she pointed: in the distance, the van (headlights still out) wound a crooked, landmine-dodging path across the plowed fields, occasionally crossing a pool of light made by the intermittent spotlights. Whoever was driving followed a pre-set arrangement; the sharp turns were clearly mapped-out. Finally, Braun's van reached the barbed wire fence that stood, tall and menacing, along "the line". Two figures, young men, hopped out of the rear door, jogged over to the fence, and began fiddling with something at a post.

"I don't know those two," Ann said after a moment, "I guess Jo and Birgit - and Braun - they must be inside the van."

"Do we go to them now, or what?" Sam asked.

"No!" Ann was alarmed at the thought. "They don't know us from Jesus right now, and even Him they probably wouldn't trust."

The two at the fence pulled back on the post, opening a "gate", a non-improvised hole, in the barbed-wire.

"Then what do we - ?"

Braun's van drove through the opening onto the West German side of the border; the two men at the wire began returning the fence to its former status.

"We'll follow 'em at a distance till morning. They're bound to stop for food or something." Ann sounded a bit like she was trying to convince herself as well. "Once they've stopped, I'll introduce myself - then you."

"Uh-huh," Sam was watching, trying to learn who they were. At least one of the two men at the fence he remembered: the boy who cried into McMasters' face, all upset about his friend that the MP had shot. They were only a hundred yards away, maybe closer, down a small hill now. The one who was not the crying boy gave a final tug at the fence post - whatever he was checking held - then the two climbed back into the van.

"There's Birgit! I knew it!" Ann cried *sotto voce* at the quick glimpse of a woman offered by the opening-and-closing of the rear doors to let the two re-enter.

"We'll wait." Sam said the words calmly; Ann had no conflict to disagree with.

Braun's van crossed a small field below them, making for a farm road. In the middle of the field the headlights popped back on: Braun was clearly travelling away from Sam and Ann's hidden position. Reaching the dirt road, the van rounded the corner of a low hill and disappeared from sight.

Sam started up their own van's engine. "Now we'll fol-"

Braun's van came roaring back down the farm road, directly towards them.

"What the -?!" Ann cried.

"Hold on!" Sam jammed the stickshift into gear, stamping on the accelerator. Headlights still out, the yellow van skidded straight ahead with a jerk, crossing the road and pulling unceremoniously into the middle of a thicket of trees with a scrape of paint along the entire right side.

The piercing headlight beams from Braun's van swept over their old position instants later, followed by the van itself roaring past. Within seconds it was over the next hill and out of sight, leaving only darkness and the idling sound of the yellow van's motor behind.

Sam and Ann both had their windows rolled down, tensely straining to hear how far away Braun's van was. In the country night, the churning engine echoed clearly its progress. Far enough away not to be coming back soon. They began to laugh nervously.

"And we wanted to meet them!" Sam chuckled.

"Well, not *here* anyway," Ann drew a mock gesture of

disdain at their woody surroundings, "not elegant enough - oh!" Alarm hit her and Sam at the same moment. "Oh, shit!"

"Can't lose them now!" Sam yelled, slamming the yellow van into reverse gear and removing another meter of dirty paint in the process. But they were out of the thicket and headed along the dirt road in less than five seconds.

"Keep the lights off for a while if you can, Sam."

"Righteous, lady."

Sam was thinking the same thing. He jumped gears from reverse to second, then was in third before they were twenty yards into their pursuit. Fortunately, the dirt road stood out clearly to his night-adjusted eyes; they went fifty klicks per hour over the same farm machine-battered surface they had made only sixty klicks on in the afternoon. Hopefully, whoever was driving in Braun's van was not trying for any speed records.

But even if they weren't, they were far ahead. Sam drove in silence over rolling hill after hill, following the direction Braun's van had taken, without any indication that he was still going the right way. They lost track of the other van by sound as soon as their own accelerating motor filled their ears. There was nothing to see. To both of their credits, neither Sam nor Ann blamed the other for the impending possibility of losing their quarry. There was no other choice but to do it this way: in lieu of a direct contact with Braun, Ann had done the best she could - and had found Braun for Sam. But both knew that, in Braun's shoes, the sight of two strangers suddenly appearing out of the darkness would have provoked a violent reflex. Daylight and a public place had to be their introductory companions. If they didn't lose Braun first. Sam took chances on the dirt road that risked spinning out into more than one drainage ditch.

Without saying it aloud, he gambled that Braun's van would be heading for the autobahn south of Fladungen, the same link to the rest of West Germany he and Ann had traversed the day before. What was the town? *Bad*-something, or *Heustreu*? If they did not catch up with the other van by then, then the autobahn would whisk Braun away beyond finding in seconds. Intentionally, Sam took the risk of discovery as a granted and turned on his headlights, using the extra illumination to accelerate to the frantic level.

They found Braun's van five kilometers later, topping a rounded hill still another kilometer distant - but easily in sight.

"All right! We got 'em."

At Ann's insistence, Sam doused the headlights again: it was safe to drive slower now, instead of playing catch-up they simply had to tag along. 'Best not to be seen following. Only when they skirted the suburbs of a small town did Ann suggest that - the autobahn sign being clearly displayed - at this point it would be *natural* to see another car or two on the road. She had experience on this point: no one in the van ahead would be concerned about another vehicle following them from the town to the highway.

And she was right on both counts: two others joined them on the road, a small Volkswagen and a produce truck, and Braun's van did not alter its course a degree. Rather, traffic at intersections becoming a fact of life even at this early hour, Sam and Ann found themselves cruising only a hundred meters behind Braun and his people, the Volkswagen between them, putt-putting nervously in several tentative attempts to pass around Braun's van and beat the small convoy to the highway by thirty seconds.

"Assholes on the road even here," Sam muttered.

"Try France, you'll love it," Ann commented dryly.

"I been a foot-walker there."

"I'm happy to have met you alive, then. Bastards." She smiled lazily, explaining: "I would have said 'sons of bitches', but I like female dogs too much. They're heading west."

Braun's van had passed the first autobahn entrance turn-off to signal its intentions for the second, heading further away from their former refuge, west. It was easy to follow them up to the highway and blend into the light traffic. The produce truck did likewise, as did the obnoxious Volkswagen.

"You sure they don't go crazy trying to figure out if anybody's following 'em?" Sam asked.

"That's just it: you *do* go crazy if you think about it too much..." she let the concept drift off, remembering her own fears of discovery. "You try not to think about it."

"Yeah - and I suppose having a gun in your hand don't hurt in the security department."

"About the guns, Sam..."

The sky behind them was beginning to brighten.

"Mmm."

"We've got the drop-off point set up." Ann tried stretching the muscles in her shoulders, avoiding direct contact with Sam, to touch upon the delicate point: "I need to tell them when you'll be prepared to deliver..."

The autobahn sign pointed them back in the direction of

Frankfurt and points beyond. Sam still had not decided whether to jettison the whole idea and jump off at the safety of base. "'You gotta have 'em now?"

"No, and I didn't want you to think about it before we met Braun. But we're almost there now, when they stop for food or gas, and -" Suddenly Ann's voice was filled with concern. "-I don't want you making any mistakes when you fill your part of the bargain. I want you safe more than I want any guns."

"I'm sure you're talking for everyone, right?" It would be easy to turn off at Frankfurt, jump out of the van, be gone before Ann could know what he was doing.

"I mean -" she was stuttering on words, her strongest allies. She tried to sound bravado, limiting her concern to "professional" matters:

"I mean - There are ways you can do it right, and ways you can get caught right away. Don't go -"

Braun's van continued past the last Frankfurt exit.

"- don't go and, and - make mistakes." Ann turned her head and stared out the passenger side window. Sam continued to follow the other van.

* * * * * * * * * *

Anger is a contrary emotion. It is hard to direct – even more difficult to maintain with any degree of passion. And anger without passion is a comic farce. Hate is easier. There's a cold dispassion to true hatred. It doesn't have to be all-consuming and emotion overwhelming. Hatred can be directed with pointed accuracy. It can be intellectually justified. It can be action. Or so it was for Braun.

When did I first understand what Josef had done? Braun himself could not say for certain the moment, sometime in 1965, when Isa's help evolved into something with meaning for him. Isa - poor, plain goose Isa, with her grey-brown jackets and limpid hair, slightly too-plump breasts fronting a body that was altogether much more modest than those twin projectiles implied. *She so thought she was "using" me,* Braun remembered with as much fondness as he could muster for his former Stasi minder. And in the end, sleeping with him almost every night, Isa did not realize herself that he would have done what he was doing now whether or not he was funded by the East. By the year 1968, when youth's rebellion broke out in riots all over Europe, Braun commanded his cadres without need - or direction - from his ostensible "superiors".

Isa's minder understood, though: he replaced her cruelly with a more hard-minded substitute who quickly evaluated the practical implications of the situation that had developed: Braun hated Western capitalism for shielding a person like Josef Sinder and helping him to prosper - Braun led his student followers in strikes aimed at destroying that system. Violent strikes. In the turbulence of '68, Braun's acts did not stand out as singular. That Braun was acting on his own, the new minder concluded, was immaterial. The effect was the same - and there was even an honest wall of "deniability" between the Stasi and its *agent provocateur.*

Josef, why would you do this? Brown asked, jumping back to the present tense of 1972 repeatedly. *Did you* really *do this?* Like

191

the Stasi who had trained him over the months in the techniques of moving through West Germany covertly, Braun found only the rumors, never the facts. This uncertainty alone was enough to prevent him from ever enjoying the delicious, warm taste of true anger. Instead, with a slow gnawing, cold hate numbed his emotions with the same cancerous efficiency as they had been deadened in the camps.

Except that, in one of the camps, there had been the Rabbi.

"You like Jews so much, stay with them!" had been his first sentence of incarceration. The Rabbi was a babbling young farmer from some godforsaken Jewish town in Poland called Czosnek – garlic. That's what he smelled of, too: garlic. Grown up in a family that tilled garlic fields, raising his own crops of the stinking bulbs himself, the Rabbi hadn't the sense to run into the Krakow ghetto when the invaders came. There, at least, he would have been protected from deportation to the camps for another two years. No, the Rabbi had been grabbed up in the middle of his field, weeding out the rows of garlic plants. His luck was in not being used for target practice right then and there by the incredulous German soldiers. "There's no one to bury the Yid if we shoot him, and he'll stink up the field if we leave him," argued the *über*-sergeant, himself a peasant farmer who looked forward to making that particular field his spice pantry for the next several months. Near the decrepit house that the Rabbi called home, there was planted a small garden of herbs: dill, basil, pepper - even a small tomato plant. Tomatoes! And there was a cherry tree! The city-born soldiers under his command did not realize the luck they

had stumbled onto. "Ship off the Yid to some place where they work - he's got a strong back," the sergeant ordered, involving himself in the important business of convincing his officers to bivouac *here* instead of in the town.

The Rabbi was uneducated, but not unlearned. He was always nervous, but not incoherent. He spoke all the time, but not without meaning. He spoke in thesis-antithesis rhythms that eventually drove everyone near him almost crazy with annoyance.

"God may seem cruel, but he is teaching us. This is so horrible, but we deserve it. We may die, but we may grow. We despair of the present, but we can still hope. We —"

"Shut up, Rabbi... please."

"I'm not a rabbi, I only quote from the Talmud."

"I'm not Jewish, I don't care."

"You are a man, God cares."

"If God cares, why does he allow this?"

The Rabbi always broke at this, looking at Braun with honest disillusion.

"I think... He has forgotten. He was close to us once, He made us in His image, but we disappointed Him and He cast us away. In punishing us, I think, God has forgotten how to be human."

The Rabbi would turn his eyes away from Braun, sad in that simple, most honest way that peasants can sometimes achieve.

"I wish I knew how to touch God – and remind Him..."

They shot the Rabbi one day when he sprained his ankle and didn't get up fast enough. Braun could never, totally, stop feeling whenever he remembered the twisted body lying by the side of the road: the Rabbi's eyes were still open, and it looked for all the world as if he had almost - but not quite - found the damn answer.

Which was, maybe, the answer that Braun had found. It took him four years of random violence, bursts of action without - quite - finding a sense to it. Then he remembered the Rabbi and knew what he would do: he would *scrape* the heart of God with his fingernails until there was feeling again.

Braun looked at his hand, relaxed, fingers half-bent - a claw - and he wondered if this was how Lucifer was born.

* * * * * * * * *

Braun's vehicle did not stop for gasoline or food or rest.

The turnoff for Bonn was passed. Then, at the ring encompassing Köln, they circled the city. To Sam and Ann it was a weird turnaround: Braun's van was almost exactly retracing their journey to the border only a day earlier. Would Braun and his people continue on to Amsterdam? Ann began to wonder if Jurgen (or, more likely, Dineka) had passed on her interest in Braun to her Berliner K-Group contacts. There had not been enough time, though. Not enough time. Maybe - in a week or so…

Braun's van took the autobahn towards Aachen.

Unconsciously, Ann let out a sigh of relief: she did not appreciate coincidence. Whatever else, the people in front of her were not headed for Amsterdam. Not yet.

"They'll probably be stopping fairly soon," she advised Sam. "Places are starting to open up."

It was still early in the morning, but commuter traffic

was heavy; the highway into Aachen, only a few kilometers from the southeast Dutch border, was crowded with trucks. It became more difficult for Sam to keep Braun's van in sight, losing the freshly-painted blue vehicle for several seconds at a time as large multi-wheelers pulled between the yellow van and its leader. "I'll *try* to stay close," Sam snapped after Ann made a number of suggestions to that effect. They were both on edge from the hours of travel and anticipation.

As if in acknowledgement of their exhaustion, Braun's vehicle left the autobahn at the first exit marked for Aachen. Aachen: founded by Charlemagne. Once the capital of Frankish Europe, now a provincial city fighting to grow large. The vans were still very far from the *centrum*; the Eifel mountains crowded around them here: steep-roofed, half-timbered houses perching on narrow stone foundations hovered three and four stories above them in perilous equilibrium.

"Jesus!" Ann breathed in awed doubt of the buildings' stability.

"Those things fall over, don't they?" Sam added in support of her opinion. He guided the yellow van on its descent into the rocky valley bordering a river, along which Braun's van ran over the well-paved road with familiarity. Despite this intrusion of natural obstacles to the city's modern expansion, Aachen's outer edges quickly dominated. The two vehicles proceeded into increasingly commercial districts.

It was only a few minutes past seven a.m.

Braun's van entered a small square - probably the *centrum* of a former satellite town to Charlemagne's capital, overtaken now by Aachen's expansion to an incorporated subservience not unlike feudal derogation. Keeping a full block's distance behind, Sam slowed down, then double-parked, when Braun's van pulled to a stop near a street corner, a natural enough action, there being a Stop sign at the spot.

Still…

"I guess this is food time," Ann hazarded the opinion.

"Certainly no gas stations around," Sam agreed.

There was also a bank.

"Oh, shit!" Sam exclaimed, as a woman and three men - including Braun - emerged from the rear of the blue van carrying weapons. One of the weapons, Sam recognized, was a Howitzer 105: "capable of piercing up to three inches of armor, and accurate enough at five hundred yards to hit the same spot twice consistently." Holding tightly onto the steering wheel, Sam recited the manual specs by rote, a litany of textbook descriptions: this had been his weapon of choice in the war games. He did not notice that Ann, much more nervous, had an automatic pistol in her hand and anxiously touched the door handle as if she were about ready to jump out of the van.

Sam turned off the engine and hoped that Braun and his people did not notice them double-parked on the opposite corner of the square. It was an iffy proposition: the square was relatively unpeopled so early in the day, the bank itself - *Sinder und Sohnen* - closed and dark. Sam considered taking Ann and bolting from the van to seek shelter further away. He did not move.

"What're they doing?" Ann's voice intruded upon Sam's thoughts.

His reply was tensely sarcastic: "Besides robbing a bank?"

"I can see what they're goin' to do," she snapped, "but what are they-"

The flash of explosion came first, but the shocking crash came an instant later to cut off her words. The dirty yellow van rocked gently from the concussion.

Dust and smoke obscured the wall of the bank.

Somehow - as in chess, as in the war games - Sam's mind began observing details even as his pulse rate soared from the unexpected impact of adrenaline and shock waves. He noticed that the blue van was, actually, fairly distant from the bank - and that Braun, a woman and a man - Birgit and Jo, Ann had identified them - used the van for protection against the aftershock of the explosion. The one with the howitzer ("Wolf or Alex," Ann said, "I don't know them apart, just their names."), having fired the charge, half-protected himself from flying debris behind a corner of the van, too. Wolf/Alex shook himself free from the effects of the explosive's concussion waves, then began reloading the howitzer. Braun stepped away from the van, followed by Birgit, and began firing his weapon at an unseen target.

Sam craned his neck, pressing his forehead against the windshield, to see a German policeman fall to his knees on the pavement, scarcely a half block away from where the yellow van hiding himself and Ann was double-parked. A replay of the Frankfurt bank robbery: would the terrorists start shooting at him again, too? To have come so far -

Braun and Birgit took hurried steps back to the side of their blue van; the howitzer fired again. The bank wall exploded open.

In the ensuing seconds of concussive deafness, a second German policemen darted from his hiding place in a doorway, aiming for his wounded friend. The terrorists' attention was occupied by the gaping hole emerging from the smoky explosion, breaching the bank vault inside the building. The second policeman reached for his colleague with one hand, foolishly fired a popgun of a pistol with the other. What he hit - on the run, without proper aim - was anyone's guess; not any of Braun's people at any rate. Braun fired a quick burst from his automatic weapon, pausing a second beforehand *to* take aim: a line of bullets spattered the brick street in front of the second policeman who quickly changed directions, abandoning his luckless friend, and ran back to a safe corner.

Braun's people were well-rehearsed, much better coordinated than they had been in Frankfurt. Fascinated as a mouse is by a rattlesnake, Sam and Ann sat frozen in their places, witnessing the unfolding tactics of attack: Birgit ran forward to the center of the small square in an aggressive defense position, freeing Braun to concentrate his attention on the bank; Jo helped the other man ("Wolf" Ann said under her breath, "yeah, that's Wolf.") dump the howitzer into the rear of the blue van, then both young terrorists dashed over to the hole in wall; at a nod from Braun, they pushed their way through the hole and into the bank vault. Sam's eyes caught sight of a peripheral activity.

"Don't do it - !" he whispered, almost to himself, at the realization that the second policeman had apparently decided that the woman terrorist was less dangerous than the men: the Aachen policeman ran forward from his position of safety, rapidly firing his pistol, diving to the ground, trying once more to reach his wounded partner.

Birgit sank to a kneeling position, fired several single-spaced shots from her AK-47.

Rolling on the ground, the German policeman tried to stay ahead of the bullets kicking up sparks on the ground around him, miraculously succeeding. Birgit flipped a lever on her automatic rifle, changing the pattern of fire from single-shots to short, clustered bursts.

The policeman must have finally realized the extremity of his position: he jumped to his feet, holding his pistol with two hands in a pathetic attempt to bring it to accurate aim on the woman.

"Fuckin' idiot!" Sam cried.

Birgit released a long, scattershot-aimed burst of gunfire at the German. She did not wait to see him fall back on his ass from the impact of the three shots that punctured his solar plexus; he sat there, a surprised look on his face, almost comical, dead - while she sprinted over to the bank wall and began helping Alex take shopping-net bags full of hundred mark currency from Wolf and Jo, transfering the money from vault to van.

"Fuckin' - !" Sam cried again, re-seeing stupid McMasters pull the same failed trick in Frankfurt, "- you don't go up against a AK-47!"

Braun, assured that the bank robbery was successfully nearing completion, directed his attention back out to the square. Any moment reinforcements from the Aachen police would be arriving; at the first hint of a distant siren, his van would be gone. Destroy the vault and leave in anonymous, mediocre speed; one undistinguished service van among the hundreds of others in the morning commercial traffic.

But for now, attention.

Braun let his eyes linger on each of the dozen passersby who had been caught on the street when the assault on the bank began: two shopkeepers over there, sweeping their sidewalks before the attack, cowering against their display windows; a trio of women; another such trio; a yellow van with a Negro boy and white girl -

"He sees us..." Ann said in awe, afraid to acknowledge Braun's recognition of their presence. She could not know that he saw only himself in the mismatched pair.

"You see, mein fraulein, moja cudowna, droga Rachel," the pale young man whispered sweetly to his dark love, "fears are impossible to believe on a fine Sunday morning, yes?"

Her seventeen year-old smile was tentative, uncertain.

"You are with me," her Silesian suitor cooed, assured in his own seventeen year-old way of the power of youth and love. "This is 1937, not the Middle Ages: politicians talk, only talk. There are no more witch hunts, or pogroms, or..."

This was not making Rachel any calmer. Only the warm sun seemed to have any positive effect. And the children. Another band of children raced across the square, filling it with enough loud laughter to convert even dour Hitler to their cause. Rachel's lover was filled with a sudden inspiration.

"Sing, Rachel, sing - for our kinder who will be -"
A smile fluttered across the corners of her lips.
"Sing -"

They were finished inside the vault. Wolf hopped out through the hole, followed by Jo, who paused at the opening only long enough to pluck an incendiary grenade from his jacket, pull the pin, and toss it behind him into the vault. He ran with a ferocious fear behind the van to join the others there, throwing himself on the ground as a phosphorus-based explosion burst out of the hole to make the entire square white-blind for a moment - at least for those whose open eyes were unprepared for the lightening blast.

The terrorists *were* prepared; while Sam was shaking his head violently to clear his vision, Braun took a position in the driver's seat of the blue van and the others settled-in behind him. It was just barely possible for Ann to see the vehicle drive out of the square without haste.

"We've got to follow them, Sam!" she cried anxiously, exhilarated.

"Not two feet behind!" he protested.

"We've got to join them - Now! - before the police!" The "Ee-wah! Ee-wah!" of approaching police sirens seemed more of an echo than anything with a real source. Still, it was a threat. Sam started the yellow van and slid in the clutch with a jolt.

"They'll blow us away if we get to 'em right now!" he shouted in reiteration of the need for caution.

Ann acknowledged the probability that Braun's people were unapproachable at the moment, no matter how much the approachee admired them. "Well, follow them!" she snapped grudgingly.

"I am!" Sam angrily retorted, nervousness making his hands slide the H-gear into second again instead of fourth. The yellow van sped across the square in pursuit of Braun's in a roar of overworked engine strain. Sam turned down the same off-street the terrorists had taken from the square.

"There they are! See?!" Ann pointed. Sam could *not* see: his attention was concentrated on maneuvering the narrow street. A block ahead of them Braun was calmly blending his vehicle in with the heavy flow of commercial traffic leading from one of Aachen's main industrial districts. A second later, it had turned a corner and was out of view.

"Faaas-terrr!" Ann urged desperately. Sam rammed the yellow van as fast as he could towards the line of heavy traffic. Collision was seemingly apparent. A slow-shifting truck left a gap in the traffic flow which the yellow van occupied with only centimeters to spare. Ann did not complain about the jolt of brakes that prevented them from rear-ending the car in front.

Braun's van could barely be seen ahead of them. That it could be seen at all was cause for a moment's rejoicing. Police sirens screamed around them - at both ends of the crowded line of traffic - but the *polizei*'s automobiles were nowhere to be seen, hidden behind tall trucks and sharp corners, converging on the deserted, wrecked square where only a burning bank, shocked citizens and two dead colleagues awaited them.

A Mercedes pulled into the street ahead of Sam, blocking his way crosswise.

"Motherfuck-!"

He did not give the Mercedes' driver opportunity to right himself into the traffic flow; Sam jerked the steering wheel into a hard turn and cut-off the other driver - as well as the street's middle lane - to steer around the Mercedes and still in pursuit of Braun's van.

The blue vehicle was stopped by the traffic as well, idling patiently behind a large trailer-truck hauling furniture. Both van and truck occupied the far right lane; both waited for a small convoy of police cars to pass through the intersection in front. The yellow van from Holland steadily gained on them.

And Sam wondered how much he really wanted to succeed.

He guided his vehicle aggressively toward the terrorists - the blue van was still far ahead, but clearly in sight now - all the while feeling reluctance claw at his every hand movement. This was Braun ahead.

A second trailer-truck, then a third, came between the two vans, slicing-off visual contact. Sam tried to switch lanes, but even Ann's frantic leaning out the window and signaling/pleading with the car hanging onto their right rear fender to let them segue-in could not make the trailer immediately next to them move any faster. Slowly they eased their way over - but the flow of traffic had already carried them past the intersection.

Braun's van had made the turn.

Sam and Ann's vehicle was tied up in a snarl of traffic now, the entire area engulfed by yet another wave of police sirens bearing down on the sight of recent violence. A sharp contrast to the quiet flow of automobiles and trucks onto the autobahn which the terrorists' van easily joined. Aachen was left far behind in minutes.

Ann leaned back in her seat; beside her Sam sat rigid, arms held straight out, grasping the steering wheel. Without intentionally mimicking him, Ann stretched out her arms straight, too, resting her hands on the dashboard. Only then, for the first time, did Sam notice the automatic pistol clutched in her right hand.

"What're you doing with that!?"

Ann hastily put the weapon back into its deep burial place within her shoulder bag. "I didn't know if the police'd be after us," she answered without embarrassment. They both angrily refused to look one another in the face.

"Damn!" Sam hit the steering wheel with a tight fist.

"You couldn't have followed closer," Ann grudgingly conceded. "You were right not to try."

But Sam's thoughts were far away from worries about having lost Braun's trail.

"Damn I gotta know!" he said loudly to himself. He did not know exactly *what*, but -

He nervously pounded on the steering wheel. Abruptly, Sam turned off the engine. "I don't need this," he barked, seized with a new line of complete thought. He turned on Ann:

"Was it the same bank?"

"Bank?"

"'Bank this Sinder dude owns!"

"Yes…" Ann answered, disoriented by the subject being questioned. "It was. He can't have many of them left."

Sam was no longer interested in Sinder's banks. "Where you say he was?"

"Who?! Sam, stop taking so fas-"

"Sinder. In Köln, right?!"

"Yes. Sinder - yes: a big place. Outside the city, of course."

Sam's resolution was immediate. "Gotta go there."

The jammed traffic began to move forward in fitful lurches. Sam re-started the motor.

"...Go there..." he repeated, working out the thought from inspiration to strategy. He had never before successfully embraced the option of moving so many pieces before. It would be interesting to see how far he got this time. He had to try.

Facts

Every time the identical routine: Replace the license plate, change the exterior markings, make the van look the same yet "different". Alex liked the routine, the repetition made him forget about Karl, dead Karl, best cook and friend. Nothing "funny" between Alex and Karl, no (let the Berliners think what they want, desire what they could not have) - just the loyalty of roommates and conversations after midnight between lonely students. Alex removed the Hamburg plate, placed a München license over the empty bumper, and began screwing it on conscientiously. Manual skills were not his forte: he had to concentrate upon the minor task - and not think about Karl.

Jo laughed expansively at Wolf's snide joke and held open wide the cabin door: they would join Alex in transforming the van from a monotone seriousness to a decorous two-tone. He was in a rhythmic mood and quoted Bartan, his former roommate and (underrated) "revolutionary poet":

> "And so it goes
> with industrial nations
> to hit
> the end
> of the road!"

Alex laughed delightedly along with Jo and Wolf at the double-edge meaning that the verse now held for them; his clumsy fingers knocked loose the single screw holding the license to the bumper and it clanged noisily to the ground.

Wolf snatched it up and used it to pantomime a guitar. "I -can't - get - no - sat-is-fac-tion," he sang *a cappella* in German.

"No satisfaction!" Alex chimed in in English.

"NO SATISFACTION!" all three roared, drowning the melody of the song in their enthusiasm. Wolf tossed the license plate back to Alex, urging the fumble-fingers to hurry up so they could cover the bumper with newspapers preparatory to repainting the lower half of the van. Alex tried his best, which was slow enough for aggravation.

But Jo would not let himself be aggravated, not this afternoon, here in the mountains, only half-a-day after their most recent triumph. Despite a frostiness to the air telling of snow soon coming to the upper altitudes, the fir trees still gave the slopes facing this temporary refuge a green and bluish tint. Jo did not see them, his thoughts ranging distantly further. Still in good-humor, he shared those thoughts aloud with the mildly bickering Wolf and Alex:

"Use the military mind against the militarist oppressors." He raised his forefinger and thumb like a pistol, shooting down the oppressors, "One, two, three."

"Four."

Jo turned at the sound: Birgit stood in the doorway, wearing glasses and holding a notebook, to which she referred, explaining with her usual pedantic specificity:

"Four. There were four banks. And now there is no more banking firm by the name of Sinder and Sons."

This was Birgit's conscious continuation of the long test of revolutionary wills between herself and Jo. Jo did not concede to let the matter drop.

"Yes, I know that. To destroy an entire capitalist institution, that was the goal, that is the success." He turned those accomplishments against her with a taunt: "And now you will write about it, yes?"

"Yes."

"The journalists always write." Jo said the words directly to her, then turned his head slightly to share the idea with the others.

Birgit was not distressed. "I write, yes. But not until we are finished."

She stepped from the doorway out into the small yard, closer to the discomfort she had spread among the young men: they all knew that they had unfinished business.

Birgit sat down in the van's open side door. Despite the back-and-forth of wills with Jo, she was not aggressive - not today, with its rush-forward highs - but shared their enthused feelings:

"We've still got to keep them from rebuilding it all, don't we?"

"Damn Sinder! He *would* rebuild it, too!" Jo angrily agreed, his *burgher*-class accent fighting the *Sturm und Drang* of his soul. "He would build it upon his sons' blood - he'll probably make a profit from their insurance!" He smashed his hand against the side of the van, causing a dent to appear and sending a tingling shock through his forearm.

"No!" Jo fought to keep his tone low and controlled: even the slightest hint of passion always aroused derisive comparisons with the fascist Hitler. Jo was no fascist. "We still have to destroy Sinder. Braun was right."

His pale eyes met Birgit's - and again he felt the suppressed desire to please the older woman, to be like the man she admired. To be better. Birgit did not smile derisively when she answered:

"And I will write about it then. And Braun *is* right -"

The others did not disagree.

"- And *we* will have done something. And others will read about it. And -"

She really, truly, was happy at the thought.

" - and help us… They *have* to help us."

Was this a plea, or an order? A plan or a hope?

"It is the only way to fight the oppressors."

"They will join us," Jo reassured her with the confidence of inexperience.

Birgit smiled at this: she had always felt more at ease with the generation a decade younger than herself - except with Braun, of course, who was another fifteen years older. She liked the Stones. *Satisfaction.* Even in German it worked.

"When I'm driving in my car

And a man comes on the radio -"

But Birgit's was a sweet voice, and Alex needed to add a coarse male reality to the rock 'n rock 'n rrooolll:

"And he's telling me more and more

About some use-less in-for-ma-tion -"

An-gry! In English!

"Supposed to *try* my *i-ma-gi-na-tion!*

I can't get no

No, no, no!"

It was a chanted chorus now:

"I CAN'T GET NO

NO, NO, NO!"

Braun watched them through the small square of cabin window, letting his right hand fall unceremoniously onto Frederick's thick neck: the Great Schnauzer growled with the contentment of a fed wolf as the strong fingers dug through his fur, massaging.

"SATISFACTION!

NO SATISFACTION!!!"

The frustrated lyrics invaded Braun's fingers: he pulled Frederick back by a thick fold of skin, then knelt down to face the leering fangs.

"Ha!"

Braun released the huge dog's neck and Frederick grabbed his arm in response. Man and animal began a rough, dangerous tumble about the floor, wrestling for control of the unseen bone called "dominance." Affection and deadly intention mixed in equal portions. Braun took both hands and put them around Frederick's throat, pushing the Great Schnauzer back; Frederick arched his backbone to an impossible angle, flinging himself and Braun off-balance and onto the hardwood floor with a minor crash.

Outside, they were too busy full-lunged singing to hear.

Now, in a turnabout, Braun put his own teeth to the dog's flesh, at the throat again, growling meaningfully and coming out with a mouthful of loose fur. Braun spat it out and laughed at his own stupidity; Frederick looked up at his master with deep love. They continued to wrestle a minute more, less aggressively now, though animal exuberance and sharp claws produced more than a few scratches - which the human answered with a pinch here, a tail-pull there, that created a few distressed yelps in revenge.

But their "battle" was almost concluded when Jo's voice echoed through the closed door with particular, clichéd vehemence:

"And then Justice! as we fight the oppressors and Burn, baby, Burn!"

To this heartfelt, plagiarized sentiment Braun reacted sarcastically, pulling the dog's huge head up close to his own so that they sat nose-to-nose squatting on the floor. "Justice!?" he addressed Frederick in his most professorially rhetorical tone of voice, "There is no justice in the world."

He let the Great Schnauzer slide to a lying position now and roughly began fondling him. Frederick had heard the sentiment before, but Braun needed to say it aloud once again - and it would not do to let the followers hear their leader speak so:

"...Men shall come and men shall go, and only those blessed with their damned passivity shall survive. Those with life, with a spirit for life, are destined to perish the earliest."

Frederick's soulful eyes asked the appropriate question: "For what?"

"For some damned ideal that life must be lived to the fullest."

The Great Schnauzer licked Braun's hand carefully, his lowered head asking the next question: "And what is the fullest?"

"Frederick, I tell you: This 'living life to the fullest' is some blasted evil conception of eating, drinking, and talking that anyone can do and most choose to do boringly."

Braun sighed into the dog's face. "Damned passivity and a taste for ignorance. Don't let them fool you, Frederick. They have no desire to live life to the fullest, but would rather feed off our successes and failures and cluck-cluck their tongues when we finally bite the dust. Don't worry about them. They'll survive…"

He stood up now, abandoning Frederick to a deep, untroubled, animal sleep. Through the small window he could see Wolf strapping on a guitar at the encouragement of the others; Alex had produced a pair of drumsticks and was setting up the old license plate between his legs as a percussive device.

"We won't…" Braun whispered very quietly, so as not to disturb the contented dog at his feet. But Frederick opened a single, questioning eye to his master.

"…Don't worry about that, either," Braun smiled, bending down to caress the animal's huge head.

"TWIST AND SHOUT
(Twist and shout)"

Alex and Wolf screamed through the mountains with their wild mantra - Beatles' version, certified Gold –

"TWIST AND SHOUT
(Twist and shout)
C'MON, C'MON, C'MON, BA-BY
(Come on, baby)

C'MON AND WORK IT ON OUT
(Work it on out)"

Rock and roll, after all, worked best in English: even Jo and Birgit agreed on this "revolutionary" point, joining the near-hysterical Alex on the shouted lead, letting Wolf carry the follow-through alone.

"YOU KNOW YOU LOOK SO GOOD
(Look so good)
YOU LOOK SO FINE
(Look so fine)
C'MON, C'MON, C'MON, BA-BY"

Braun did not let himself worry about their attracting attention: they would be on their way in two hours, maybe less. Long before any authorities could pinpoint their location among the echoing mountains.

"DON'T YOU KNOW THAT YOU'RE MINE!
ah - aH - AH - AAHHH

* * * * * * * * * *

The entrance to Sinder's compound was imposing - and security since the morning's attack on his Aachen bank, his last bank, was tightened almost to the breaking point. Sam and Ann had to submit to a thorough scrutiny to enter the front gate: each was patted down for concealed weapons, both forced to produce identification. It was only the fact of Sam's G.I. travel documents that allowed them in at all. None of the private security guards could figure who had the authority to bar business appointments and, while the two young people had no appointment, Sam's military papers implied a hastily arranged late afternoon meeting. The black private was smart enough to say nothing that would make them think otherwise.

And Ann was saying nothing at all.

Two security guards led them into the modernistic building, passing through the front entrance into an anteroom dividing Josef Sinder's office from the rest of the world. They were only admitted a few feet into the spacious lobby - clearing front gate security was only the first hurdle to surmount in Sam's quest to speak with the president and owner of the now-defunct Sinder and Sons - but when Sinder's personal assistant tried to converse with them it became immediately obvious that the language barrier could not be surmounted. Ann made no effort to assist. The assistant indicated a handful of comfortable armchairs further into the anteroom, nodded to the security guards that they could leave, then left himself in search of a translator: the police and journalists had all left by noon, but there was still a confusion of affairs to handle.

Sam followed the assistant's pantomimed advice and walked deeper within the room, though he did not allow himself to sit. He was too tired. He knew he would sink into an exhausted stupor, if not full sleep, if he touched down on one of the armchairs. Ann stood by the entrance door.

"Come in," Sam beckoned.

"Why? It's your business here, not mine." She had grown

increasingly reluctant as they drove to Sinder's enclave, thirty kilometers outside of Köln. Ann did not want her clear perceptions muddied by shades of grey.

"You could help me with the language," Sam answered, not bothering to keep the bite of exhaustion-tinged annoyance out of his voice.

"I can't stand the smell of the place," Ann spat back with her own bite. "I'll wait for you."

Sinder's personal assistant and a translator appeared as the departing Irishwoman charged out the door.

"Does the young lady-" the translator began to offer.

"No!" Sam turned back to the two men hurriedly. "It's my business: I came to talk to Josef Sinder about the stories."

The translator, an older man whose English skills dated back to studies in London in the 1930s, attempted to convey the rushed words to Herr Sinder's personal assistant, a statement which puzzled them both. Sam, indeed, puzzled them both: a nineteen year-old American Negro in the middle of the central office of Sinder & Sons. The two Germans self-consciously debated the young man's fate - there was really no question of allowing him in to see Herr Sinder: the grieving father and broken financial lord was not to be disturbed. But how to phrase the rejection once the imprudent security guards had let the American get this far? (The young woman had been so much more "convenient," leaving abruptly as she did.) Josef Sinder had instilled in his personnel a sense of polite civility that was presently at war with his assistant's and translator's desire to simply tell the stranger "Go away". They kept their voices low and uninflected and Sam could not make out the gist of their conversation through any nuance of emotion.

Finally, however, suitable response was settled upon. Proud of their decision, the two men turned to face Sam as one, neither noticing the door to Herr Sinder's office silently opening a crack.

The translator gave a deferential nod to the personal assistant as he explained to Sam: "Her Sinder does not give interviews to student journalists."

"No. I want to know about the stories."

The translator was confused by the method of the young American's refusal to be put off. "Know *what?*"

"Know about the war. Know if it's true…" Sam's voice trailed off - he had not thought out that much *what*, indeed, he wanted to ask, to know.

The translator related this confused conversation to his colleague. The personal assistant lost all pretense of civility. "I have no need of idiotic Americans sitting here!" he snapped.

"If you will just -" the translator cooed to Sam, trying to maintain a polite tone of conversation, "- give me your name and address, perhaps we can arrange an appointment next-"

"I know who killed his children!" Sam exploded, frightening the two Germans with his enthusiastic bulk and dark-ness. The translator shared a nervous glance with the personal assistant, who stretched his hand towards the security alarm button.

"I know who killed my children, too," Josef Sinder said in calm, quiet English. He stood in the now-fully opened doorway to his office, filling the space. He turned his back on the anteroom, disappearing from view. Only his voice crept out, muttering in German: "I will speak with him. Leave us alone."

An awkward moment in the anteroom: Sam did not understand the invitation. He stood before Sinder's two employees, uncertain.

The personal assistant stared resentfully at the Negro. "Go on," the translator said at last, recovering the momentum of his position.

As Sam hesitantly stepped towards the office doorway, Sinder's voice once again drifted out: "Please close the door behind you," he said absently, this time in English. Sam forgot to anyway; behind him Herr Sinder's personal assistant hurriedly rushed forward to pull it closed.

Sam had never been in a room with glass walls: it was fortunate that they were there, for the only illumination in the room came from the outside's dying sunlight. Sam's eyes were immediately attracted to a huge desk dominating the office - but Sinder was not there. A heavy sense of shadow hung over the room. For a moment there were just the dark silhouettes of two men to consider: no color, no cultural, no language differences between them. Sinder was not particularly interested in turning to formally greet the American boy; Sam, for his part, did not approach the German as if he expected any welcome. They were both stopped randomly in the room as if in the middle of a conversation between two familiar acquaintances - or comfortable enemies. Sinder stood with his back to Sam; Sam let his hands slide into his pockets and waited, feet apart. Conversation had not yet begun, and it was as if Sam had just said something and Sinder needed to take a few seconds to consider a response.

Those seconds taken, Sinder took a fleeting interest in several objects in the room as he spoke:

"I am well aware of why the terrorists have singled out my firm, and I know who they are." His accent was clean; it fought only with his conflicting desires to be philosophic, anguished and vengeful. "I have paid very highly for that information - and now you come to me with the same information. Is this philanthropy?"

"No."

Sinder abruptly pushed his face towards Sam's. "I know all of their names. I even know the grades they last received in school. Do you know that much?"

"No."

"But you know they are killing my sons."

"Yes. That's all they're doing."

Sinder turned his face away: he would allow the American to see his anger, nothing else. "Actually," he fought down a sob, disguising it as a stoic breath, "I have no more sons living. I have a grandson..."

Why did he admit this to a stranger? Why did he let this Negro in? He needed to talk. Sinder took a quick breath and said with almost disaffected ease: "My reports say that their intent is to destroy a single capitalist institution. Completely. And, as of this morning, they have succeeded."

"I know. I saw them this morning."

Like the cobra fascinated by the mongoose, Sinder asked with interest: "How did they do it?"

Sam let his professional mind respond. "With a Howitzer

105, a armor piercing weapon, two AK-47s and a incendiary bomb - prob'ly attached to a grenade."

It was important to talk. "I didn't have anymore children to kill, did I?" Sinder could not stop the sob this time.

Sam heard the tears. "That man hates you," he said quickly. "Did you do it?"

"They crucified Ernst!" Sinder still refused to let the young soldier see his face. But he had to tell someone, tell the wall, about Ernst: "He had very delicate hands from the rough soap we had to use after the war, and I taught him to write by wrapping my hand around his."

"What about the other kids?"

"Hmmm?" Sinder could see little Ernst's chapped hands, covered in petroleum jelly, struggling to hold the slippery pencil.

Sam could not tell where his interrogator's persistence came from. "What about the other kids, the ones who were sold to the Germans?"

"Sold to the Germans." For this Josef Sinder could face the other man, to explain. "I am German. We are all German - oh, you're not - but *we* were all... living every day... with a pain - here - from..."

He pointed to his stomach, and it was the correct place to point, but it was not, not...

"Not fear. Not fear. Those who are afraid break down and starve to death - or say stupid things. Then the Gestapo come and they have a reason for breaking down. But usually they don't, then. Usually they then become very calm and it is over - for them.

"But if they had talked to you the pain became worse, because if *they* thought *you* had *listened,* had *agreed* - ! And they knew - enough to suspect, and not enough to know the truth."

Sam had heard the same argument in Detroit. "No, man, they knew it was wrong."

"Nobody knew it was 'wrong'." Sinder answered, a sing-song ridicule to his voice. "You hear a bomb screaming down in the night and you don't say "Oh, yes, they have a perfect right to blast us into oblivion.'"! You see the inevitable happening to a ghetto and you know that gold will buy food for those who have a chance to live. Who have a *chance* to live, not the quixotic fantasy of - Two sons, murdered in... in..."

"You did it?" Sam's voice was unexpectedly hoarse.

"Did what?" Josef Sinder was growing impatient with explanation.

The impatience spurred Sam to anger. "I want to know, man, how you could, how anyone could-"

"Know *what*!?" Sinder roared. "You can't *know,* because nobody *knew*! Because nobody wanted to do anything that they did for half-a-dozen years and lost track of things that they would never do in a lifetime."

"Tell me anyway." Sam's voice was hard.

The hardness caused Sinder to falter: What was there to explain if it could never be understood? To explain that the Gestapo knew everything anyway? That there was never any doubt about the fate of foolish hopes?

"I will... later," he muttered, "I... will. But not today."

"Braun thinks you did it."

Sinder looked up at Sam with the rabbit-eyes of the accused. It was a momentary panic only: his absorption in self-pity became overwhelming immediately. With numb fingers Sinder found the buzzer at its familiar position on his desk. "Not today," he repeated.

The door to the anteroom opened immediately, Sinder's personal assistant and translator standing careful guard for his summons.

"This gentleman and I are through for now," he dictated in careful German. "Make him an appointment for... whenever - if he wants it. He is Herr -" He switched to English, directing the distracted question at the American: "What is your name?"

"Sam." Sam did not try very hard to elaborate.

"Sam..." Josef Sinder considered the name of his impromptu confessor. "... We will talk, Mister Sam... We will..."

Sam did not expect to see the man again.

In that, he was wrong.

* * * * * * * * *

"Did you tell him anything?"

Ann sat in the driver's seat and interrogated him with the same hard edge to her voice he had employed on Josef Sinder only minutes earlier. Stepping into the van through the passenger's door, Sam was shaken out of his private thoughts by the question.

"Tell him? No, I didn't try."

His cool distraction frightened Ann.

"Try! I was thinking of your telling Sinder something by accident! Were you *trying* to tell him things?!"

"No. And he knew more than we do anyway."

Ann sat back hard into the bench seat. "Bloody fascist and his-"

"Shut up." Sam turned angry, confused eyes on the Irishwoman - who did *not* accede to his wishes:

"Why don't *you* shut up, Sam!? Why?" she shot back, "Why! Why don't you just tell me if you found out what you wanted to know? He did it, didn't he? He did it-"

"He did it," Sam cut her off.

Consoled that the facts did, indeed, bear out her convictions, Ann remained silent for a long minute, staring at the security-gated entrance to Sinder's compound across the road. Satisfied emotion well-up inside her, though, and she finally had to burst out:

"Fascist pig."

"He's not a fascist!" Sam cried, the confusion in his eyes more pronounced than before. "It's not that simple!"

"It's that simple if you believe in the truth!"

"What fuckin' truth?! What fuckin', simple-"

The explosion smashed his words in mid-air: the compound security gate ceased to exist. An alarm bell began to ring insistently. Ann hopped up and down on her seat like a child at the circus, turning to Sam with a smile of exhilaration.

"They're doing! They're bloody doing it, Sam!"

Wolf threw down the anti-tank weapon behind the newly-painted van, while Birgit and Jo leapt forward, automatic weapons spewing bullets into the now-destroyed gated entrance.

Under the exuberant cheers of Ann rooting their efforts

on, Sam repeated in disbelief: "They're gonna kill him? They're fuckin' gonna kill him!?"

Four violent bank robberies had drilled them to an almost military precision. Standing on each side of the shattered entrance, using its solid walls for cover, Birgit and Jo pinned down the security guards inside the compound with heavy alternating waves of gunfire. Suddenly - and Sam could see it was a planned coordination - both Birgit and Jo stepped into the entrance, firing at the same time - while Alex and Wolf ran between them into the compound, across the short yard, up to the closed front doorway. There, like seasoned veterans, they crammed themselves into the shallow recess.

It was not enough protection: a security guard, hiding behind a tree safe from Birgit's covering fire, had a clear shot at the entrance - his automatic pistol let out a short, frustrated bark before jamming, enough to send three bullets into Wolf's chest.

Braun lobbed a small grenade near to the tree, unconcerned with pinpoint accuracy; the explosion took off the security guard's left leg at the knee, the concussion threw him into Jo's line of fire.

Braun stepped between Birgit and Jo at the entrance gate, bringing to bear an intermittent, aimed, gunfire at the yard while those two dashed to join Alex - who began to rage at the closed front door as his reaction to Wolf's death. The security alarm, still insistently throbbing, rattled into the background of everyone's nerves.

For all her encouraging excitement, Ann sat frozen in the Dutch van, a powerless bystander. "Don't... don't..." Sam whispered, seeing inside the compound clearly through the broken gate, and though Ann knew he was not talking to her, she heeded the advice: from Alex's mad passion to Braun's cool deliberation, there was a personal, private air about the attack. No polemical rhetoric could disguise that fact, no matter how loudly or how often the participants themselves might say otherwise. Braun was able to jog much slower than the others across the yard, shielded by an angry, persistent cover of gunfire from the other three. Birgit's snub-nosed automatic weapon found a second security guard with a clear shot at the front door and wasted him accordingly.

Braun did not hesitate, nor slow the force of his momentum, as he approached the front door, launching a flying shoulder at the bullet-chipped heavy wood: it burst open with a crash. Now, unlike the yard run, Braun sprinted hell-bent for the other wall across the room, dashing just ahead of the interior guards' unprepared crossfire. Behind him, Alex and Jo jumped through the entrance and began spraying the corners of the room; Birgit knelt in the entrance, aiming at the thick lock on the metal door of Sinder's office. Braun slammed into the opposite wall, bounced back, whirling around, firing blindly at the side walls where his attackers stood.

Sinder's elderly translator was hit immediately, a victim of the security guards' misdirected crossfire. There were only two security guards inside the anteroom; they died under Alex's wild bursts. The lock on Sinder's office door melted under the bullets' hammering blows: the metal door stood solid and strong, but the catch gave way and the heavy plane began to sway open. Birgit stood up, pleased at her accomplishment.

The shot was from outside. It hit her in the spine.

"Braun?" she called out, her eyes wide with wonder at the body-numbing effect of realizing she had just been killed.

He was almost ready to jump into Sinder's office, to face his lifetime's purpose: with an effort Braun held himself back and looked across the anteroom at the blond woman who loved him.

"Birgit!" Jo cried, turning from his triumph over a security guard to see her death.

"Braun?" Birgit asked again, not knowing why, as life left her eyes.

They stayed anchored on Braun's eyes, though, for the long second it took Birgit to crumple to the ground. He tried to think of her, but saw only dark-eyed Rachel.

A handful of pistol shots flew out from the interior of Sinder's office: the door had swung fully open now. Braun fell to his stomach in the doorway and fired up at the lone security guard standing in the rear of the room, knocking him into one of the glass walls. The glass did not break; it was more impact resistant than the metal door.

Sinder sat at his desk. His personal assistant stood nervously in a corner. Braun checked to see if either held a weapon - their hands were in view, empty - then he stood up, remaining in the doorway.

"Alex, Jo."

Alex appeared at Braun's elbow. "Birgit is dead," he whispered, his own hysterical rage dampened by the body count. Braun nodded acknowledgement of what he heard, but Alex plucked at his sleeve, insistent. "Birgit's *dead*." He succeeded in getting Braun to turn his head and look.

Jo knelt over Birgit's body, amazed that she could be dead.

Braun did not waste another moment considering it. He faced back into the office and squeezed off a short burst into Sinder's chest. His eyes took on a blank expression, carefully observing the moment.

Then he turned away, back into the anterior room. Crossing the anteroom, he tugged at Jo's shoulder in passing. Jo rose to join him, Alex bringing up the rear. As he arrived at the entrance door, Braun - who had been accelerating his foot speed - shouted over the rattling alarm bell:

"Stop firing and more of you will live!"

With that he broke into a run across the compound, followed closely by Jo and Alex.

It took a moment for the remaining security guards to understand what was happening - and by the time they did it was too late: straggling bullets began to kick the ground and walls behind the three, but they were already at the front gate. Their newly-painted van was there as they had left it. Braun jumped behind the steering wheel; Jo and Alex in through the open rear door - the vehicle was moving before they could close it. As the van disappeared in the distance, scattered shots followed lamely.

To Sam it always remained something of a mystery, unclear, whether he actually *heard* what happened next - or simply remembered the words from his own bank robbery experience. He *understood* the confused words, that much he knew: Sinder's personal assistant shouting over the telephone, trying to give descriptions of people he had seen only at a terrified glance, "I don't know, I don't remember! How can I remember! It is here! Come see! Here! Here!" Oddly, Sam knew, he could not have heard the first telephone call to the *polizei* because he and Ann were still sitting numbly in the Dutch van as the security guards tentatively stepped out through the destroyed gate and took their futile potshots at the long gone terrorists.

There was no question of following Braun. Not today. Logic did not play a part in their decision, only simple instinct. Survival instinct. Or maybe Sam remembered that from another time, too: he and Ann did not talk. Instead, after a security guard looked across the road at them - it was one of the two guards who had originally escorted them in only twenty minutes earlier - Sam responded to the mute appeal for help. Wordlessly, he abandoned the van for the chaos of the compound.

He almost did not make it inside.

Shocked that Sam would return to Sinder's enclave, Ann hurriedly slid across to the driver's side and called out the window:

"Sam! Get the hell back in here! The police will be here any minute!"

He could see more of the destruction inside the compound now, standing just inside the entrance.

"Sam! I can't be here when they come!" Ann started up the ancient motor with a scrape of ignition.

He was not on the run. Sam stepped deeper into the compound, over to the body of the first dead security guard. In his gun and military-type uniform, the German looked nothing at all - and everything like - McMasters.

"I'll be in Amsterdam!" Ann shouted out in angry frustration, driving the Dutch van away and trying not to cry at Sam's leaving her. Police sirens could be heard in the distance; she drove in the opposite direction from Braun's van.

Someone finally turned off the security alarm bell; its absence was as painful as its throbbing rattle. Sam knelt to help another, wounded, security guard. His months of weekly Field Aid drills kicked-in to automatic pilot and he used his jacket to cover the man, then raised the victim's feet higher than his head, helping to fight impending shock. The security guard was not bleeding badly, which was good since Sam had nothing with which to staunch the flow of blood beyond direct hand pressure. He held his palm on the man's oozing shoulder until another security guard appeared carrying a roll of gauze. He eased Sam away from his wounded comrade and took over the task of attending to the injury, leaving Sam free to look around the yard. A small fire had been set off by the initial gate explosion: some-one was trying to put it out. Other than that, the yard was quiet.

In the doorway, an angry security guard roughly handled Birgit's body, checking first to see if she was still alive and dangerous, then pulling the blond woman's corpse away from the opening and over to where the long-haired male terrorist, Wolf, lay stretched out as he fell, across an autumn-dried flower bed.

Sam did not know either Birgit or Wolf except from a distance - or from behind a gun pointing in his direction. He stepped through the doorway into the anteroom.

Herr Sinder's translator had not died. His critical wounds caused the man to moan loudly at the pain, but there was nothing those hovering around him could do beyond attending to the makeshift tourniquet attached to his right arm: the ugly wound at his neck could only be covered with cloths, which became quickly blood-soaked, and were then replaced by others. A woman, probably the housekeeper her clothing indicated, spoke calmly over the telephone, describing his wounds in a manner that implied some sort of medical person was on the other end of the line. In response to some unheard instruction, she directed the security guard helping the translator to cover him with a jacket - as Sam had done for the wounded man outside - and raise his feet higher than his head. Herr Sinder's personal assistant could be heard screaming incoherently into his own telephone inside the office.

In contrast to the damage to the other places - and the battered condition of the metal door - Sinder's office appeared relatively untouched. The body of the dead guard sat slouched against an unscratched window wall. Josef Sinder leaned back in his desk chair, dead expression lost in the late afternoon shadows. Those were the only two touches of violence to the office - that and the hysterical shouts of Herr Sinder's assistant at the telephone. *Polizei* sirens crept into the room, indicating that Herr Sinder's rescuers would soon be swarming in.

Sam walked up to Sinder's body: a family man sitting in a chair. Sam kept his words low, between himself and Josef Sinder.

"You did it, didn't you. You fuckin' started it all for a buck - workin' for the Man…"

Ann did not succeed in keeping her eyes free from tears. She cried freely now, safely away from the *polizei*'s dangerous scrutiny, pulled over at a small restaurant where, later, she would eat dinner, telephone Dineka in Amsterdam to tell her where the van was, then make her way somehow back to Paris - an itinerary she would tell no one. Ann did not know if she could trust Sam anymore or, even if she could, if he knew enough not to betray her accidentally.

"...fuck'em over for a buck..." Sam whispered to the dead child-seller.

Frankfurt

He was back in Frankfurt and he heard them talking all around. Sam only heard the talking, he couldn't make himself care what they said.

Private conversations:

"Jesus,! 'Been here half'n hour now! What they think I want to do with my day?"

"They got your day, they just got nothin' to do."

Sergeant conversations:

"We could repaint the barracks."

"Did that three months ago, and it'd take a day to requisition the paint."

"We could - No, nothing."

"What?"

"Couldn't think of anything intelligent. What're you thinking of?"

"I'm thinking of retiring - but got another five years still to go…"

More private conversation:

"King be dead… Knight still on the board. No game. Every Pawn be dead. Fuckin' Queen Ann still alive. Fuckin' stupid

Sam still here, too. McMasters, you bullshit artist, what you forget to tell me? Huh!"

Sergeant to private:

"It's *Nam*, private: we're going to Nam. It's not a place on a map anymore, it's gonna be home for the tour."

"Yeah, but Nixon says he's ending the draft - ?"

"You're on the wrong side of the intention, kid. 'Could be worse, 'could be in Hanoi: Nixon's boy Kissinger (or is it Kissinger's boy Nixon) got 'em dropping a shitload more bombs down their asses than the last ten years combined. 'Shoulda done it in '65."

Behind the color barrier:

"Lindell, you know what you're doing, right?"

"Yeah, corp'rl."

"Then you got nothing to worry about. I did a tour three years ago, just after the TET Offensive - 'guys who knew the rules made it."

"Yeah, I know the rules: white man rules.

"The *Man*'s rules, Lindell."

"The Man's rules, the Man's war."

"You going anywhere else, nigger?"

"You a corp'rl, you tell me."

"I'm telling you how to stay alive-"

"But-"

"But, blood, I know where you from, I know where we

from, and the only way we got for ourselves to get out a-live is to fight this war and get Uncle Sam's bread."

"Right on."

"Righteous.

"Fuckin' gonna show Vietcong Charlie."

"Cover my black ass, I cover yours."

Tactical conversation:

"You stick metal in your shoes and then the pungi sticks can't-"

"What the hell are pungi sticks?!"

"Like stakes, bro: Charlie shits on 'em. You step on these pungi shit sticks, an'-"

"Aw, fuck! That metal work?"

"'Guy told me it did."

General conversation:

"Williams explained it to me, sir."

"I've heard the tape, Captain: your man hardly said a thing."

"General, it wasn't just Private Williams I talked to: Herr Sinder's assistant said he had nothing to do with it - just a coincidence - and the head of security said he used first aid to help the wounded. If anything my private *helped* them."

"And the girl? Sinder's security cameras show Williams was with a girl - and *she* has known connections with the Irish Republican Army."

"Williams didn't know that, sir."

"How do you know that, Captain? How-do-you-know? From what I heard on the tapes, Williams just muttered something about 'she was wrong, fucking wrong' -"

"'Everybody's fucking wrong'."

"Eh?"

"That's what he told me, General: 'Everybody's fucking wrong'. Something about Herr Sinder selling Jewish babies during the war and-"

"Oh, shit! Don't tell me Williams got sucked into swallowing some Commie propaganda crap?!"

"Whatever it was, he didn't buy it, sir: not if he thinks '*Everybody*'s wrong'."

"Yeah, Captain, he'll be a great one to have on your team over in 'Nam"

"Williams is good, sir, I've seen him on maneuvers. He thinks."

"Then he shouldn't be a private. When do you ship out?"

"'Day after Christmas."

"Three weeks. Keep him on base. It's your ass, Captain."

"I understood that from the beginning, General."

If you watch from the outside long enough, the details blur and everything becomes clear.

Sam did not listen to the others' nervous conversation *ad nauseam* about Viet Nam. He tried. He tried to be excited by the prospect - or scared - or even care. All of the emotions played their alternating games inside his stomach, but none surfaced higher than his chest; none captured his imagination, took over his thoughts. There was no surprise about being shipped out to Nam: the minute Sam read that the bombing of Hanoi had started again he understood that *that* was going to happen; McMasters had explained the kind of twisted strategy motoring the Paris peace talks months ago. And the presidential election, of course. First, the promise of peace - undercut the "peace" Democrat McGovern - then smash the North Viets in the face to show 'em that peace don't come easy. We got *pride*, man, don't fuck with U-S US!

No, don't.

Don't think about Ann Shea or Braun or Sinder, either. Nor especially not McMasters, dumb fuck Regular Army getting himself killed and pulling Sam into all this.

Dumb fuck.

The words didn't seem right when talking about McMasters. McMasters never used words like that, it didn't do right by his memory to use them on him. *Unlucky fool.* Closer, not perfect. *Luck's Pawn.* Chess, yeah, McMasters would like that. But he weren't never no Pawn. (Weren't no King, neither, for that matter.) Knight? Castle? McMasters was a Castle, a Rook: straightforward and strong. No twist-turning Knight he. Luck's Castle. He let Sam be the Knight.

Which meant the board wasn't closed yet. No stalemate: the Knight wasn't limited to straightline action. Sam hid his duffel bag six hours earlier and strolled out of the barracks on the Monday night with all of the innocence of the half-hundred others idling over to the PX. No pass, Williams, he had been told - and that was without even asking. Maybe if they hadn't said a thing to him Sam would have curled up on his bunk every night and slept through the remainder of the tour in Germany. Only a couple more weeks.

But they said "No."

And whatever else they said that shouldn't have been it. Not since Adam and Eve had a flat-out "No" ever worked. And Sam had a far better reason to indulge his curiosity than an apple on a tree.

He used up a pocketful of marks on the German pay telephone set up just inside the camp gate, watching the money tick away in increments of wasted time as he called Paris every fifteen minutes. He missed lights-out. Sam stood by the telephone and shivered in the late night air. Whatever else, he was AWOL now, Absent With Out Leave. He was also about to be put on hold again.

"Eh?" he called into the long distance spitfire of French coming out at him through the receiver. "I'll wait," he attempted to interject, then gave up and repeated slowly and distinctly, "See-if-she-is-there-yet. I-will-wait-"

He tossed in another handful of coins, almost his last available change.

"-for-as-long-as-it-takes. *Merci*, thanks."

And then the line was empty, the shuffling step of the concierge's heavy slippers on cold linoleum, reluctantly climbing the stairs, was unable to cross the telephone lines to reach Sam's ears. But at least the line was not dead, as had happened twice before. Sam was grateful for that minor blessing. He bounced up and down in front of the telephone in small celebration - or to keep warm - one hand in his pocket, the other holding the receiver, then switching hands, finally cradling the receiver between his shoulder and his ear and putting both hands deep into his jacket pockets.

The Duty Sergeant over at the gate stepped out of his heated guard box to shout to the dancing man, "It's after eleven, soldier!"

Sam waved his arm in acknowledgement: he had implied to the Duty Sergeant three hours earlier that he was the possessor of an overnight pass hoping to get a ride instead of taking the tram into Frankfurt. If nothing else, his vigil at the phone had convinced the Duty Sergeant that the private was sincere, that he really *had* a pass. Nobody would sit outside freezing off their tail end (on a Monday night, no less) just to try to flash a fake pass. Sam had not calculated this reasoning, but he knew from conversations with McMasters that pass inspection was lax on weekday nights.

The telephone in Paris was picked up.

"Hello?!" Sam hurriedly called into it, afraid that some passerby in the hallway would absently hang up the phone or try to use it himself. "I am still waiting! Did you find-"

"Hello, Sam."

The music of Ann's accent carried the distance.

There was too much to say.

"You weren't in Amsterdam," Sam said simply, starting from the beginning.

"You went there for me?"

"Yeah."

There was still too much to say: skip to the end.

"I've got three for you -" The Duty Sergeant was close enough to hear the conversation if he chose; Sam did not finish the sentence.

Ann understood. "When can I get them?"

"Right now."

"You're in Paris?"

"No."

"The gu-, *they*'re in Paris?"

"No."

"Look, Sam, I'm not going to start playing Twenty Questions."

"I need your help one more time. Can you be in Frankfurt by morning - with a car?"

Ann stood barefoot on the cold linoleum of the Parisian hallway outside the concierge's door and calculated the favors she could call in at that dark hour. "I can get another van - probably," she decided. "Where will you be?"

"Bergenstrasse. It's on Bergenstrasse: I don't remember the number, but it's the only hotel there. I'll be waiting."

He hesitated, determined to say something else, unable to. Ann thought of adding her own sentiment to fill the gap. "Good-bye," one of them said, finally. It didn't matter which one.

Sam stepped away from the pay telephone and over to the guard box. The Duty Sergeant emerged, cradling a thermos of coffee between his palms.

"Made it, didn't I?" Sam smiled.

"Just barely," The Duty Sergeant pulled Sam's duffel bag

out of the guard box, handing it over. "They comin' for ya?"

"Nope. Goin' in free and single."

"One tram left, comes by any minute." The Duty Sergeant retreated to his heated cube of wood. "Hell of a time to go out sightseeing."

"Tell me about it," Sam agreed, sighting the tram pulling into the stop a hundred meters down the road. The Duty Sergeant did not make any attempt to check his pass as the young private ran to catch the last public transportation into Frankfurt for the night.

* * * * * * * * *

It wasn't a hotel exactly, although the title bestowed that honorific upon the establishment: "Hotel" Sinfel was a middle-sized pension whose owners had realized in the late '60s the income-vs.-tax bite fiscal advantage of the identity change. Tourists - American and every other ilk - knew that you had to pay more at a hotel than at a pension or hostel. Still, the owners ran Hotel Sinfel like it was an extension of their own home, which, in fact, it was - which was why Sam had to face the sleep-heavy visage of Frau Heller when he knocked on the door at five minutes to midnight. Frau Heller did not believe in night clerks. She did have faith in deutschmarks, francs, dollars, traveler's checks and American Express. She overcame her drowsy annoyance to let Sam rent one of her three available rooms for the remainder of the night ("Checkout nine hours," she repeated three times, lest the American soldier fail to understand that she paid her *gastarbeit*

Yugoslavian maid for mornings only.)

She could have said "six hours" for all Sam cared: he did not intend to stay longer, even though he was bone-tired.

But the weariness was physical. Emotionally, Sam was wired. Standing out in the cold night had sapped his energy, worrying about whether or not he would be able to locate Ann, freezing off the carbohydrates of his starch-rich G.I. dinner meal. Now, still wearing a heavy fatigue jacket and feeling the cozy warmth of Frau Heller's high-ceilinged room ooze into his bones, Sam's heart began to pump faster than the sleep-persuading exhaustion could handle. Behind drooping eyelids his pupils narrowed into pinpoints of concentration. McMasters would have been proud of the way, subconsciously, his protégé had been thinking several moves ahead of his decisive action this night. Knight to Queen-four, Pawn to King-three, Bishop - wait, ready: not Checkmate yet, not even Check. But ready. Soon.

The pieces of metal, heavy tape and rubber he had assembled over the previous days fell onto Frau Heller's goose feather comforter with quiet thuds. Sam pulled off his olive drab woolen gloves, itchy but warm Regular Army issue: in the crevice next to the little finger of his left hand the bullet was safely cradled. It had not been difficult to "lose" a shell during rifle practice, the problem had been in finding a piece of short pipe in which the bullet would fit snugly, the narrow rim of the casing firmly pressed against the pipe's circular opening. As Sam had not decided to call Ann yet, there was the added disincentive of a clear lack of motivation. "Why am I doin' this?" he would ask himself silently, sharing his thoughts with no one - as if talking with the Nam-nervous others would give him any feedback he could use. Nobody to rap with. No McMasters. No Ann Shea. At one point Sam felt like the only person in the world who would understand him would be Braun, Sinder-killer Braun. "Why'm I lookin' for a piece a strong pipe, Mister Braun?" Sam said aloud to a pile of plumbing scrap behind the kitchen mess hall the afternoon he found the right sized section. He knew he would talk to Braun. After the zip gun was ready.

It is not difficult to assemble a zip gun, particularly if you already know the design. Sam's momma had made him stay away from the obvious killer boys in Detroit, but she couldn't do enough to counter the neighborhood they had descended to after coming up from Alabama in '55. Sam saw the zips and the blades at school lunch from the time he was in sixth grade, first as pint-sized boasts of accomplishment ("Look what I done made!" "Wow!"), then as junior high displays of threat ("He come after me with a blade, I off him, I off the mother!"). By high school the zip was a sign of desperation: the power bloods had real guns, flooding the streets direct from Viet Nam to your local neighborhood, care/of your legless vet deposited back in the tenements after Uncle Samuel had used him up. Or the whole-bodied vets. Or, why be color blind?, Sam saw enough R.A.-issue weaponry during his high school days to figure out that the local National Guard white boys - who were never going to see Nam - were doing a decent side business on the streets. Hard to get into the Guard if you didn't have connections; hard to make a decent profit out of the war.

It fit together pretty easy: slide the bullet into the pipe

opening, attached a thick piece of rubber securely onto the pipe with strong tape, jam a short nail into the rubber - and there you have it. Shooting is simple, just point the pipe where you want the bullet to go, pull back on the rubber banded nail, let it go... Pow! When that nail snaps into the back of the shell there is a fifty-fifty chance the bullet is gonna snap into action. One shot, of course, but from three feet it's hard to miss. From six feet it's hard to hit. So you've gotta be close.

Sam slid the zip gun under his left sleeve, along his forearm. It was impossible to see the thin weapon. He let his arm drop: the zip fell easily into his hand. It was ready. He could sleep now.

Sam sat in the single armchair the Hotel Sinfel provided each room and did not sleep. His eyes never fully closed as he stared blankly at the thin, patterned rug Frau Heller had thrown over the parquet floor. Somewhere down the narrow street at the end of Bergenstrasse an early morning worker started his car with much effort and draining of battery. It was at least another hour after that before the sun came up. Sam did not look at his watch to check. When the sound of starting cars became regular, he rose from the chair, slid out of his jacket and began stripping himself of the soldier's leave uniform that had seen him safely out of base. He pulled from his duffel bag a pair of flare-bell jeans, a wide collared hot pink shirt and a heavy sweater Ann had helped him buy in Paris. The zip gun fit even more comfortably on his arm with the added support of the sweater's elasticity; now it would not fall out of its improvised "holster" unless he pulled at it. It was an added bonus: Sam had not thought of it, he only brought the sweater for warmth. And disguise. He could wear the Army jacket, though: every third person in Europe under the age of twenty-five wore U.S. Army jackets. Even Ann probably would. He would see. Sam left a deutschmark tip on the bed and left the Hotel Sinfel. It was almost seven o'clock by his watch, oh-seven-hundred military time, which he looked anxiously at every five minutes for the next hour-plus until a beat up van turned onto Bergenstrasse and came to a stop by the far corner.

Sam could see Ann through the front windshield, sitting behind the steering wheel, trying to scout out the location of Bergenstrasse's sole hotel. She looked past him twice before realizing it. At the same moment Sam began walking down the center of the narrow street towards her, the van moved forward to pick up its passenger.

Sam had not slept, but Ann was the more tired of the two: dark circles from all-night driving had given her the look of bruised eyes. Wary eyes. Ann could not fathom Sam's intentions, not after the visit to Sinder, and her thoughts had violently argued the point on the road from Paris. Sam understood her uneasiness: he felt the same way about himself.

"I'll drive," he offered, standing outside the driver's-side window. Ann slid over without protest. Sam handed her a folded piece of paper before climbing behind the wheel. "Your guns are there. Three of 'em, in pieces - it's up to your people to put 'em together."

Ann wanted to close her eyes in relief, but couldn't. "I trusted you to do it, Sam."

"Really?... I didn't." They made eye contact for the first time since meeting. Ann could close her eyes now: she was afraid of the answer to her next question.

"Are you going back?" she asked. She could not keep the slight Irish music out of her voice, and it made her angry inside to be so soft.

"For the record or for real?"

A slight laugh. "Make it for the record."

"I'm always going back. Don't trust me not to."

He'd said it: Ann heard the words. She opened her eyes at the sound of Sam's confusing confession, letting the disturbance in her eyes show clearly to him. She loved him, and it did no good to know that he was not wholly hers. An almost-smile bent her lips enough for Sam to see. He could have kissed her then and wanted to very much. But not enough. There was not enough traffic on Bergenstrasse to disturb the long minute the two stared at one another.

"Well?…" Ann asked at last.

"Where's Braun?"

"Berlin."

That had been the agreement: guns for Braun. A meeting in exchange for weapons. The guns were needed. Braun would understand.

Berlin

Sam wanted a radio. Bad. The van Ann had arranged this time made the earlier Dutch van seem regal and luxury-class by comparison. On the speed limit-free German autobahn he was rarely able to urge the vehicle above eighty kilometers per hour - on down-slopes and (very rare) flatlands. The route to Berlin should have landed them in the city by mid-day; it was almost noon now and they were just pulling up to sit in the long line awaiting inspection at the East German border. Sam needed music to keep him awake. Ann slept deeply, her tumbled emotions buried under the needs of exhaustion. Sam needed to hear music - stupid music - to make him stop repeating the song that was stuck in his head:

> *One child grows up to be*
> *Somebody who likes to learn*
> *One child grows up to be*
> *Somebody who just loves to burn*

The dark yet forward-moving rhythms and occasional voice in the wilderness sliced at Sam's nerves.

> *Both childs are good to mom*
> *You see it's in the blood*
> *Both childs love their mom*
> *Blood is thicker than the mud*

Braun and Sinder and McMasters and Ann. Jewish kids and German kids and little black kids in Detroit.

It's a fam'ly affair
It's a fam'ly affair.

"Why Berlin?" Sam had asked earlier in the morning, before sleep and road-tedium overtook Ann.

"That's where Braun is holed up, that's all I know…" She said the words listlessly, her eyes focused on the countryside flashing past. It was almost winter now: except for blue-green needle-leaved conifers, a perfect match for the blue-grey sky, the rest of the landscape was stripped of color. Ann spoke without turning her head, seeing Sam's reflection in the dirty side window, "The police caught one of them already: Jo Grobleiner.…"

Sam knotted his eyebrows together, trying to put a face to the name.

"…We saw him. He had a beard…"

More than one had worn a beard; but Sam saw all of the bank robbers' faces clearly now, even the dead one that Mc-Masters shot.

"…They caught him at a concert in Munich. Pink Floyd."

Ann did not go north into Germany often, this was the first time in cold weather. The sight of the orchard trees shocked her: the full, leafy branches were stripped bare now, severely pruned for the winter to protect them from breaking in the icy rain that would pelt the land again and again. The trunks were stout, telephone-pole thick pillars reaching up a little past a man's height - then every thick branch was hacked off. Only thin, skeletal branches were allowed to remain, reaching up at the grey clouds. And not all of those: the farmers chopped the thin branches down to the trunk on more than half the trees Ann saw, in anticipation of a wet, cold winter, leaving only stubs projecting from the trunks. Amputated fingers of trees lay scattered beneath. Ann shivered at the image and denounced Jo in angry objectivity:

"Really stupid, really. Caught him crashing the gate, then pulled an I.D. on him for an old fire-bombing from '68. I don't think they even know who he is yet."

"Will he tell them about Braun?"

"They already know about Braun: he's on the other side of the Wall. Untouchable. That's how I know where to find him now."

Twice while Ann slept Sam unbuttoned the cuff on his left sleeve and let his arm drop: the zip gun fell effortlessly into his hand.

Ann had been more prepared for Sam's decision to join her than he realized. When the autobahn curved into the heavy blockade of the East German border, a sign marked the turnoff to the "Foreigners to Berlin" lane: a horde of East German guard uniforms swarmed around the checkpoint.

Sam nudged Ann awake.

"What do we do now? This isn't no walk-across border."

The line-up of cars heading to Berlin was backed up twenty-deep. East German border guards descended upon each one in groups of five, working their way back car to car, checking papers, shouting snidely to the passengers at frequent intervals.

Every third driver, it seemed, was ordered into a small building to fill out transit papers. Sam's stomach pulled a nervous stretch at the memory of Ann's earlier avoidance of the Dutch-German border crossing.

Ann did not share the same qualms. She produced a Swedish passport with Sam's photograph inside.

"No problem," she yawned, handing Sam one of her own to carry as well. "These look pretty good, they'll get us through..." Ann could not shake the sleep from her brain, yawned again, "...they always do."

Even through her sleep-haze, though, she could sense Sam's reluctant stare at his photo inside the bogus Swede passport. "I had them made up a month ago, before we left for Amsterdam," she explained. "Sweden takes American political AWOLs. It can be a real passport soon enough - if you want it."

Sam remembered when she would have done it: ten francs worth of photo machine headshots taken at the *Gare du Nord* train station in Paris, most of them with Ann's head crammed into the small square, her cheek pressed closely to his. He did not remember any "serious" pictures being taken. Close inspection of the passport photograph revealed the traces of a grin still playing in his eyes and cheek muscles. Sam had a lot of Cherokee blood swimming around in his black veins, or so Gramma W'ims always said; it showed up in his cheekbones, high and strong.

"Why didn't we use these before?" Sam asked, uncomfortable with committing himself to the false documents - especially when the commitment was with the East Germans.

"It's no good using them too often," Ann answered.

The East Germans were at their vehicle now, making rude remarks about black men with white whores, remarks that Sam and Ann understood without need for translation. The Swedish passports were handed out - and back in again - without ceremony or deep inspection. A demand was made for twenty deutschmarks - *West* German - which Ann had ready in hand. "It doesn't take papers to cross the Frenchy and Dutch borders," she added as they were waved onto the highway to Berlin, "so why use them?"

The contrast between autobahns East and West was striking: once past the border crossing the six lane ease of the West German system was replaced by a two lane affair, pock-marked with spots roughly repaired. Instead of the clear view of landscape they had enjoyed in the morning, as the van crossed the East German country-side a closed-in feeling of grayness defeated their emotions, heightening Ann's awareness of the treeless time in autumn the year had now become. In Ireland, even so late in the year, the wet green of the land would have blanketed her with its colour, fathomless jade comfort to whatever ugliness Belfast held in its daily abuses. A deep and abiding homesickness crawled into her shoulders, making her feel shrunken, ready to weep at any moment. She hid her emotions behind closed eyes and a sleepless imitation of slumber.

Until it grew dark. With the falling of the early north country night, there was no color to depress one's spirit. Ann threw off her self-pity and convinced Sam to let her drive the final hundred kilo-meters of dark highway. Despite a formula protest, Sam was asleep in seconds, leaving Ann's green eyes alone to search out the way beyond the thirty meters' cast of the headlight beams.

Berlin glowed with a Disneyland enchantment in the distance. Long before road signs indicated the divided city's presence ahead, an isolated glow reflected from the low evening clouds, signaling the presence of something definitively *not* East German riding beyond the next horizon. The countryside remained stubbornly unlit, aggressively refusing to compete with the approaching city. The Soviets had made their German client state erect its fences in a wide-cast circle around Berlin, starting as far south as Potsdam: even from there, the lights and sounds of the Western enclave changed the scenery. A moment of darkness - a sign announcing the turnoff to Berlin - then, behind a hectare of masking pine trees: the East German border crossing and the brilliance of Berlin looming behind. The bright light woke Sam before the unfriendly voices of the East German border guards had a chance to.

Their transit papers were in order; the standard search for refugees revealed no hidden compartments inside the van. They were allowed to pass into the American sector of World War II's major political creation. The Free City of Berlin.

A rush into another culture. Instead of the staid mercantilism of Frankfurt, or the ordered classicism of Paris, garish signs sprouted up along the Kurfürstendamm, the central artery of West Berlin's activity. Students roamed in herds, mixing freely with businessmen who were just leaving work. Despite the darkness and seemingly endless length of their journey, Sam and Ann had not arrived very late. Time hovered somewhere before the seventh hour of evening. A deep hunger growled up from Sam's stomach, an angry reminder of nutritional necessity. They settled on a Turkish shawarma restaurant where a deutschmark bought a lamb-filled handful of pita bread and a second DM tagged on a liter of pilsner. Sam's eyes were filled with the glitter of shops offering a richness of goods -

"It's a dying city," Ann muttered to herself, but loud enough for Sam to overhear.

"It's got money," he said in Berlin's defense, growing enthusiastic at the thought of life here.

"You think that a window full of electric kitchen machines and stereos is all there is to it? They belie the true situation, Sam: Berlin's a shell, used by both East and West as a symbol to each other about what good things they stand for. Look up and down the Kudamm here: See the Money, Sam? *That's* what they're tellin' the East Berliners that democracy is all about. Go over to the other side and see the tall statues and clean streets: they don't have any deeper message than that you can get Order for your Communist dollar. Big choice!"

She stormed across the sidewalk, jabbing her finger at window after window display. "There is no one committed to *living* in this city, it's all symbols!" She whirled back to face Sam. "I don't want to live a symbol, Sam! I don't want anything more than that they just treat each other right and that the oppressors who try to force us to do otherwise get their just comeuppance!"

She let her words fall out and die, hearing for herself the pathetic naiveté that underlay the actions that had transported her in five years from Belfast to Berlin. Ann thrust her hands into her jacket pocket and laughed harshly at herself:

"Hell, I'm such a proper little Roamin' Catholic girl,

aren't I? I'd probably go back to the Church now if only the Pope would lay off oppressing women and give us a good condom!" She pulled a hand out of its pocket to link her arm through Sam's. "Father Ann Shea! What a priest I'd make, eh, Sam?"

"I'm thinkin' you fail the celibacy bit," he answered, feeling, as he always did, surprised at these odd lapses of vulnerability set forth so openly by Ann, grateful for her ability to hide her hurt behind a joke at this moment. They headed leisurely back to the van. "Ah, I guess I'm lost no matter what," Ann mocked-sighed. "Let's go celebrate my failure to become a priest."

"Where do we find Braun?"

The laughter stayed behind them.

"I told you before," Ann said without looking up at Sam, "the other side of the Wall. He's got a place just off the Alexanderplatz. A safe house."

"Can we get there tonight?"

"I think not. It's too much trouble being in the Eastern sector at night."

"Is he expecting us?"

"No. But he knows we're coming - by now."

The hint of threat in Ann's voice was unmistakable. Sam stopped walking. Ann hugged in tighter to Sam, still not looking up. They could have been a couple admiring a display of furniture, except that they were facing away from the shop windows.

"You don't play straight with me, Sam. I can trust you - I do - but I can't take the responsibility for others."

"I don't care… I just want to meet him."

Ann thought at once of asking "Why?", then decided even

faster not to. It was too late to ask that question. Besides: *she* wanted to meet Braun, too. It was not hard to imagine why Sam would want to.

Or, in fact, it was impossible for Ann to imagine any other reasons but her own: she had spoken with Sam interminable hours in Paris, listened to him, *felt* his thoughts to be similar to hers on so many things. Now, in this wasting away city of Berlin, the only thing alive she felt was Sam standing next to her. Sam shivered reactively to a gust of December wind curling down the Ku-damm; Ann hugged in tighter.

"I'll show you a place where we can look at East Berlin," she offered, tugging gently at Sam's arm to lead him back to the van. "We can wait there till morning."

Brandenburg Gate.

In large part thanks to Ann, Sam's sightseeing in Paris had been limited to his first day of trudging past too many grand monuments to grasp. He was unprepared for the grandiose deso-lation of the Brandenburg Gate. Still too Detroit-naive American boy wide-eyed to suppress an "Ah!" gasp at the thick, columned portals rising above the Berlin Wall, topped by a huge black metal chariot drawn by fiery horses.

Surrounded by the desolation of political necessity and ablaze with orange-bright streetlights.

Ann stopped the van a half kilometer away from the Gate - as close as available street parking would allow - but the police cordons would not have allowed them much closer access at any rate. A wide, empty expanse of broad boulevard-and-plaza fronted West Berlin's side of the Wall in open contrast to the closed, dark

East Berlin side. The Brandenburg Gate. The fiery horses pulling the chariot pointed their asses to the West.

"These are the portals between East and West," Ann explained with a lavish shrug of Irish disrespect. Prosaically she added: "I don't know what it means, this symbol here, but it scares the hell out of me and makes me distrust everything but what I can touch and feel privately."

It sounded like a confession. Then Sam felt her hands slide into his and knew it for a come-on. It was not hard to respond: his own private thoughts took on a new confusion in the reflected glare of the Gate's powerful reality.

"… but what I can touch and feel privately."

Sam let his fingertips touch Ann's face with a tenderness he himself did not know he possessed. He needed to feel her delicately, minutely; to blindly grasp her close would crush the emotions he felt growing as surely as the Wall in front of them blocked so much else in the world. Everything big and impressive was the enemy: ideas, countries, Walls, wills…

"I ain't no Panther," he sensed himself breathing, drawing the white woman closer.

"I ain't no soldier," he stroked her closed eyelids.

"No guy from America, from Detroit, from… anywhere… I ain't nobody –" Did she hear his voice?

" - but me."

He could almost fall asleep at that moment, lulled by the closeness of their insular universe, save for the warm tears crossing over his high cheekbones, curving down into that part of his jaw pressed close to Ann's forehead. She felt the moisture, and wept her own mother's tears of protection for the boy-man in her arms. It could have been a thousand years ago, and she wished it was, lying in a peat hut in the hills above Cucholain - alone against the dark winter and cruel night - instead of sitting on a vinyl bench seat in the front of a van. With whispered urgings and half-closed eyes they retreated to the back of the vehicle, arranging the scattered blankets into a semblance of cocoon, descending inside, there to slide shaking young bodies against one another, recreating - for an anxious midnight - a safer, *living* world than the one glaring through the front windshield.

> *And if I could but stay awhile,*
> *A while with you I'd stay.*
> *I'd stay, Kathleen,*
> *Oh, smile!, Kathleen,*
> *For this is our last day.*

Ann hated the old song. She could not stop singing it in her head.

Behind The Wall

Frederichstrasse. Via the S-Bahn. An official crossing between East and West. Americans did not cross into East Berlin at Frederichstrasse. Sam's passport said he was not American.

Everything else about him spoke differently, though, and his heart thumped anxiously as the electrified S-Bahn train - which seemed for all the world to Sam just like the "El" in Chicago - swayed violently from side to side as it shot across West Berlin towards the East. His right hand gripped the overhead handbar hard to keep from staggering across the aisle.

His left arm was occupied hugging Ann close.

Neither one seemed willing to let go of the other. Since crisp, harsh-cold night had decided to bleed only reluctantly into a dark, grey morning, Ann or Sam had always found a free hand with which to touch the other. They were clumsy contacts, like kindergartners clutching at one another on their way to the first day of school, seeking reassurance. Oddly, neither one felt afraid, despite the intentionally frightening aspects of crossing the Wall that Cold War politics had erected. Sam's pulse raced faster than it should, but it was excitement pushing the adrenaline in. Knight to King-four: that was the move. He could not be certain what the response would be, was only vaguely aware that he had sketched out contingencies in the back of his mind, but Sam was on Braun's side of the board. He held Ann closely while the S-Bahn shuddered over another stretch of aging rails, speeding towards Frederichstrasse.

A giant "needle" pricked the sky ahead. Or, as Sam thought more specifically, a giant prick stood out over the city. They were in East Berlin now and, Ann explained after consulting a map, the pride of East Germany, the Alexanderplatz, stood nearby the Frederichstrasse S-Bahn stop they would have to exit for Passport Control. The giant prick was a late 50s/early 60s architectural monstrosity, a television tower. Neato-keeno attractive in a comic book way, Sam thought, but certainly not the monument to future progress the designers intended. Neither Sam nor Ann could suppress a sleepiness-induced giggle at the sight of it. Dour faces turned their way. No one exiting at Frederichstrasse chattered gaily.

"It's a bit early," Ann noted, leading Sam out of the train. "We'll probably hit the lines."

"What lines?"

"Those."

The checkpoint lines snaked back from the street exit almost up to the bottom of the stairs Sam and Ann descended from the rail platform. They were in a tunnel now, artificial light casting a dull glare over everything - an improvement on the overcast morning outside, but garish in its flat intensity. East German border guards paced nervously down the lines: to their minds there were too many West Berliners here - afraid, yes - but too apt to quarrel nevertheless. *Osters* were better: they kept their mouths shut and their eyes smartly downcast. (A nervous eye could attract a *Stasi* secret police report).

The guards would not have been any happier if they had known the observation running through Sam's mind.

"I could take them," he calculated, the soldier's training running like a cold instinct in the back of this thoughts, "they're no older then me and a lot smaller - 'cept for the guns." 'Cept for the guns. Yeah. Sam's drilled-in survival instinct did not dismiss the toylike submachine guns the East German guards carried menacingly at their hips. You didn't have to aim very well to hit something with a spray of bullets for every second of tense trigger clenching. Inaccurate as hell, though: that's what the McMasters man had told him once - adding that the inaccuracy was one of the weapon's attractions to the East German border guards. Yeah: nobody waiting on this line would want anyone else in line to make with the violence - not when *everybody* would be part of the target.

The border guards pulled a man out of line and began questioning him intently. It was a young German, with the long, center-parted locks and beard of a postcard Jesus Christ. A *Wester* who was not too afraid, obviously, because he shrugged his shoulders and said with a sneer "Karl Marx (something)." The remark earned him an order to empty his duffle bag out onto the grimy concrete floor. Two more guards sidled close to ensure nonvocal compliance.

"They're probably seeing if he has any illegal literature, don't you know?" Ann commented. "He's K-Group Marxist if ever I saw one. They hate the true believers here."

Illegal literature. Not what Sam carried. Weariness made him care very little for the West German Jesus Christ's plight. "Yeah, well they can search us all they want. I ain't got nothing they would care about."

"I do."

Weariness disappeared too fast for heartbeat to catch up. Sam stared down at Ann wide-eyed. "Not hash?" he mouthed the words.

"And I'm needing it, Sam." She smiled wanly and Sam realized that, damn! Ann had been talking half high to him even on the first night. Hash, grass, alcohol, buzz. Where had his eyes been?

Her wan smile carried a hint of command. "This would not be a bad time, Sam, for us to separate for a few minutes. Apart from my baggage of medicinal needs, they might try to hassle us 'cause we're together."

But it was too late to heed Ann's bit of intelligent perception: in the planned capriciousness of the East Berlin border, the waiting line was unexpectedly pumped forward in a group of twenty-together into a long room identified as CHECK-POINT. Sam was swept into the room along with Ann; there was no time to separate without calling unwanted attention to themselves. Their false passports were taken in with the others and all were directed to sit at a long bench opposite a low table where, one by one, each entrant to the East was passed along a line of uniformed Control clericals. Each person painstakingly filled out a visa application card under the unsmiling eye of a pimply clerk, the back of whose neck appeared to be a cratered tribute to the recent moonwalk by American astronauts.

"Vill-i-amz!"

Sam stood up at the approximation of his name: a young border guard appeared at the far end of the room holding his faked documents. The nineteen year-old from Detroit towered over the nineteen year-old from East Berlin. "Twelve hours. Please pay now," the boy carrying the machine gun said, indicating with an open palm and a thumb-and-forefinger rubbed together the universal sign language for money. West German deutschmarks only, *danke schön*."

Sam ponied up the required currency. Another clerical held out the stamped false passport and half-day visa. "Shea!" was called out behind Sam's back. He hesitated at the exit door, waiting for Ann.

Something was wrong.

Two guards hovered around Ann, one holding her pass-port, both asking her questions in aggressive German. Her eyes sparkling angry Irish, Ann argued back in her own broken version of the language. Sam knew from their discussion on the S-bahn that he should either continue on through the exit door or, at the most, stay where he was quietly. He could not. It was only a few steps back to the low table.

"Ann - ?" he asked tentatively.

"They want to hassle about WEST German visas, wouldn't you know!?" she answered, indicating by a tilt of her head that she had forgotten about her earlier admonition against Sam's becoming involved. Even if she had been pissed off at him, Sam knew immediately what he was going to do.

"Ann, come here!" he said in a strong, angry and comman-ding voice.

Ann was taken aback, but she obeyed. The two East Ger-mans holding her documents did nothing to stop her. "Sam, I -"

"Clear it up and come on."

It was all there for everyone to see: a very mean-looking motherfucker had just told his woman to stop wasting his time. To emphasize the point, Sam threw down a tour book on the low table with a loud slap. A very real anger crept in a low voice between clenched teeth: "Son-of-a-BITCH. You said it would be *easy* getting through!" He played it for Ann and the guards to hear, no one else. Ann found herself shaking at the vehemence in Sam's eyes.

A very large and angry black motherfucker, annoyed at delays.

Ann turned back to the two guards with a helpless look.

Courageously, the two East Germans did not take a step back from the dark giant towering over them. A quick glance down the long room, however, convinced them of two things: none of the control clerks would lift a finger to help - and their comrades-in-arms were all much too small and too too far away.

Besides, what the blackface did to the white whore was not their business.

* * * * * * * * *

Sam and Ann emerged from the closed Checkpoint Control tunnel into the diesel-clear air of the open street, arm in arm.

"You were good, Sam!" Ann was exhilarated, adrenaline pumping happily through her veins. "That was really good!"

Sam's own nervous adrenal flow had to be slowed down.

A McMasters rule. He consciously paced every step to a deliberate, moderate speed. "No, it wasn't so good," he muttered.

"What do you mean 'It wasn't'? You had them scared to wetting their pants!"

"They were scared of a nigger. And I'm no nigger... But even if I'd smiled I'd still be a nigger to them." The flow of bitter nervous energy was hard to staunch.

* * * * * * * * *

A street crossed, a corner turned. The soaring prick of the Alexanderplatz television tower sprang up in front of them. Swiveling their heads in one direction, they could see all the glory of the Marxist state laid out in kilometer-wide magnitude. Turning their heads in another direction, there in the distance stood the Brandenburg Gate - past glory of the German state. And, of course, the Wall. The Wall peeked out between trees and buildings from every perspective pointing west. None of the graffiti that marked the West Berlin side marred the *Os/*ers' view: the Iron Curtain here was pristine in its simple dangerousness. Car barriers, barbed wire, patrolling guards, machine gun posts, spotlights and concrete Wall. It was all there. Nothing more to be said. Ann consulted a street map and directed them deeper into the city, away from political symbols.

She did this wordlessly. Sam was out of words, so was she for the time being. They were both somewhat awed by the differences between the two Berlins, only a few hundred meters apart, light years distant in terms of style. West Berlin, smelling of decadence with its world-weary professional students and political posturing, was nevertheless full of color, of an energy that had infected even the exhausted Sam and Ann the night before. A polyglot mix of Germans and their *gastarbeit* Turk and Yugoslav workers - plus the visiting French/Brit/Yank "occupation army" - made the isolated city of West Berlin a living being of its own breed. Germans of both East and West persuasion could arguably say it was not truly "German." ("Hell," Sam heard McMasters say once, "even Bismarck considered Berlin, his Prussian-empire-ambitious-kaiser-housing Berlin, something different than simply 'German.' Of course, being Prussian himself, he considered it better than a German city. Of course, he was a mean bastard, too, which pretty much makes him a typical German when it comes to military politics. Figure it out for yourself, Sam.") Sam wished McMasters' voice would shut up inside his head; the running dialogue of advice, observations and plain ramblings of the dead MP ground at his concentration. He focused on the face of East Berlin.

Fewer cars here than in West Berlin. Fewer people on the streets: many uniformed men, polyestered civilians. It was all very clean - and very grey. None of the billboards of the Western sectors. ("Correction," McMasters' voice interjected, "different billboards.") Huge red banners hung from some buildings, obscuring the entire face of one, striping the face of another. Karl Marx loomed like a poster boy from a number of street-level store windows. Lenin's mug was next in popularity. The hammer-and-sickle cliché vied with the red star for third place. Ann hardly gave them a glance as she led Sam further away from the Alexander-platz, around a corner into narrower residential streets.

World War II was still an active memory here. Several blank plots indicated where buildings had never been rebuilt after the War. Cleaned-up, yes, and covered in grass now, twenty-seven years later, but the surrounding walls showed need of repair and slow decay. Despite the European design of the buildings, Sam felt a dread familiarity in the dead-end grimness of it all.

Ann walked beside him in silence for several minutes. Finally, relatively sure they were on the right track, she attempted conversation. "Been here before Sam?"

"Yeah."

"When? On leave? Do they bring the Yank soldiers here to 'see the enemy' and how poorly they live?"

"Before that. We called it downtown Detroit."

For a quick moment, Ann saw their surroundings with Sam's eyes.

"We called it Belfast."

Her hand slipped into his and squeezed it. She spoke low and for Sam only:

"We can change it, Sam, we can. We saw how to do it - like Braun: fight it. Fight for the revolution…" She let her voice fade out -

Three soldiers were coming down the street in the opposite direction. Once they had passed:

"I'm not talking 'fight for the Soviet line,' Sam, believe me on this: I'm' not talking fight for *here* - we just use here."

One of the soldiers did as was expected of him and wrote

a description of the two foreigners into his notebook. His Stasi *Oberlieutenant* would commend him for the clarity of his report.

"But, dammit, Braun has literally destroyed an oppressor institution, Sam - and we can help him do it again!"

Sam remembered a Panther talking quietly on a Detroit street corner the summer, after the riots: "'Place like this, you got no choice but to be violent." He kept his hand hooked in Ann's and stepped away from her. "You want to do that?"

There was clear admiration in Ann's green beautiful eyes. "You want to see him, you've got the guns. I'll join you."

Sam stopped walking, forcing Ann to stop as well. He swiveled his head to get a clear view of the clean, crumbling city around him. Inside his head, McMasters and the Panther were arguing something, a relief since they left Sam alone. "Join me…" he said to himself. Then, alert to every possibility: "We far from Braun?"

"Another block or two. Not far."

"Let's be there now." He did not feel nineteen and that felt weird.

* * * * * * * * *

Sam's knuckles rapped on Braun's door. Hard. A large dog began barking somewhere outside, its voice cutting through the air from not far away.

"I think - back here." Ann disappeared around the corner of the building.

Sam followed her to the corner. It was a detached building,

as were all on this particular block. The space between each domicile was scarcely wide enough for a body to squeeze through sideways, but the individuality of each residence distinguished the neighborhood as a formerly upper-bourgeois neighborhood of fin-de-siècle Berlin. Three floors to a house, four rooms to a floor. Decaying since the First World War; since the Second, subdivided with two families to a floor, six to a house. Sam squeezed through the passageway following Ann to discover a small plot of land imitating a back yard behind Braun's building. Enclosed by a low fence whose purpose was symbolic rather than efficiency, Braun was playing with his dog. It was an animal game: devoid of human sounds, a wrestling, violent tumble of bodies. Braun clutched the large beast in an embrace that asked to be bitten - but was not. He was underneath now, holding the dog's huge head in his own powerful hands, practically thrusting his face between the ferocious growling fangs. Braun growled back with equal ferocity, which elicited the yapping bark that had attracted Ann's attention.

"We're here, man," Sam said loud enough to cut through the game.

Braun, in the middle of lifting up the Great Schnauzer by his forelegs, answered in crisp English without bothering to turn around, "Yes?" His attention remained upon the dog in his arms, the animal's hind legs now dancing a tango of excitement upon the ground. The dog, unlike Braun, looked over towards the fence and barked at Sam without aggression as if to say "Join the fun! C'mon! Join the fun!" Braun released the dog, and the animal raced over to the newcomers to extend his invitation in person.

"We're here." Sam repeated, declining the offer reluctantly. His right hand crept over the fence to bury its fingers deeply in the dog's fur. Too many childhood summers on a Grandma's dirt farm in Alabama could not be forgotten. Ann looked at Braun, then Sam, uncertainly.

Braun commanded the Great Schnauzer in German: "Quiet, Frederick. Sit." The dog did as ordered, not moving as Braun stepped over to the fence. Braun noted Sam's hand absently massaging one of Frederick's ears. Then he looked closely into Sam's face.

"This is supposed to be a meeting of old friends?"

The question was genuine. It discomfited Sam a bit, but he returned the close look. This was the man who killed McMasters. This was also the man who had visited cruel justice upon Ernst Sinder for selling Jewish children to the Nazis.

"We thought you'd know someone was coming."

Braun's blank expression did not offer an immediate answer. Then he stepped over to a gate and undid its lock, inviting them into the yard with an opening gesture.

"I didn't - but you are here." He added very quietly to Ann, who was about to speak: "You probably think I keep in contact with the K-Groups, don't you?"

Ann blushed, surprised at her own embarrassment at his attention. Her words rocked with Irish rhythms: "I won't presume to know your strategy."

"No, don't. You would be anticipating me."

Frederick had followed Sam over to the gate and now, once through it, Sam was given the animal's full attention: a forceful rubbing of his huge body against Sam's leg, pushing his black, rubbery nose against the young American's hand, demanding that the hand perform its natural function of scratching a dog's head.

Locking the gate behind the visitors, Braun saw the tell-tale glimpse of grey-blue uniforms standing at the far end of the passage between his house and his neighbor's: East Berlin police, watching. They were always watching, though. In the back of his mind, two thoughts about the Black American began to play. His dogs' attraction to the young man (What was he - eighteen? Twenty-one?), this tilted his attitude towards one of approval. There was also the beginning of a recognition. The beginning only. The approval he acknowledged with a nod to Frederick. "You can play," he said in German. To Sam he translated simply: "Play."

To Ann's surprise, the command was obeyed. Sam needed the release. He began a chase-and-charge game as desperate (if not as violent) as Braun's had been. Rushing at the animal like a mock-bear, arms widespread, roaring above Frederick, Sam invited the hair on the dog's back to stand up, his stubby tail to churn furiously. Suddenly Sam ran away! With a look of happy surprise, the strong-legged Great Schnauzer sprang after him, colliding into Sam in the crowded chase. Sam cut a figure-8 around the tiny back yard, forcing Braun and Ann against the fence, then ran back between animal and humans, shouting at Braun's dog with encouraging words his father must have known from a rural childhood far removed from Detroit. Through the narrow passageway, Braun could see the police observers swell in number from two to four.

Ann, approaching like an admiring fan, wanted to give

Braun the good news about Sam's defection: "I have brought -"

"Observers?" Braun knew *what* Ann was, if not *who* specifically. His sarcasm was directed at her sloppiness. "Do you bring your observers with you, or did you just attract them along the way?"

Ann followed Braun's subtle glance to see the East Berlin police gathering in front of the building.

"Small little dangerous soldiers…" Braun muttered to himself, then turned his head to stare directly at them. All four policemen stepped out of sight. "…desperate soldiers."

He turned to Ann with the command, "Let us go inside." Across the small back yard, he called to Sam in comfortable invitation: "Inside, sir?"

Sam, identifying with Braun through the dog, gave the animal a final rough scratch. "Might as well." It was a tired, comfortable reply.

Braun pointed them through a door leading to a minuscule square of hallway: an unstylish wall had been erected from back to front of the house lengthwise, dividing each floor into right- and left-side flats. Braun crowded into the small parterre behind them, leaving Frederick outside with the comment: "No, not now. Go lie on the grass instead of my rug." It was spoken in English and the dog looked at his master quizzically. Braun smiled at the American: the words had been for Sam's amusement. But, inside the house now, Sam was too wired to be amused; he did not smile back. Braun let his own smile fade and directed Ann to a right-side door. "It is open, then straight ahead. There is a room with chairs."

They walked down a long, narrow hall - the original wide hallway cut in half - passing a large kitchen, a narrow lavatory, and a bedroom lined with overflowing bookshelves, to arrive at a large salon characterized by a *Jungendstil* chandelier and several overstuffed armchairs. More book cabinets lined the walls, all shelves crammed to capacity-plus.

Ann gravitated to the front window. The large glass panels were heavily curtained; she could look onto the street without being seen from outside. Sam lifted a dusty book with the imprint of a chess piece pressed into the spine. A pawn. The book was in German, but inside he could recognize the chess move notation McMasters had taught him. Only a few pages had been cut open.

Shit, Sam thought, *I know more about chess than he does. Pawn to King's Knight-Eight: I can become any piece I want now. Check.*

Braun entered the salon. Sam did not hesitate:

"I came to kill you, you know that."

Ann twisted her head from the window. Braun stared hard at Sam, finally remembering: "There was a black soldier... in Frankfurt..."

"His name was McMasters."

"Sam, what the hell are you talking about?" Ann screeched. "Killing! Are you a bloody police?!"

Sam fingered the zip gun in his sleeve, slipping the metal tube loose from his arm. "No," he answered Ann, his eyes on Braun.

"- the soldier killed one of my people..." Still remembering.

"He was my friend."

For all of her emotion, Ann's feet were rooted to one spot. Everything was falling apart. A repeat of Belfast and the London bombs: people were not understanding, Sam was not understanding. "It had to be an accident, Sam! For the good of the people - !"

"That's not enough!" Sam shouted angrily back at her.

"It is enough! It's enough to know that this man here is part of a revolution - and there's no bloody part in it for private revenge."

Sam wanted to scream back at her a hundred arguments. They choked in this throat trying to find a way out together. Finally, quietly, "Yes, there is," was all he could answer. He let the zip gun slide out of his sleeve into his left hand. Deftly, the fingers of his right hand fitted-in the single bullet to the tube. He drew back the thick rubber band firing pin and pointed the weapon at Braun.

Braun's reaction was different than Sam expected: he stepped closer to the young American, next to one of the overstuffed armchairs. An easier target. Both of them ignored Ann. "He was your friend?"

"Yes."

"I am sorry." There was no telling if Braun was sincere or not; his expression indicated thoughts miles distant.

Then his eyes refocused to the present - on Sam: "Did you know you were going to kill me?"

"I - ... no." No, maybe from weakness of strategy, or weakness of intent. Sam knew that his actions had never been as single-minded as revenge would dictate.

Braun saw the truth playing in Sam's eyes - they were only a meter apart, after all. A sardonically-tinged "Good" emerged from his lips.

"I'll kill you, Sam."

The pistol Ann pointed at Sam's head was of IRA issue: which meant a British service revolver stolen or lifted off a dead Tommy. "I will, hear me now, I've done it before." She still stood at the window, the gun heavy in her hand. Sam's survival instinct dictated his answer: she was close enough for the zip gun.

"I could kill you, too, Ann..." He let the zip gun's aim tilt down towards the floor, to a halfway position between Ann and Braun. His planned hatred of Braun collided with other emotions. "... I could kill either one of you - if I wanted." Bitterly sure of himself: "If I fuckin' wanted."

He was not afraid of Ann's gun: he would be faster than her and have it to use on Braun. "But - " he stuttered.

"I don't want-"

"- to kill." Braun finished the sentence, laughing at the irony: "You are an American soldier." Still chuckling with relief, he turned to Ann. "Would you have killed him?"

To her own surprise, words did not spring easily to Ann's lips in response. "Yes," she said at last. "It would have been necessary." She added a second hand to the pistol grip to aim it at Sam with more emphasis. A pair of praying hands. There was sadness in her voice, but no sense of indecision. "Yes," she repeated.

In one smooth movement, Braun pulled a small submachine gun from beneath the cushion of the overstuffed armchair. The equation of weaponry was all in his favor. To Ann he asked: "You would be with me, then?"

"Yes."

With familiar hands Braun cocked the submachine gun bolt into action and squeezed a burst of three rounds into the front window. Ann and Sam jumped back from the shattered glass, shocked.

There was no such surge of visible adrenaline in Braun. "I believe the police will be here in force soon enough," he said conversationally. In response to the question "Why?" screaming in his visitors' eyes, he added: "They really have no need of me any longer. This is as good a time to make an end of it as any."

Despite the distance of the long corridor and the length of the building, Braun's dog could be heard howling in ferocious anxiety at the back door, scratching furiously at it to be closer to his master. Through the shattered window, the four East Berlin police who had been observing the house could be seen hiding behind parked cars. One of the four scurried away for reinforcements, the remaining three held drawn weapons pointed at Braun's window. Braun's attention was on the dog's barking:

"I must let Frederick in, yes. Come with me, American soldier." To Ann, frozen in disbelief at the sudden changes, he had a different command: "Be with me, then, and keep them away."

"You crazy bastard," she whispered between clenched teeth.

"No, my parents were married."

A tear squeezed from the corner of her eye as her face contorted in confused anger. "Fucking-"

A police whistle echoed from a distant corner of the

block of houses, stopping her obscene protest. "Stand away from the window, Braun instructed patiently. "Ann, I believe that is your name," his calm voice soothed the nervousness in the room. "Ann, I want you to aim at the car engines: these are East German automobiles, some of them are made of *papier maché* and fiberglass only. You can make a very beautiful boom-boom. My apology: I do not remember the word for 'boom-boom' in English."

Ann relaxed her arm, letting the pistol lower towards the floor. Braun was looking her directly in the eyes.

"Why should I do this for you," she asked.

"Because I need your help - and you have no place else to go, anyway."

"I could run with Sam."

"No, Ann: you were prepared to kill him a moment ago - it would never be the same with him. We have no places to live without running, you and me, and such running is not life. Shoot through the window, now. Please. And wait for me."

Without looking to see if she complied with his directions, Braun pushed Sam out of the salon and down the dark hall to the narrow bathroom: the door, once opened, blocked the hallway completely, cutting off the light from the single overhead lamp at the end of the hall. Sam felt Braun's free hand fumble familiarly along the wall to find the light switch; Braun's other hand was still occupied in keeping the submachine gun alert, at these close quarters, pressed into Sam's ribs. The bathroom light, switched on, blinded Sam and simultaneously relieved the pressure of the gun barrel: Braun stepped into the narrow bathroom and onto the rim of a deep tub. Above their heads was a square window which Braun first unlatched, then ripped off its hinges by pulling it violently down into the bathtub.

"The passage between houses on this side does not connect to the front street. Follow it and turn left: you will be on Alexanderplatz in four hundred meters."

Sam stood unmoving in the bathroom doorway. Why...?"

Braun stepped from the bathtub rim over to an unsteady balance atop the toilet bowl. "Out, out. Conversation later." He grabbed at Sam's arm and pulled him up towards the high window. Sam found himself scrambling awkwardly through: he knew that his exit would be, at best, a controlled, headlong fall to the ground. Braun saw it, too, and held out an arm for Sam to grasp for balance. Instead, Sam held on with a lock-grip.

"Go!" Braun urged.

"No! Why? Tell me!"

Urgency made Braun speak with more intensity than he wanted.

"To make justice," he answered hurriedly. "Is not that what everything is about? To make scales even and crimes paid. Sinder's crimes, mine – Even. Debt paid. Ha!" He slapped his palm down on Sam's hand. "Account closed! You do not kill, you go free: the lady will kill, will die, will balance out - No!"

"No!" Braun closed his eyes as if in pain - or deep thought, trying to remember an idea long forgotten.

"I wanted to -" he let the words squeeze out, "- hurt -

"No!"

Braun's eyes remained closed, but the tension left his

face. A tear of relief leaked onto a cheek. His eyes opened, he smiled, and began speaking again: the urgency left Braun's voice, replaced by an amused twang.

"To make a point," he said, the amusement disintegrating into a growing, contained passion. "A very little point...

"A touch in God's heart - so that He will not forget what He has done to us. He could not forgive us in the beginning, and now -"

Braun said nothing more for a moment, then he pointed the gun barrel at Sam's hand grasping his own. "I will shoot your arm if that is what it takes to make you leave."

Sam released his grip, and Braun let him tumble headfirst out the window: the passage between buildings was too narrow for a clean fall, and a broken neck was replaced by a bruised shoulder, skinned knee and two chafed wrists.

Braun stuck his head out the window, holding out the gun for Sam to see. The American was not moving, staring up at Braun, needing something more. "This vengeance," Braun tried not to sound vulgarly decadent: "it really does not have much taste."

He pointed the weapon again at Sam, to make certain that the young soldier was escaping as ordered, then returned to the front salon.

Ann had followed Braun's advice: she knelt at a corner of the window, firing single shots at the automobiles the East Berlin police hid behind. A contingent of six joined the original set; return gunfire began, intermittent and still unorganized by a higher-ranked strategy.

A honking siren told Braun that more reinforcements

would soon be arriving. He stepped next to Ann at the window, offering her another pistol, a vintage World War II Luger. "Are you ready to fight the oppressor?" he asked rather bemusedly.

Grimness and fright marked her features as she looked up at him. "Do you really care?" Bullets began to whistle through the window, pockmarking the wall behind them.

A loud yelp reminded Braun that Frederick was still in the back yard, frustrated at the inability to be with his master. *It will be better to turn him loose*, Braun thought. He hurried to the back of the house, crouching low to duck the occasional stray round that found its way down the hall. At the rear door he rushed out into the backyard, opened the gate and waved an arm towards the Great Schnauzer to leave. Frederick ran in circles around Braun's legs instead. Braun ran out the gate, Frederick followed, and then Braun doubled back into the yard, closing the gate. The dog tried to follow him back. "Go on then!" Braun shouted, throwing a stick far out into the alley near the passage where the black soldier had gone. In the far corner, down the block to the right, Braun saw some of the East German soldiers starting to gather for a rear attack. "Remember to stay low," he called to Frederick, then caught himself in a smile: the dog was already ignoring his master, intent on catching the stick.

Oddly, Sam felt the absence of the dog's barking as much as the growing increase in distant gunfire. He emerged from the passage and onto the next street behind Braun's. He made the sharp left as directed and was on still another street: the Alexanderplatz tower was a sharp arrow in the sky ahead. Dozens of people were on the sidewalk here, all with their faces angled toward the sounds of shooting. Instinctually, Sam turned to look back, too. There was Braun's dog, holding a stick? Frederick saw Sam, too, recognized a friend, and trotted after the young man walking rapidly away. Sam followed Braun's advice and kept walking, walking, forcing himself to ignore the gunfire.

Braun released his shots in bursts of three: tat-tat-tat, tat-tat-tat. An isolated policeman, one stupid enough to raise his head at the wrong moment, purchased one of the rounds with his life, rising to full height with the impact before arching back to hit the ground. A vanload of East German soldiers blocked each end of the street now, unloading their dozen paramilitary troops in neat lines of controlled advance. Braun leaned a shoulder against the interior wall and sent a burst down one long-distance lane to scatter them: there was no chance of hitting anyone from that distance, but it gave the soldiers a necessary dose of humility.

Unconsciously, after months of field training, Sam recognized the differences in weaponfire. The distortions of distance and city echo made no difference in distinguishing Braun's automatic weapon from the East Germans'. Ann's solitary pistol shots stood out starkly in the odd, unplanned silences that developed between salvos from each side. Sam continued to walk towards the Alexanderplatz as instructed.

A small fire began to lick at the hood of one of the East German cars Ann had shot. A *Trabant*. With a smile of satisfaction she saw the flames take hold on the epoxied *papier maché* fenders, then encase the entire vehicle. East Berlin policemen hurried away from the scorching tongues of flame, driven into the open where

Braun's tat-tat-tat struck several, sending them into a skidding dance to the pavement. With a whoosh the Trabant's gas tank exploded, sending even more policemen rushing from the fire's epicenter - inspiring a vengeful hail of bullets from the newly-arrived paramilitary.

Ann fell back from the window: the Luger was empty anyway. She clicked the trigger several times absently, then looked over at Braun, who would lead the successful revolution she had always desired to follow.

Braun had stopped firing, too, but he was not out of ammunition. Nor was he taking a respite from the heavy gunfire the police and paramilitary were now pouring into his building. In a few minutes, one, maybe two, maybe half-a-dozen soldiers would sprint down the passage on the left side of the house, closing in from the rear. He leaned against the side of the window and did not see them as East Berlin police or paramilitary. Their uniforms in his eyes bore SS lightning bolts.

and the bodies of the children, the thousands of children, he saw buried by bulldozers

Braun stepped into the center of the window and began firing rapid bursts, furious bursts, with concentrated care, overpowering, for a moment, the East German assault.

* * * * * * * * *

Sam was at the corner of the Alexanderplatz now. Braun's dog had caught up with him, but no one seemed to notice. Why would they? Something dangerous was happening, close enough to be interesting, far away enough to be safe. Now, like every pedestrian in sight, Sam again turned his head to face the echoed airplay of rapid shots, then wave-upon-wave of gunfire, then…

The grey morning had finally seeped into a light mist, laying a patina of moisture over everything. Oil-filmy rainbows of pale color sheened the streets. Isolated shots followed the deluge, then ended without fanfare. Everyone stared at the empty sound for a minute, expectant. When nothing followed, they went their individual ways. Whatever thoughts, excitements, speculations there were would not be voiced. The Stasi would be listening. Gradually, although it had never gone away, Sam heard the bustle of West Berlin's distant traffic fade into his consciousness, leapfrogging the Wall to land in the Alexanderplatz, where traffic, steady as it was, seemed to proceed with orderly quiet.

A Soviet tour group walked in locked-arm phalanx across the wide expanse of wet concrete, apparently aiming towards a pedestaled bust of Karl Marx that, from Sam's perspective, resembled a bronze cabbage on a stick. The rest of the Alexanderplatz was empty: those pedestrians who had stopped to listen to the gunplay at Braun's dwelling were all hurried away, leaving only Sam, Braun's dog, and a few desolate food vendors to remain shivering in the crap-wet weather. The dog – what was his name? Frederick? – nuzzled Sam's hand, urging him to pay attention. A gnawing dizziness reminded Sam that he had not eaten for almost eighteen hours. He chose the nearest vendor, an open-air sausage stand, and pointed himself towards it. If he ate food and breathed slow, deep breaths, he would not faint. Or cry.

There was a red-faced woman in a white smock standing miserably behind the counter. She was too uncomfortable to feel anything remarkable about a black American appearing as her first customer of the day. The sausages, bratwurst, were split open lengthwise, grilled from below; if the vendress could have thrust her hands into the fire herself, she would have. While Sam surveyed the meager selection of "breakfasts," she hovered her hands above the sausages in a circling motion, as if conjuring the spirit of Marxist Democracy to keep herself warm. Sam knew of brats from Detroit, where *Oktoberfests* infiltrated the city from the suburbs every autumn. He counted out the correct change for two sausages in West German deutschmarks and handed them across the counter. The vendress's eyes gleamed at the unexpected prize: on the black market these coins would bring four times their "official" exchange value with *Ost* currency. Despite the cold nipping at her sinuses, she smiled at the Black man: these little treasures were why she had paid bribes to work at a stand in the Alexanderplatz.

"*Bitte.*"

"*Danke schön.*"

"*Auf wiedersehen.*"

Then she was behind him, as Sam drifted away from the television tower and towards the Wall. He would go back over Checkpoint Charlie, invisible from here but, he knew from maps read and remembered, not far away. Like finding your way in the war games: straight to the Wall, then parallel south till you find it. Like a Rook playing chess: straight line to the King's row, then left. Check. Checkmate. At any rate, the Queen was dead, the King was dead. Game over.

(McMasters never said "won" - he never expected anything to end, especially war.)

A nail in the heel of Sam's shoe struck a cobblestone with a loud Crack! like a pistol in a girl's hand. That was the Brandenburg Gate far ahead.

* * * * * * * * *

Sam stopped walking for a moment, remembering the two sausages in his hands. He took a bite from the warmer of the two; it tasted different than anything he had ever eaten before. Not bad. The dog Frederick pressed against his leg. Sam gave a piece of sausage to Frederick, who scarfed it down with familiarity. The traffic sounds from across the Wall were loud now. Sam looked through the Brandenburg Gate at the West; he turned his back on that to examine the East.

"Not Detroit," he said to Frederick, who seemed to agree, and they began walking towards the Wall to go home.

THE END

Made in the USA
San Bernardino, CA
18 February 2016